MADELON

MORE WILDSIDE CLASSICS

MADELON

MARY E. WILKINS

WILDSIDE PRESS

*Love is the crown, and the crucifixion, of life,
and proves thereby its own divinity.*

MADELON

This edition published 2005 by Wildside Press, LLC.
www.wildsidepress.com

CHAPTER I

There was a new snow over the village. Indeed, it had ceased to fall only at sunset, and it was now eight o'clock. It was heaped apparently with the lightness of foam on the windward sides of the roads, over the fences and the stone walls, and on the village roofs. Its weight was evident only on the branches of the ever-green-trees, which were bent low in their white shagginess, and lost their upward spring.

There were evergreens — Norway pines, spruces, and hem-locks — bordering the road along which Burr Gordon was com-ing. Now and then he jostled a low-hanging bough and shook off its load of snow upon his shoulders. Then he walked nearer the middle of the street, tramping steadily through the new snow. This was an old road, but little used of late years, and the forest seemed to be moving upon it with the unnoted swiftness of a pro-cession endless from the beginning of the world. In places the branches of the opposite pines stretched to each other like white-draped arms across the road, and slender, snow-laden saplings stood out in young crowds well in advance of the old trees. At times the road was no more than a cart-path through the forest; but it was a short-cut to the Hautville place, and that was why Burr Gordon went that way.

Everything was very still. The new-fallen snow seemed to muffle silence itself, and do away with that wide susceptibility to sound which affects one as forcibly as the crashing of can-non.

There was no whisper of life from the village, which lay a half-mile back; no roll of wheels, or shout, or peal of bell. Burr Gordon kept on in utter silence until he came near the Hautville house. Then he began to hear music: the soaring sweetness of a soprano voice, the rich undertone of a bass, and the twang of stringed instruments.

When he came close to the house the low structure itself, overlaid with snow, and with snow clinging to its gray-shingled sides like shreds of wool, seemed to vibrate and pulse and shake, and wax fairly sonorous with music, like an organ.

Burr Gordon stood still in the road and listened. The constit-uents of the concert resolved themselves to his ear. There was a wonderful soprano, a tenor, a bass, one sweet boy's voice, a bass-viol, and a violin. They were practising a fugue. The soprano rang out like the invitation of an angel,

> "Come, my beloved, haste away,
> Cut short the hours of thy delay,"

above all the others — even the shrill boy-treble. Then it followed, with noblest and sweetest order, the bass in —

"Fly like a youthful hart or roe,
Over the hills where the spices grow."

The very breath of the spices of Arabia seemed borne into the young man's senses by that voice. He saw in vision the blue tops of those delectable hills where the myrtle and the cassia grew; he felt within his limbs the ardent impulse of the hart or roe. He stood with his head bent, listening, until the music ceased; the blue hills sank suddenly into the land of the past, and all the spice-plants withered away.

There was but a few minutes' interval; then there was a chorus —

"Strike the Timbrel."

Burr Gordon, listening, heard in that only the great soprano, and it was to him like the voice of Miriam of old, summoning him to battle and glory.

But when that music ceased he did not wait any longer nor enter the house, but stole away silently. This time he travelled the main road, which intersected the old one at the Hautville house. The village lights shone before him all the way. He was half-way to the village when he met his cousin, Lot Gordon. He knew he was coming through the pale darkness of the night some time before he was actually in sight by his cough. Lot Gordon had had for years a sharp cough which afflicted him particularly when he walked abroad in night air. It carried as far as the yelp of a dog; when Burr first heard it he stopped short, and looked irresolutely at the thicket beside the road. He had a half-impulse to slink in there among the snowy bushes and hide until his cousin passed by. Then he shook his head angrily and kept on.

However, when the two men drew near each other Burr kept well to his side of the road and strode on rapidly, hoping his cousin might not recognize him. But Lot, with a hoarse laugh and another cough, swerved after him and jostled him roughly.

"Can't cheat me, Burr Gordon," said he.

"I don't want to cheat you," returned Burr, in a surly tone.

"You can't if you do. Set me down anywhere in the woods when there's a wind, and I'll tell ye what the trees are if it's so dark you can't see a leaf by the way the boughs blow. The maples strike out stiff like dead men's arms, and the elms lash like live snakes, and the pines stir all together like women. I can tell the trees no matter how dark 'tis by the way they move, and I can tell a Gordon by the swing of his shoulders, no matter how fast he slinks by on the other side in the shadow. You don't set much by me, Burr, and I don't set any too much by you, but we've got to swing our shoulders one way, whether we will or no, because our father and our grandfather did before us. Good Lord, aren't men in leading-strings, no matter how high they kick!"

"I can't stand here in the snow talking," said Burr, and he tried to push past. But the other man stood before him with another laugh and cough. "You aren't talking, Burr; I'm the one that's talking, and I've heard stuff that was worse to listen to. You'd better stand still."

"I tell you I'm going," said Burr, with a thrust of his elbow in his cousin's side.

"Well," said Lot, "go if you want to, or go if you don't want to. That last is what you're doing, Burr Gordon."

"What do mean by that?"

"You're going to see Dorothy Fair when you want to see Madelon Hautville, because you don't want to do what you want to. Well, go on. I'm going to see Madelon and hear her sing. I've given up trying to work against my own motions. It's no use; when you think you've done it, you haven't. You never can get out of this one gait that you were born to except in your own looking-glass. Go and court Dorothy Fair, and in spite of yourself you'll kiss the other girl when you're kissing her. Well, I sha'n't cheat Madelon Hautville that way."

"You know — she will not — you know Madelon Hautville never —" stammered Burr Gordon, furiously.

Lot laughed again. "You think she sets so much by you she'll never kiss me," said he. "Don't be too sure, Burr. Nature's nature, and the best of us come under it. Madelon Hautville's got her place, like all the rest. There isn't a rose that's too good to take a bee in. Go do your own courting, and trust me to do mine. Courting's in our blood — I sha'n't disgrace the family."

Burr Gordon went past his cousin with a smothered ejaculation. Lot laughed again, and tramped, coughing, away to the Hautville house. When he drew near the house the chorus within were still practising "Strike the Timbrel." When he opened the door and entered there was no cessation in the music, but suddenly the girl's voice seemed to gain new impulse and hurl itself in his face like a war-trumpet.

Burr Gordon kept on to Minister Jonathan Fair's great house in the village, next the tavern. There was a light in the north parlor, and he knew Dorothy was expecting him. He raised the knocker, and knew when it fell that a girl's heart within responded to it with a wild beat.

He waited until there was a heavy shuffle of feet in the hall and the door opened, and Minister Fair's black servant-woman stood there flaring a candle before his eyes.

"Who be you?" said she, in her rich drone, which had yet a twang of hostility in it.

Burr Gordon ignored her question. "Is Miss Dorothy at home?" said he.

"Yes, she's at home, I s'pose," muttered the woman, grudgingly. She distrusted this young man as a suitor for Dorothy. The girl's mother had long been dead, and this old dark woman, whose very thoughts seemed to the village people to move on barbarian pivots of their own, had a jealous guardianship of her which exceeded that of her father.

Now she filled up the doorway before Burr Gordon with her majestic, palpitating bulk, her great black face stiffened back with obstinacy. It was said that she had been born in Africa, and had been a princess in her own country; and, indeed, she bore herself like one now, and held up her orange-turbaned head as if it were crowned, and bore her candle like a flaming sceptre which brought out strange gleams of color and metallic lustres from her garments and the rows of beads on her black neck.

Burr Gordon made an impatient yet deferential motion to enter. "I would like to see her a few minutes if she is at home," said he.

The woman muttered something which might have been in her native dialect, the words were so rolled into each other under her thick tongue. Her small, sharp eyes were fairly malicious upon the young man's handsome face.

"I don't know what you say," he said, half angrily. "Can't I see her?"

"She's in the north parlor, I s'pose," muttered the black woman; and she stood aside and let Burr Gordon pass in, following him with her hostile eyes as he opened the north-parlor door. Dorothy Fair sat with her embroidery-work at the mahogany table, whereon a whole branch of candles burned in silver sticks. She was working a muslin collar for her own adornment, and she set a fine stitch in a sprig before she rose up, either to prove her self-command to herself or to Burr Gordon. She had also held herself quiet during the delay in the hall.

Dorothy Fair came of a gentle and self-controlled race of New England ministers; but now her young heart carried her away. She stood up; her embroidery, with her scissors and bodkin, slid to the ground, and she came forward with her fair curls dropping around a face pink and smiling openly with love like a child's, and was, seemingly half of her own accord, in Burr Gordon's arms with her lips meeting his; and then they sat down side by side on the north-parlor sofa.

Dorothy Fair's face was very sweet to see; her blue eyes and her soft lips were innocent and fond under her lover's gaze. Her little white hand clung to his like a baby's. There was a sweet hollow under her chin, above her fine lace collar. Her soft, fair curls smelt in his face of roses and lavender. The utter daintiness of this maiden Dorothy Fair was a separate charm and a fascination full of subtle and innocent earthiness to the senses of a lover. She appealed to his selfish delight like a sweet-scented flower, like a pink or a rose.

Lot Gordon had been only half right in his analysis of his cousin's wooing. When Burr sat with his arm around this maiden's waist, with his face bent tenderly down towards the soft, pink cheek on his shoulder, this sweetness near at hand was well-nigh sufficient for him, and Dorothy's shy murmur of love in his ear overcame largely the memory of the other's wonderful song. A bee cares only for the honey and not for the flower, therefore one flower is as dear to him as another; and so it is with many a lover when he gets fairly to tasting love. The memory of the rose before fades, even if he never wore it. Then, too, Burr Gordon had a sense of approbation from his shrewder self which sustained him. This Dorothy Fair, the minister's daughter, of gentle New England lineage, the descendant of college-learned men, and of women who had held themselves with a fine dignity and mild reserve in the village society, the sole heiress of what seemed a goodly property to the simple needs of the day, appealed to his reason as well as his heart. He remained until near midnight, while the old black woman crouched with the patience of a watching animal outside the door, and he wooed Dorothy Fair with ardor and delight, although her softly affectionate kisses were to Madelon Hautville's as the fall of snow-flakes to drops of warm honey. And although after he had gone home and fallen asleep his dreams were mixed, still when he waked with the image of Madelon between himself and Dorothy, because sleep had set his heart free, it was still with that sense of approbation.

Madelon Hautville was not considered a fair match for a young man who had claims to ambition. The Hautville family held a peculiar place in public estimation. They belonged not to any defined stratum of the village society, but formed rather a side ledge, a cropping, of quite another kind, at which people looked askance. One reason undoubtedly was the mixture of foreign blood which their name denoted. Anything of alien race was looked upon with a mixture of fear and aversion in this village of people whose blood had flowed in one course for generations. The Hautvilles were said to have French and Indian blood yet, in strong measure, in their veins; it was certain that they had both, although it was fairly back in history since the first Hautville, who, report said, was of a noble French family, had espoused an Iroquois Indian girl. The sturdy males of the family had handed down the name and the characteristics of the races through years of intermarriage with the English settlers. All the Hautvilles — the father, the four sons, and the daughter — were tall and dark, and straight as arrows, and they all had wondrous grace of manner, which abashed and half offended, while it charmed, the stiff village people. Not a young man in the village, no matter how finely attired in city-made clothing, had the courtly air of these Hautville sons, in their rude, half-woodland garb; not a girl, not even Dorothy Fair, could wear a gown of brocade with the grace, inherited from a far-away French grandmother, with which Madelon Hautville wore indigo cotton.

Moreover, the whole family was as musical as a band of troubadours, and while that brought them into constant requisition and gave them an importance in the town, it yet caused them to be held with a certain cheapness. Music as an end of existence and means of livelihood was lightly estimated by the followers of the learned professions, the wielders of weighty doctrines and drugs, and also by the tillers of the stern New England soil. The Hautvilles, furnishing the music in church, and for dances and funerals, were regarded much in the light of mountebanks, and jugglers with sweet sounds. People wondered that Lot and Burr Gordon should go to their house so much. Not a week all winter but Burr had been there once or twice, and Lot had been there nearly every night when his cousin was not. And he stayed late also — this night he outstayed Burr at Dorothy Fair's. The music was kept up until a late hour, for Madelon proposed tune after tune with nervous ardor when her father and brothers seemed to flag. Nobody paid much attention to Lot; he was too constant a visitor. He settled into a favorite chair of his near the fire, and listened with the firelight playing over his delicate, peaked face. Now and then he coughed.

Old David Hautville, the father, stood out in front of the hearth by his great bass-viol, leaning fondly over it like a lover over his mistress. David Hautville was a great, spare man — a body of muscles and sinews under dry, brown flesh, like an old oak-tree. His long, white mustache curved towards his ears with sharp sweeps, like doves' wings. His thick, white brows met over his keen, black eyes. He kept time with his head, jerking it impatiently now and then, when some one lagged or sped ahead in the musical race.

Three of the Hautville sons were men grown. One, Louis, laid his dark, smooth cheek caressingly against the violin which he played. Eugene sang the sonorous tenor, and Abner the bass, like an organ. The youngest son, Richard, small and slender as a girl, so like Madelon that he might have been taken for her had he been dressed in feminine gear, lifted his eager face at her side and raised his piercing, sweet treble, which seemed to pass beyond hearing into fancy. Madelon, her brown throat swelling above her lace tucker, like a bird's, stood in the midst of the men, and sang and sang, and her wonderful soprano flowed through the harmony like a river of honey; and yet now and then it came with a sudden fierce impetus, as if she would force some enemy to bay with music. Madelon was slender, but full of curves which were like the soft breast of a bird before an enemy. Sometimes as she sang she flung out her slender hands with a nervous gesture which had hostility in it. Truth was that she hated Lot Gordon both on his own account and because he came instead of his cousin Burr. She had expected Burr that night; she had taken his cousin's hand on the doorlatch for his. He had not been to see her for three weeks, and her heart was breaking as she sang. Any face which had appeared to her instead of his in the doorway that night would have been to her as the face of a bitter enemy or a black providence, but Lot Gordon was in himself hateful to her. She knew, too, by a curious revulsion of all her senses from unwelcome desire, that he loved her, and the love of any man except Burr Gordon was to her like a serpent.

She would not look at him, but somehow she knew that his eyes were upon her, and that they were full of love and malice, and she knew not which she dreaded more. She resolved that he should not have a word with her that night if she could help it, and so she urged on her father and her brothers with new tunes until they would have no more, and went off to bed — all except the boy Richard. She whispered in his ear, and he stayed behind with her while she mixed some bread and set it for rising on the hearth.

Lot Gordon sat watching her. There was a hungry look in his hollow blue eyes. Now and then he coughed painfully, and clapped his hand to his chest with an impatient movement.

"Well, whether I ever get to heaven or not, I've heard music," he said, when she passed him with the bread-bowl on her hip and her soft arm curved around it. He reached out his slender hand and caught hold of her dress-skirt; she jerked away with a haughty motion, and set the bowl on the hearth. "You'd better rake down the fire now, Richard," said she.

The boy jostled Lot roughly as he passed around him to get the fire-shovel. Lot looked at the clock, and the hand was near twelve. He arose slowly.

"I met Burr on his way down to Parson Fair's," he said.

Madelon covered up the bread closely with a linen towel. There was a surging in her ears, as if misery itself had a veritable sound, and her face was as white as the ashes on the hearth, but she kept it turned away from Lot.

"Well," said he, in his husky drawl, "a rose isn't a rose to a bee, she's only a honey-pot; and she's only one out of a shelfful to him; she can't complain, it's what she was born to. If she finds any fault it's got to be with creation, and what's one rose to face creation? There's nothing to do but to make the best of it. Good-night, Madelon."

"Good-night," said Madelon. The color had come back to her cheeks, and she looked back at him proudly, standing beside her bread-bowl on the hearth.

Lot passed out, turning his delicate face over his shoulder with a subtle smile as he went. Richard clapped the door to after him with a jar that shook the house, and shot the bolt viciously. "I'll get my gun and follow him if you say so, and then I'll find Burr Gordon," he said, turning a furious face to his sister.

"Would you make me a laughing-stock to the whole town?" said she. "Rake down the fire; it's time to go to bed."

She looked as proudly at her brother as she had done at Lot. The resemblance between the two faces faded a little as they confronted each other. A virile quality in the boy's anger made the difference of sex more apparent. He looked at her, holding his wrath, as it were, like a two-edged sword which must smite some one. "If I thought you cared about that man that has jilted you — and I've heard the talk about it," said he, "I'd feel like shooting *you.*"

"You needn't shoot," returned Madelon.

The boy looked at her as angrily as if she were Burr Gordon. Suddenly her mouth quivered a little and her eyes fell. The boy flung both his arms around her. "I don't care," he said, brokenly, in his sweet treble — "I don't care, you're the handsomest girl in the town, and the best and the smartest, and not one can sing like you, and I'll kill any man that treats you ill — I will, I will!" He was sobbing on his sister's shoulder; she stood still, looking over his dark head at the snow-hung window and the night outside. Her lips and eyes were quite steady now; she had recovered self-control when her brother's failed him, as if by some curious mental seesaw.

"No man can treat me ill unless I take it ill," said she, "and that I'll do for no man. There's no killing to be done, and if there were I'd do it myself and ask nobody. Come, Richard, let me go; I'm going to bed." She gave the boy's head a firm pat. "There's a turnover in the pantry, under a bowl on the lowermost shelf," said she; and she laughed in his passionate, flushed face when he raised it.

"I don't care, I will!" he cried.

"Go and get your turnover; I saved it for you," said she, with a push.

Neither of them dreamed that Lot Gordon had been watching them, standing in a snow-drift under the south window, his eyes peering over the sill, his forehead wet with a snow-wreath, stifling back his cough. When at last the candlelight went out in the great kitchen he crept stiffly and wearily through the snow.

CHAPTER II

Lot Gordon lived about half a mile away in the old Gordon homestead alone, except for an old servant-woman and her husband, who managed his house for him and took care of the farm. Lot himself did not work in the common acceptance of the term. His father had left him quite a property, and he did not need to toil for his bread. People called him lazy. He owned nearly as many books as the parson and the lawyer. He often read all night it was said, and he roamed the woods in all seasons. Under low-hanging winter boughs and summer arches did Lot Gordon pry and slink and lie in wait, his fine, sharp face peering through snowy tunnels or white spring thickets like a white fox, hungrily intent upon the secrets of nature.

There was a deep mystery in this to the village people. They could not fathom the reason for a man's haunting wild places like a wild animal unless he hunted and trapped like the Hautville sons. They were suspicious of dark motives, upon which they exercised their imaginations.

Lot Gordon's talk, moreover, was an enigma to them. He was no favorite, and only his goodly property tempered his ill repute. People could not help identifying him, in a measure, with his noble old house, with the stately pillared portico, with his silver-plate and damask and mahogany, which his great-grandfather had brought from the old country, with his fine fields and his money in the bank. He held, moreover, a large mortgage on the house opposite, where Burr Gordon lived with his mother. Burr's father and Lot's, although sons of one shrewd father, had been of very different financial abilities. Lot's father kept his property intact, never wasting, but adding from others' waste. Burr's plunged into speculation, built a new house, for which he could not pay, married a wife who was not thrifty, and when his father died had anticipated the larger portion of his birthright. So Lot's father succeeded to nearly all the family estates, and in time absorbed the rest. Lot, at his father's death, had inherited the mortgage upon the estate of Burr and his mother. Burr's father had died some time before. Lot was rumored to be harder, in the matter of exacting heavy interest, than his father had been. It was said that Burr was far behind in his payments, and that Lot would foreclose. Burr had a better head than his father's, but he had terrible odds against him. There was only one chance for his release from difficulty, people thought. All the property, by a provision in the grandfather's will, was to fall to him if Lot died unmarried. Lot was twenty years older than Burr, and he coughed.

"Burr Gordon ain't makin' out much now," people said; "the paint's all off his house and his land's run down, but there's dead men's shoes with gold buckles in the path ahead of him."

Burr thought of it sometimes, although he turned his face from the thought, and Lot considered it when he took the mortgage note out of his desk and scored another installment of unpaid interest on it. "If a man's only his own debtor he won't be very hard on himself," he said aloud, and laughed. Old Margaret Bean, his housekeeper, looked at him over her spectacles, but she did not know what he meant. She prepared many a valuable remedy for his cough from herbs and roots, but Lot would never taste them, and she made her old husband swallow them all as preventatives of colds, that they should not be wasted. Lot was coughing harder lately. To-night, after he returned from the Hautvilles', he had one paroxysm after another. He did not go to bed, but huddled over the fire wrapped in a shawl, with a leather-bound book on his knees, all night, holding to his chest when he coughed, then turning to his book again.

When daylight was fully in the room he blew out the candle, and went over to the window and looked out across the road at the house opposite, which had always been called the "new house" to distinguish it from the old Gordon homestead. It was not so solid and noble as the other, but it had sundry little touches of later times, which his father had always characterized as wasteful follies. For one thing, it was elevated ostentatiously far above the road-level upon terraces surmounted by a flight of stone steps. It fairly looked down, like any spirit of a younger age, upon the older house, which might have been regarded in a way as its progenitor.

The smoke was coming out of the kitchen chimney in the ell. Lot Gordon looked across. Burr was clearing the snow from the stone steps over the terraces. There had never been any lack of energy and industry in Burr to account for his flagging fortunes. He arose betimes every morning. Lot, standing well behind the dimity curtain, watched him flinging the snow aside like spray, his handsome face glowing like a rose.

"I suppose he is going to the party at the tavern to-night," Lot murmured. Suddenly his face took on a piteous, wistful look like a woman's; tears stood in his blue eyes. He doubled over with a violent fit of coughing, then went back to his chair and his book.

This party had been the talk of the village for several weeks. It was to be an unusually large one. People were coming from all the towns roundabout. Burr Gordon had been one of the ringleaders of the enterprise. All day long he worked over the preparations, dragging out evergreen garlands from under the snow in the woods, cutting hemlock boughs, and trimming the ball-room in the tavern. Towards night he heard a piece of news which threatened to bring everything to a standstill. The dusk was thickening fast; Burr and the two young men who were working with him were hurrying to finish the decorations before candlelight when Richard Hautville came in. Burr started when he saw him. He looked so like his sister in the dim light that he thought for a moment she was there.

Richard did not notice him at all. He hustled by him roughly and approached the other two young men. "Louis can't fiddle to-night," he announced, curtly. The young men stared at him in dismay.

"What's the trouble?" asked Burr.

"He's hurt his arm," replied Richard; but he still addressed the other two, and made as if he were not answering Burr.

"Broke it?" asked one of the others.

"No; sprained it. He was clearing the snow off the barn roof and the ladder fell. It's all black-and-blue, and he can't lift it enough to fiddle to-night."

The three young men looked at each other.

"What's going to be done?" said one.

"I don't know," said Burr. "There's Davy Barrett, over to the Four Corners — I suppose we might get him if we sent right over."

"You can't get him," said Richard Hautville, still addressing the other two, as if they had spoken. "Louis said you couldn't. His wife's got the typhus-fever, and he's up nights watching with her — won't let anybody else. You can't get him."

"We can't have a ball without a fiddler," one young man said, soberly.

"Maybe Madelon would lilt for the dancing," Burr Gordon said; and then he colored furiously, as if he had startled himself in saying it.

The boy turned on him. "Maybe you think my sister will lilt for you to dance, Burr Gordon!" cried he, and his face blazed white in Burr's eyes, and he shook his slender brown fist.

"Nobody wants your sister to lilt if she isn't willing to," Burr returned, in a hard voice; and he snatched up a hemlock bough, and went away with it to the other side of the ball-room.

"My sister won't lilt for you, and you can have your ball the best way you can!" shouted the boy, his angry eyes following Burr. Then he went out of the ball-room with a leap, and slammed the door so that the tavern trembled.

The young men chuckled. "Injun blood is up," said one.

"You'll be scalped, Burr," called the other.

Burr came over to them with an angry stride. "Oh, quit fooling!" said he, impatiently. "What's going to be done?"

"Nothing can be done; we shall have to give the ball up for to-night unless you can get Madelon Hautville to lilt for the dancing," returned one, and the other nodded assent. "That's the state of the case," said he.

Burr scraped a foot impatiently on the waxed floor. "Go and ask her yourself, Daniel Plympton," said he. "I don't see why it has all got to come on to me."

"Can't," replied Daniel Plympton, with a laugh. "Remember the falling out Eugene and I had at the house-raising? I ain't going to his house to ask his sister to lilt for my dancing."

"You, then, Abner Little," said Burr, peremptorily, to the other young man. He had a fair, nervous face, and he was screwing his forehead anxiously over the situation.

"Can't nohow, Burr," said he. "I've got to drive four miles home, and milk, and take care of the horses, and shave, and get dressed, and then drive another three miles for my girl. I'm going to take one of the Morse girls, over at Summer Falls. I haven't got time to go down to the Hautvilles', and that's the truth, Burr."

"You'll have to go yourself, Burr," said Daniel Plympton, with a half-laugh.

"I can't," said Burr, "and I won't, if we give the ball up."

"What will all the out-of-town folks say?"

"I don't care what they say — they can play forfeits."

"Forfeits!" returned Daniel Plympton with scorn. "What's kissing to dancing?" Daniel Plympton was somewhat stout but curiously light of foot, and accounted the best dancer in town. As he spoke he sprang up on his toes as if he had winged heels. "Forfeits!" repeated he, jerking his great flaxen head.

"Well, you can go yourself, then, and ask Madelon Hautville to lilt," said Burr.

"I tell you I can't, Burr — I ain't mean enough."

"Well, I won't, and that's flat."

"I've got to go home, anyway," said Abner Little. "What I want to know is — is there going to be any ball?"

"Oh, get your girl anyhow, Ab," returned Daniel, with a great laugh; "there'll be something. If there ain't dancing, there'll be kissing, and that'll suit her just as well. And if she can't get enough here, why there's the ride home. Lord, I'd get a girl nearer home! You've got to drive six miles out of your way to Summer Falls and back. As for me, the quicker I get a girl off my hands the better. I'm going to take Nancy Blake because she lives next door to the tavern. Go along with ye, Ab; Burr and I will settle it some way."

But it looked for some time after Abner Little left as if there would be no ball that night. They could not have any dance unless Madelon Hautville would sing for it, and both Daniel Plympton and Burr Gordon were determined not to ask her.

At half-past seven Madelon was all dressed for the ball, and neither of them had come to see her about it. She and all her brothers except Louis were going. They wondered who would play for the dancing, but supposed some arrangements would be made. "Burr Gordon will put it through somehow," said Louis. "Maybe he'll ride over to Farnham Hollow and get Luke Corliss to fiddle." Louis sat discontentedly by the fire, with his arm soaking in cider-brandy and wormwood.

"Farnham Hollow is ten miles away," said Richard.

"His horse is fast; he'd get him here by eight o'clock," returned Louis.

Madelon was radiant. In spite of herself, she was full of hope in going to the ball. She knew Dorothy Fair would not be present, since her father was the orthodox parson, and she had seen her own face in her glass. With her rival away, what could not a face like that do with a heart that leaned towards it of its own nature? Madelon dimly felt that Burr Gordon had to resist himself as well as her in this matter. She had tended a monthly rose in the south window all winter, and she wore two red roses in her black braids. Her cheeks and her lips were fuller of warm red life than the roses. She lowered her black eyes before her father and her brothers, for there was a light in them which she could not subdue, which belonged to Burr Gordon only. No costly finery had Madelon Hautville, but she had done some cunning needle-work on an old black-satin gown of her mother's, and it was fitted as softly over her sweet curves as a leaf over a bud. A long garland of flowers after her own design had she wrought in bright-colored silks around the petticoat, and there were knots of red ribbon to fasten the loopings here and there. And she wore another red rose in her lace tucker against her soft brown bosom. Madelon wore, too, trim black-silk stockings with red clocks over her slender ankles, and little black-satin shoes with steel buckles and red rosettes. Every one of her brothers, except the youngest, Richard, must needs compare her in his own heart, to her disparagement, with some maid not his sister, but they all viewed her with pride. Old David Hautville's eyes, under his thick, white brows, followed her and dwelt upon her as she moved around the kitchen.

Madelon had got out her red cloak and her silk hood, and it was nearly time to start when there was a knock on the door. Madelon's face was pale in a second, then red again. She pushed Richard aside. "I'll go to the door," said she.

She knew somehow that it was Burr Gordon, and when she opened the door he stood there. He looked curiously embarrassed, but she did not notice that. His mere presence for the moment seemed to fill all her comprehension. She had no eye for shades of expression.

"Come in," said she, all blushing and trembling before him, and yet with a certain dignity which never quite deserted her.

"Can I see you a minute?" Burr said, awkwardly.

"Come this way."

Madelon led the way into the best room, where there was no fire. It had not been warmed all winter, except on nights when Burr had come courting her. In the midst of it the great curtained bedstead reared itself, holding its feather-bed like a drift of snow. The floor was sanded in a fine, small pattern, there were white tasselled curtains at the windows, and there was a tall chest of drawers that reached the ceiling. The room was just as Madelon's mother, who had been one of the village girls, had left it.

Madelon glanced at the hearth, where she had laid the wood symmetrically — all ready to be kindled at a moment's notice should Burr come. "I'll light the fire," said she, in a trembling voice.

"No, I can't stop," returned the young man. "I've got to go right up to the tavern. Look here, Madelon —"

"Well?" she murmured, trembling.

"I want to know if — look here, won't you lilt for the dancing to-night, Madelon?"

Madelon's face changed. "That's all he came for," she thought. She turned away from him. "You'd better get Luke Corliss to fiddle," she said, coldly.

"We can't. I started to go over there, and I met a man that lives next door to him, and he said it was no use, for Luke had gone down to Winfield to fiddle at a ball there."

"I don't feel like lilting to-night," said Madelon.

The young man colored. "Well," said he, in a stiff, embarrassed voice, and he turned towards the door, "we won't have any ball to-night, that's all," he added.

"Well, you can go visiting instead," returned Madelon, suddenly.

"I'd rather go a-visiting — here!" cried Burr, with a quick fervor, and he turned back and came close to her.

Madelon looked at him sharply, steeling her heart against his tender tone, but he met her gaze with passionate eyes.

"Oh, Madelon, you look so beautiful to-night!" he whispered, hoarsely. Her eyes fell before his. She made, whether she would or not, a motion towards him, and he put his arms around her. They kissed again and again, lingering upon each kiss as if it were a foothold in heaven. A great rapture of faith in her lover and his love came over Madelon. She said to herself that they had lied — they had all lied! Burr had never courted Dorothy Fair. She believed, with her whole heart and soul, that he loved her and her alone. And, indeed, she was at that time, at that minute, right and not deceived; for Burr Gordon was one of those who can encompass love in one tense only, and that the present; and they who love only in the present, hampered by no memories and no dreams, yield out love's sweetness fully. All Burr Gordon's soul was in his kisses and his fond eyes, and her own crept out to meet it with perfect faith.

"I will lilt for the dancing," she whispered.

The Hautvilles were going to the ball on their wood-sled, drawn by oxen. David was to drive them, and take the team home. It was already before the door when Burr came out, and Madelon asked him to ride with them, but he refused. "I've got to go home first," he said, and plunged off quickly down the old road, the short-cut to his house.

Madelon Hautville, in her red cloak and her great silk hood, stood in the midst of her brothers on the wood-sled, and the oxen drew them ponderously to the ball. The tavern was all alight. Many other sleds were drawn up before the door; indeed, certain of the young men who had not their especial sweethearts took their ox-sleds and went from door to door collecting the young women. Many a jingling load slipped along the snowy road to the tavern that night, and the ball-room filled rapidly.

At eight o'clock the ball opened. Madelon stood up in the little gallery allotted to the violins and lilted, and the march began. Two and two, the young men and the girls swung around the room. Madelon lilted with her eyes upon the moving throng, gay as a garden in a wind; and suddenly her heart stood still, although she lilted on. Down on the floor below Burr Gordon led the march, with Dorothy Fair on his arm. Dorothy Fair, waving a great painted fan with the tremulous motion of a butterfly's wing, with her blue brocade petticoat tilting airily as she moved, like an inverted bell-flower, with a locket set in brilliants flashing on her white neck, with her pink-and-white face smiling out with gentle gayety from her fair curls, stepped delicately, pointing out her blue satin toes, around the ball-room, with one little white hand on Burr Gordon's arm.

CHAPTER III

Suddenly all Madelon's beauty was cheapened in her own eyes. She saw herself swart and harsh-faced as some old savage squaw beside this fair angel. She turned on herself as well as on her recreant lover with rage and disdain — and all the time she lilted without one break.

The ball swung on and on, and Madelon, up in the musicians' gallery, sang the old country-dances in the curious dissyllabic fashion termed lilting. It never occurred to her to wonder how it was that Dorothy Fair, the daughter of the orthodox minister, should be at the ball — she who had been brought up to believe in the sinful and hellward tendencies of the dance. Madelon only grasped the fact that she was there with Burr; but others wondered, and the surprise had been great when Dorothy in her blue brocade had appeared in the ball-room.

This had been largely of late years a liberal and Unitarian village, but Parson Fair had always held stanchly to his stern orthodox tenets, and promulgated them undiluted before his thinning congregations and in his own household. Dorothy could not only not play cards or dance, but she could not be present at a party where the cards were produced or the fiddle played. There was, indeed, a rumor that she had learned to dance when she was in Boston at school, but no one knew for certain.

Dorothy Fair was advancing daintily between the two long lines, holding up her blue brocade to clear her blue-satin shoes, to meet the young man from the opposite corner, flinging out gayly towards her, when suddenly, with no warning whatever, a great dark woman sped after her through the dance, like a wild animal of her native woods. She reached out her black hand and caught Dorothy by the white, lace-draped arm, and she whispered loud in her ear.

The people near, finding it hard to understand the African woman's thick tongue, could not exactly vouch for the words, but the purport of her hurried speech they did not mistake. Parson Fair had discovered Mistress Dorothy's absence, and home she must hasten at once. It was evident enough to everybody that staid and decorous Dorothy had run away to the ball with Burr Gordon, and a smothered titter ran down the files of the Virginia reel.

Burr Gordon cast a fierce glance around; then he sprang to Dorothy's side, and she looked palely and piteously up at him.

He pulled her hand through his arm and led her out of the ball-room, with the black woman following sulkily, muttering to herself. Burr bent closely down over Dorothy's drooping head as they passed out of the door. "Don't be frightened, sweetheart," whispered he. Madelon saw him as she lilted, and it seemed to her that she heard what he said.

It was not long after when she felt a touch on her shoulder as she sat resting between the dances, gazing with her proud, bright eyes down at the merry, chattering throng below. She turned, and her brother Richard stood there with a strange young man, and Richard held Louis's fiddle on his shoulder.

"This is Mr. Otis, Madelon," said Richard, "and he came up from Kingston to the ball, and he can fiddle as well as Louis, and he said 'twas a shame you should lilt all night and not have a chance to dance yourself; and so I ran home and got Louis's fiddle, and there are plenty down there to jump at the chance of you for a partner — and —" the boy leaned forward and whispered in his sister's ear: "Burr Gordon's gone — and Dorothy Fair."

Madelon turned her beautiful, proud face towards the stranger, and did not notice Richard at all. "Thank you, sir," said she, inclining her long neck; "but I care not to dance — I'd as lief lilt."

"But," said the strange young man, pressing forward impetuously and gazing into her black eyes, "you look tired; 'tis a shame to work you so."

"I rest between the dances, and I am not tired," said Madelon, coldly.

"I beg you to let me fiddle for the rest of the ball," pleaded the young man. "Let me fiddle while you dance; you may be sure I'll fiddle my best for you."

A tender note came into his voice, and, curiously enough, Madelon did not resent it, although she had never seen him before and he had no right. She looked up in his bright fair face with sudden hesitation, and his blue eyes bent half humorously, half lovingly upon her. She had a fierce desire to get away from this place, out into the night, and home. "I do not care to dance," said she, falteringly; "but I could go home, if you felt disposed to fiddle."

"Then go home and rest," cried the stranger, brightly. "'Tis a strain on the throat to lilt so long, and you cannot put in a new string as you can in a fiddle."

With that the young man came forward to the front of the little gallery, and Madelon yielded up her place hesitatingly.

"But you cannot dance yourself, sir," said she.

"I have danced all I want to to-night," he replied, and began tuning the fiddle.

"I'm sure I'm much obliged to you, sir," Madelon said, and got her hood and cloak from the back of the gallery with no more parley.

The young man cast admiring glances after her as she went out, with her young brother at her heels.

"I'm going home with you," Richard said to her as they went down the gallery stairs.

"Not a step," said she. "You've just been after the fiddle, and they're going to dance the Fisher's Hornpipe next."

"You'll be afraid in that lonesome stretch after you leave the village."

"Afraid!" There was a ring of despairing scorn in the girl's voice, as if she faced already such woe that the supposition of new terror was an absurdity.

They had come down to the ball-room floor, and were standing directly in front of the musicians' gallery. The young fiddler, Jim Otis, leaned over and looked at them.

"I don't care," said Richard, "I won't let you go alone unless you take my knife."

Madelon laughed. "What nonsense!" said she, and tried to pass her brother.

But Richard held her by the arm while he rummaged in his pocket for the great clasp-knife which he had earned himself by the sale of some rabbit-skins, and which was the pride of his heart and his dearest treasure, and opened it. "Here," said he, and he forced the clasp-knife into his sister's hand. Otis, leaning over the gallery, saw it all. Many of the dancers had gone to supper; there was no other person very near them. "If you should meet a *bear*, you could kill him with that knife — it's so strong," said the boy. "If you don't take it I'll go home with you, and it's so late father won't let me come out again to-night."

"Well, I'll take it," Madelon said, wearily, and she passed out of the ball-room with the knife in her hand, under her cloak.

When she got out in the cold night air she sped along fast over the creaking snow, still holding the knife clutched fast in her hand. She began to lilt again as she went, and again Burr and Dorothy danced together before her eyes. She passed Parson Fair's house, and the best-room windows were lighted. She thought that Burr was there, and she lilted more loudly the Virginia reel.

After Parson Fair's house was some time left behind, and she had come into the lengthy stretch of road, she saw a shadowy figure ahead. She could not at first tell whether it was moving towards or from her — whether it was a man or a woman; or, indeed, whether it were not a forest tree encroaching on the road and moving in the wind. She kept on swiftly, holding her knife under her cloak. She had stopped singing.

Presently she saw that the figure was a man, and coming her way; and then her heart stood still, for she knew by the swing of his shoulders that it was Burr Gordon. She threw back her proud head and sped along towards him, grasping her knife under her cloak and looking neither to the right nor left. She swerved not her eyes a hair's-breadth when she came close to him — so close that their shoulders almost touched in passing in the narrow path.

Suddenly there was a quick sigh in her ear — "Oh, Madelon!" Then an arm was flung around her waist and hot lips were pressed to her own.

The mixed blood of two races, in which action is quick to follow impulse, surged up to Madelon's head. She drew the hand which held the knife from under her cloak and struck. "Kiss me again, Burr Gordon, if you dare!" she cried out, and her cry was met by a groan as he fell away from her into the snow.

CHAPTER IV

Madelon stood for a second looking at the dark, prostrate form as one of her Iroquois ancestors might have looked at a fallen foe before he drew his scalping-knife; then suddenly the surging of the savage blood in her ears grew faint. She fell down on her knees beside him. "Have I killed you, Burr?" she said, and bent her face down to his — and it was not Burr, but Lot Gordon!

The white, peaked face smiled up at her out of the snow. "You haven't killed me if I die, since you took me for Burr," whispered Lot Gordon.

"Are you much hurt?"

"I — don't know. The knife has gone a little way into my side. It has not reached my heart, but that was hurt unto death already by life, so this matters not."

Madelon felt along his side and hit the handle of the clasp-knife, firmly fixed.

"Don't try to draw it out — you cannot," said Lot, and his pain forced a groan from him. "I'll live, if I can, till the wound is healed for the sake of your peace. I'd be content to die of it, since you gave it in vengeance for another man's kiss, if it were not for you. But they shall never know — they shall never — know." Lot's voice died away in a faint murmur between his parted lips; his eyes stared up with no meaning in them at the wintry stars.

Madelon ran back on the road to the village, taking great leaps through the snow, straining her eyes ahead. Now and then she cried out hoarsely, as if she really saw some one, "Hullo! hullo!" At the curve of the road she turned a headlong corner and ran roughly against a man who was hurrying towards her; and this time it was Burr Gordon.

Burr reeled back with the shock; then his face peered into hers with fear and wonder. "Is it you?" he stammered out. "What is the matter?"

But Madelon caught his arm in a hard grip. "Come, quick!" she gasped, and pulled him along the road after her.

"What is the matter?" Burr demanded, half yielding and half resisting.

Madelon faced him suddenly as they sped along. "I met your cousin Lot just below here and he kissed me, and I took him for you and stabbed him, if you must know," she sobbed out, dryly.

Burr gave a choking cry of horror.

"I think I — have killed him," said she, and pulled him on faster.

"And you meant to kill me?"

"Yes, I did."

"I wish to God you had!" Burr cried out, with a sudden fierce anger at himself and her; and now he hurried on faster than she.

Lot was quite motionless when they reached him. Burr threw himself down in the snow and leaned his ear to his cousin's heart. Madelon stood over them, panting. Suddenly a merry roulade of whistling broke the awful stillness. Two men were coming down the road whistling "Roy's Wife of Alidivalloch" as clearly soft and sweet as flutes, accented with human gayety and mirth.

On came the merry whistlers. Burr sprang up and grasped Madelon Hautville's arm. "He isn't dead," he whispered, hoarsely. "Somebody's coming. Go home, quick!"

But Madelon looked at him with despairing obstinacy. "I'll stay," said she.

"I tell you, go! Somebody is coming. I'll get help. I'll send for the doctor. Go home!"

"No!"

"Oh, Madelon, if you have ever loved me, go home!"

Madelon turned away at that. "I'll be there when they come for me," said she, and went swiftly down the road and out of sight in the converging distance of trees, with the snow muffling her footsteps.

When she reached home she groped her way into the living-room, which was lighted only by the low, red gleam of the coals on the hearth. Her father's gruff voice called out from the bedroom beyond: "That you, Madelon?"

"Yes," said she, and lighted a candle at the coals.

"Have the boys come?"

"No."

Madelon went up the steep stairs to her chamber, but before she opened her door her brother Louis's voice, broken with pain, besought her to come into his room and bathe his sprained shoulder for him. She went in, set the candle on the table, and rubbed in the cider-brandy and wormwood without a word. Louis, in the midst of his pain, kept looking up wonderingly at his sister's face. It looked as if it were frozen. She did not seem to see him. Nothing about her seemed alive but her gently moving hands.

Suddenly he gave a startled cry. "What's that? Have you cut your hand, Madelon?" Madelon glanced at her hand, and there was a broad red stain over the palm and three of her fingers.

"No," said she, and went on rubbing.

"But it looks like blood!" cried Louis, knitting his pale brows at her.

Madelon made no reply.

"Madelon, what is that on your hand?"

"Blood."

"How came it there?"

"You'll know to-morrow." Madelon put the stopper in the cider-brandy and wormwood bottle; then she covered up the wounded arm and went out.

"Madelon, what is it? What is the matter? What ails you?" Louis called after her.

"You'll know to-morrow," said she, and shut her chamber door, which was nearly opposite Louis's. His youngest brother Richard occupied the same room, having his little cot at the other side, under the window. When he came in, an hour later, Louis turned to him eagerly.

"Has anything happened?" he demanded.

The boy's face, which was always so like his sister's, had the same despair in it now. "Don't know of anything that's happened," he returned, surlily.

"What ails Madelon?"

"I tell you I don't know." Richard would say no more. He blew out his candle and tumbled into bed, turned his face to the window and lay awake until and hour before dawn. Then he arose, dressed himself, and went down-stairs. He put more wood on the hearth fire, then knelt down before it, and puffed out his boyish cheeks at the bellows until the new flames crept through the smoke. Then he lighted the lantern, and went to the barn to milk and feed the stock. That was always Richard's morning task, and he always on his way thither replenished the hearth fire, that his sister Madelon might have a lighter and speedier task at preparing breakfast. Madelon usually arose a half-hour after Richard, and she was not behindhand this morning. She entered the great living-room, lit the candles, and went about getting breakfast. Human daily needs arise and set on tragedy as remorselessly as the sun.

Madelon Hautville, who had washed but a few hours ago the stain of murder from her hand, in whose heart was an unsounded depth of despair, mixed up the corn-meal daintily with cream, and baked the cakes which her father and brothers loved before the fire, and laid the table. She had always attended to the needs of the males of her family with the stern faithfulness of an Indian squaw. Now, as she worked, the wonder, softer than her other emotions, was upon her as to how they would get on when she was in prison and after she was dead; for she made no doubt that she had killed Lot Gordon and the sheriff would be there presently for her, and she felt plainly the fretting of the rope around her soft neck. She hoped they would not come for her until breakfast was prepared and eaten, the dishes cleared away, and the house tidied; but she listened like a savage for a foot-fall and a hand at the door. She had packed a little bundle ready to take with her before she left her chamber. Her cloak and hood were laid out on the bed.

When she sat down at the table with her father and brothers, all of them except Richard and Louis stared at her with open amazement and questioned her. Richard and Louis stared furtively at their sister's face, as stiff, set, and pale as if she were dead, but they asked no questions. Madelon said, in a voice that was not hers, that she was not sick, and put pieces of Indian cake into her untasting mouth and listened. But breakfast was well over and the dishes put away before anybody came. And then it was not the sheriff to hale her to prison on a charge of murder, but an old man from the village big with news.

He was a relative of the Hautvilles, an uncle on the mother's side, old and broken, scarcely able to find his feeble way on his shrunken legs through the snow; but, with the instinct of gossip, the sharp nose for his neighbors' affairs, still alert in him, he had arisen at dawn to canvass the village, and had come thither at first, since he anticipated that he might possibly have the delight of bringing the intelligence before any of the family had heard it elsewhere. He came in, dragging his old, snow-laden feet, tapping heavily with his stout stick, and settled, cackling, into a chair.

"Heard the news?" queried Uncle Luke basset, his eyes, like black sparks, twinkling rapidly at all their faces.

Madelon set the cups and saucers on the dresser.

"We don't have any time for anybody's business but our own," quoth David Hautville, gruffly. He did not like his wife's uncle. He was tightening a string in his bass-viol; he pulled it as he spoke, and it gave out a fierce twang. Louis sat moodily over the fire with his painful arm in wet bandages. Richard was whittling kindling-wood, with nervous speed, beside him. Eugene and Abner were cleaning their guns. They all looked at the eager old man except Richard and Louis and Madelon.

"Burr Gordon has killed Lot so's to get his property," proclaimed the old man, and his voice broke with eager delight and importance.

Madelon gave a cry and sprang forward in front of him. "It's a lie!" she shouted.

The old man laughed in her face. "No, 'tain't, Madelon. You're showin' a Christian sperrit to stan' up for him when he's jilted ye for another gal, but 'tain't a lie. His knife, with his name on to it, was a-stickin' out of Lot's side."

"*It's a lie!* I killed him with my brother Richard's knife!"

The old man shrank back before her in incredulous horror. The great bass-viol fell to the ground like a woman as David strode forward and Abner and Eugene turned their shocked, white faces from their guns.

"I killed him with Richard's knife," repeated Madelon.

Richard got up and came around before her, thrusting his

hand in his pocket. He pulled out his own clasp-knife, and brandished it in her face. "Here is my knife," he cried, fiercely — "my knife, with my name cut in the handle. Say you killed Lot Gordon with it again!"

Madelon snatched the knife out of her brother's hand and looked at it with straining eyes. There, indeed, was a rude "R. H." cut in the horn handle. She gasped. "What does this mean?" she cried out.

"It means you have lost your wits," answered Richard, contemptuously; but his eyes on his sister's face were full of pleading agony.

"What knife did you give me when I started home last night?"

"I gave you no knife."

Old Luke Basset asserted himself again. "The gal's lost her balance," he said. "It was Burr Gordon's knife, with his name cut into it, that was stickin' out of Lot Gordon's side."

"Is Lot Gordon dead?" Louis demanded, hoarsely.

"No, he ain't dead, but the doctor thinks he can't live long. Ephraim Steele and Eleazer Hooper were a-goin' home from the ball when they come right on Lot layin' side of the road and Burr a-tryin' to draw his knife out, so it shouldn't testify against him."

"It's a lie!" Madelon groaned. "Burr Gordon did not kill him. It was I! He met me, and tried to — kiss me, and — the knife was in my hand — Richard made me take it because I was coming home alone, and there had been rumors of a bear."

"I did not," persisted Richard, doggedly. "I did not make her take my knife. Here is my knife, with my name cut in the handle."

Madelon turned on him fiercely. "You did, you know you did!" said she.

"Here is my knife, with my name cut on the handle."

"You gave me a knife as I was coming out of the tavern."

"No, I did not."

"You did, and I killed him with it. It was not Burr! I ran for help, and I met Burr, and I told him what I had done, and he went back with me to Lot. Then he sent me home when he heard somebody coming. Ask Lot Gordon if I did not kill him; if he can speak he can tell you."

"There won't neither him nor Burr say a word," said the old man, "but there was Burr's knife a-stickin' into Lot's side, with his name cut into it."

Madelon turned sharply to Louis. "You saw the blood on my hand when I was rubbing your arm last night," she said.

He made no reply, but stared gloomily at the fire.

"Louis, you saw Lot Gordon's blood on my hand?"

Louis sprang up with an oath, and pushed past her out of the room.

"Louis," Madelon cried, "tell them!"

"She is trying to shield Burr Gordon!" Louis called back, fiercely, and the closing door shook the house like a cannon-shot.

"Where is Burr?" Madelon demanded of old Luke Basset.

"The sheriff took him to New Salem to jail this morning," he replied, grinning.

Madelon gave a great cry and started to rush out of the room, but her father stood in her way.

"Where are you going?" he asked, sternly.

"I am going to get my hood and cloak, and then I am going to Lot Gordon's." Her father stood aside, and she went out and upstairs to her chamber. She took up the red cloak which lay on her bed, and examined it eagerly to see if by chance there was a blood stain thereon to prove her guilt and Burr Gordon's innocence, but she could find none. She had flung it back when she struck. She looked also carefully at her pretty ball gown, but the black fabric showed no stain.

When she went down-stairs with her cloak and hood on old Luke Basset was gone, and so were her brothers. Her father stood waiting for her, and he had on his fur cap and his heavy cloak. He came forward and took her firmly by the arm. "I'm going with you to Lot Gordon's," said he. And they went out together and up the road, he still keeping a firm hand on his daughter's arm, and neither spoke all the way to Lot Gordon's house.

When they reached it David Hautville opened the door without touching the knocker, and strode in with Madelon following. Old Margaret Bean was just passing through the entry with a great roll of linen cloths in her arms, and she stopped when she saw them.

"How is he?" whispered David, hoarsely.

"He's pretty low," returned Margaret Bean, at the same time nodding her head cautiously towards the door on her right. Long, smooth loops of sallow hair fell from Margaret Bean's clean white cap over her cheeks, which looked as if they had been scrubbed and rasped red with tears. Her own gray hair was strained back out of sight — not to be discovered, even when there was a murder in the house.

"Does he know anybody?" queried David Hautville.

"Just as well as ever he did." Margaret Bean rubbed a tear dry on her cheek with her starched apron.

"We've got to see him, then."

"I dunno as you can — the doctor —"

"I don't care anything about the doctor! We've got to see him!" David's voice rang out quite loud in the hush of murder and death which seemed to fill the house. Margaret Bean stood aside with a scared look. David Hautville threw open the door on the right, and he and Madelon went in.

Lot Gordon's eyes turned towards them, but not his head. He lay as still in bed as if he were already dead, and his long body raised the gay patchwork quilt in a stiff ridge like a grave.

Madelon went close to him and bent over him. "Tell who stabbed you," said she, in a sharp voice.

Lot looked up at her, and a red flush came over his livid face.

"Tell who stabbed you."

Lot smiled feebly, but he did not speak.

Margaret Bean came in, with her old husband shuffling at her heels. A great face, bristling with a yellow stubble of beard, appeared in the door. It belonged to the sheriff, Jonas Hapgood, who had just returned from taking Burr to New Salem. Madelon cast a desperate glance around at them. "Lot Gordon," she cried out, "tell them — tell them I was the one who stabbed you, and set Burr free!"

There was a chuckle from Jonas Hapgood in the door. "Likely story," he muttered to Margaret Bean's husband, and the old man nodded wisely.

"Tell them!" commanded Madelon. She reached out a hand as if she would shake Lot Gordon into obedience, wounded unto death although he was, but Lot only smiled up in her face.

Then David Hautville bent his stern face down to the sick man's. "Lot Gordon, tell the truth before God, daughter of mine or no daughter of mine," said he, in his deep voice. Lot only followed Madelon with his longing, smiling eyes.

"Speak, Lot Gordon!"

The wounded man turned his eyes on David and made a feeble motion, scarcely more than a quiver of his hand, which seemed to express negation.

"Can't you speak?"

Again Lot made that faint signal.

"He ain't spoke sence they brought him home," said Margaret Bean — "not a word to the doctor nor nobody."

"I couldn't get a word out of him," announced the sheriff, stepping farther into the room. "In course, there was Burr's knife and Burr himself over him when the others came up, and that was proof enough; but still we kinder thought we'd like to have Lot's word for it afore he died, in case it came to hangin' with Burr; but I guess he's past speakin'. I miss my guess if he can sense anything we say."

"Tell them — tell them I was the one who stabbed you, and Burr is innocent!" Madelon pleaded; but he smiled back at her unmoved.

Jonas Hapgood's great body shook with mirth. "Likely story a gal did it," he chuckled.

"I did do it!" returned Madelon, fiercely, turning to him. "I guess you don't want your beau hung."

"I tell you I killed this man. I am the one to be hung!"

CHAPTER V

The sheriff turned to David Hautville. "Guess you'd better take your gal home," he said, his red, bristling cheeks broad with laughter. "Guess she's kind of off her balance, she feels so bad about her beau."

David's black eyes flashed haughtily at Jonas Hapgood, who straightened his face suddenly. He deigned not a word to him, but he turned to his daughter with a stern air. "Whether it is one way, or whether it is the other way," said he, "we go neither by staying here. Come home."

"I won't go!"

David looked sharply at his daughter's face. Jonas Hapgood's doubt was over him too. He wondered, with a great spasm of wrath, if she could be accusing herself to shield this man who had played her false.

He grasped her arm again. "Come," he said, "I'll have no more of this," and Madelon went out with her father. Full of spirit as she was, she had always been strangely docile with him. He had ruled all his children with a firm hand from their youth up, and tuned their wills to suit his ear as he did his viol strings.

"I'll have no foolery," he said to her, gruffly, when they were out on the road. "I'll have no putting yourself in the wrong to save a man that's given you the go-by. If ye be fooling me, ye can stop it now if you're a daughter of mine." He shook his head fiercely at her.

But Madelon answered him with a burst of wrath that equalled his own. "I stabbed him because I took him for the man who jilted me a-trying to kiss me, with Dorothy Fair's kiss on his lips. *Me!*" she cried; and she raised her hand as if she would have struck again had Burr Gordon and his false lips been there.

Her father looked at her gloomily, then strode on with his eyes on the snowy ground. He was still in doubt. David Hautville had that primitive order of mind which distrusts and holds in contempt that which it cannot clearly comprehend, and he could not comprehend womankind. His sons were to him as words of one syllable in straight lines; his daughter was written in compound and involved sentences, as her mother had been before her. Fond and proud of Madelon as he was, and in spite of his stern anxiety, her word had not the weight with him that one of his son's would have had. It was as if he had visions of endless twistings and complexities which might give it the lie, and rob it, at all events, of its direct force.

Indeed, Madelon strengthened this doubt by crying out passionately all at once, as they went on: "Father, you must believe me! I tell you I did it! I — don't let them hang him! Father!" All

Madelon's proud fierceness was gone for a moment. She looked up at her father, choking with great sobs.

David smiled down at her convulsed face. "She's nothing but a woman," he thought to himself, and he thought also, with a throb of angry relief, that she had not killed Lot Gordon. "Come along home and red up the house, and let's have no more fooling," he said, roughly, and strode on faster and would not say another word, although Madelon besought him hard to assure her that he believed her, and that Burr should not be hanged, until they reached the Hautville house. Then he turned on her and said, with keen sarcasm that stung more than a whip-lash, "'Tis Parson Fair's daughter and not mine that should come down the road in broad daylight a-bawling for Burr Gordon."

Madelon started back, and her face stiffened and whitened. She shut her mouth hard and followed her father into the house. The great living-room was empty; indeed, not one of the Hautville sons was in the house; even Louis was gone. David took his axe out of the corner and set out for the woods to cut some cedar fire-logs. Madelon put the house in order, setting the kitchen and pantry to rights, going through the icy chambers and making the high feather beds. In her own room she paused long and searched again, holding up her red cloak and her ball dress to the window, where they caught the wintry light, for a stain of blood that might prove her guilt; but she could find none.

Madelon prepared dinner for her father and brothers as usual, and when it was ready to be dished she stood in the doorway, with the north wind buffeting her in the face, and blew the dinner-horn with a blast that could be heard far off in the woods.

Presently her father emerged from under the snowy boughs with his axe over his shoulder, and shortly afterwards Eugene and Abner came, in Indian file, with their guns. Eugene was carrying a fat rabbit by its long ears. Louis and Richard did not come at all. David asked sternly of their brothers where they were, but neither Eugene nor Abner knew. They had not seen them since David and Madelon left for Lot Gordon's that morning.

Madelon set the food before her father and her brothers, and took her place as usual, and ate as she might have filled a crock with milk or cakes, tasting nothing which she put into her mouth. She did not during the meal say another word concerning the tragedy in which she was living, but there was a strange silent vehemence and fire about her which seemed louder than speech. Now and then her father and her brothers started and stared at her as if she had cried out. Two red spots had come on her brown cheeks; her eyes were glittering with dark light; her lips were a firm red; her fingers stiffened with nervous clutches. She looked as if every muscle in her were strained and rigid for a leap.

After dinner Eugene and Abner went out again with their guns, and David smoked his old pipe by the fire, while Madelon put away the dishes and swept the floor. When her work was finished the pipe was smoked out, and David rose up slowly, clapped his fur cap over his white head, and took up his axe.

"Mind ye say what ye said this morning to nobody else," he said, as he went out the door.

"I'll say it with my dying breath," returned Madelon, and she caught her breath, as if it were indeed her last, as she spoke.

"Accuse yourself of murder, would ye, and be hung, and leave your own kith and kin with nobody to keep house for them, for the sake of a man that's left ye for another girl!"

"Father, I tell you that *I* did it!"

But David clapped to the door on her speech, and the awful truth of it seemed to smite her in her own face.

Madelon went up-stairs, and brushed and braided her black hair before her glass; but the face therein did not look like her own to her, and she felt all the time as if she were braiding and wreathing the hair around another's head. One of those deeds had she committed which lead a man to see suddenly the stranger that abides always in his flesh and in his own soul, and makes him realize that of all the millions of earth there is not one that he knows not better than his own self, nor whose face can look so strange to him in the light of his own actions.

Madelon put her red cloak over her shoulders as she might have put it on a lay-figure, and tied on her hood. Then she went down-stairs, out of the house to the barn, and put the side-saddle on the roan mare.

Not another woman in the village, and scarcely a man except the Hautville sons, would have dared to ride this roan, with the backward roll of her vicious eyes and her wicked, flat-laid ears; but Madelon Hautville could not be thrown.

The mare, when she was saddled, danced an iron-bound dance in the barn bay, but Madelon bade her stand still, and she obeyed, her nostrils quivering, the breath coming from them in a snort of smoke, and every muscle under her roan hide vibrating.

Then Madelon placed her foot in the stirrup, and was in the saddle, pulling the bit hard against the jaw, and the mare shot out of the barn with a fierce lash-out of her heels and an upheaval of her gaunt roan flanks that threatened to dash the girl's head against the lintel of the door.

But Madelon knew with what she had to do, and she bent low in the saddle and passed out in safety. Then she spared not the mare for nigh three miles on the New Salem road. It was ten miles to New Salem, and it did not take long to reach it, riding a horse who went at times as if all the fiends were in chase, and often sprang out like a bow into the wayside bushes, and was off with a new spurt of vicious terror. It was still far from sundown when Madelon Hautville tied the roan outside the jail where Burr Gordon lay.

Burr was sitting in his cell, which was nothing but a rough chamber with whitewashed walls and a grated window. It was furnished with a bed, a table, and a chair. He had an inkstand and a great sheet of paper on the table, and he was writing a letter when the bolt shot and the jailer entered with Madelon Hautville.

Burr looked at her with a white, incredulous face. Then he started up and came forward, but Madelon did not look at him. She turned to the jailer, Alvin Mead. "I want to see him alone," said she, imperatively.

"It's again my orders," said the jailer. He was a great man, with an arm like a crow-bar. He was reputed to have used it as one many a time at a house-raising.

"I've got to see him alone!"

"He's in here on a charge of murder, and it's again my orders," repeated Alvin Mead, like a parrot.

"I've got to see him alone!"

Alvin Mead looked at her irresolutely with his stupid light eyes; then all his great system of bone and muscle seemed to back out of the room before her. He shut the door after him, and they heard the bolt slide.

Madelon turned to Burr. "Tell them," she gasped out — "tell them it was — I!"

Burr did not speak for a minute; he stood looking at her. "Perhaps I am not any too much of a man," he said, slowly, at length, "but you ask me to be a good deal less of a man than I am."

Madelon did not seem to hear him. "I have told them I did it! I have told them all," said she, "but they won't believe me — they won't believe me! *You* must tell them."

"I will die before I will tell them," said Burr Gordon.

Madelon looked at his white face, which was set against hers like a rock; then she gave a great cry and fell down on her knees before him. "Tell them," she moaned, "or they will hang you — they will hang you, Burr!"

"Let them hang me, then!"

"Tell them; they won't believe me!"

Burr caught hold of her two arms and raised her to her feet. "See here, Madelon," said he, "don't you know —"

She looked at him dumbly.

"Don't you know — I would not tell them if they would, but — I might tell them until I was gray, and they would not believe me!"

Madelon cried out sharply, as if she in her turn had been struck to the heart.

"It is true," Burr said, quietly.

"Then if he dies without telling, there is no way of — saving you —"

Burr shook his head.

"The knife — how — came your knife there instead of Richard's?"

Burr smiled.

Bluish shadows came around Madelon's dark eyes and her mouth. She gasped for breath as she spoke. "I — have — killed you, then," said she. Suddenly she put up her white, stiffly quivering lips to Burr's. "Kiss me!" she cried out. "I beg you to give me the kiss that I might have killed you for last night!"

Burr bent down and kissed her, and she threw her arms around him and pressed his head to her bosom. "They shall not," she cried out, fiercely — "they shall not hang you! I will make them believe me! Don't be afraid, don't be afraid, Burr."

"Madelon," Burr said, huskily, "I have been double-faced and false to you, but, as God is my witness, I'm glad I've got the chance to suffer in your stead."

"You shall not! They shall believe I did it. I will make Lot Gordon tell. He shall tell before he dies!"

The bolt slid back, and Alvin Mead's great bulk darkened the doorway. Madelon turned her face towards him, with her arms still clasping Burr and holding his head to her bosom. "This man is innocent!" she cried out, with a fierce gesture of protection, as if she were defending her young instead of her false lover. "I tell you he is innocent — you must let him go! I am the one who stabbed Lot Gordon!"

Alvin Mead stared; his heavy pink jaw lopped.

"I tell you, you must let him go!" She released Burr from her arms and gave him a push towards the door. "Go out," she said; "I am the one to stay here."

But Alvin Mead collected and brought about his great body with a show of lumbering fists. "Come," said he, "this ain't a-goin to do. We can't have no sech work as this, young woman. It's time you went."

"Let him go, I tell you!" commanded Madelon, confronting him fiercely. "I am going to stay."

"They won't let you come again if you don't go quietly now," Burr whispered, and he laid his hand on her nervous shoulder.

"I ruther guess we won't have no sech doin's again," said Alvin Mead, with sulky assent.

"You must go, Madelon."

Madelon tied on her hood. Her white face had its rigid, desperate look again.

"I will make them believe me yet, and you shall be set free," she said to Burr, with a stern nod, and passed out, while Alvin Mead stood back to give her passage, watching her with sullen and wary eyes. He was, in truth, half afraid of her.

CHAPTER VI

When Madelon, returning from New Salem, came in sight of her home the first thing which she noticed was her father in the yard in front of the house.

David Hautville's great figure stood out in the dusk of the snowy landscape like a giant's. He was motionless. The roan mare's gallop had evidently struck his ear some time before, and he knew that Madelon was returning. He did not even look her way as she drew nearer, but when she rode into the yard he made a swift movement forward and seized the mare by the bridle. She reared, but Madelon sat firm, with wretched, undaunted eyes upon her father. David Hautville's eyes blazed back at her out of the whiteness of his wrath.

"Where have you been?" he demanded, in a thick voice.

"To New Salem."

"What for?"

"To see Burr, and beg him to confess that I killed Lot."

"You didn't."

"I did."

"Fool!" David Hautville jerked the bridle so fiercely that the mare reared far back again. He jerked her down to her feet, and she made a vicious lunge at him, but he shunted her away.

"I'll fasten you into your chamber," he shouted, "if this work goes on! I'll stop your making a fool of yourself."

"It is Lot Gordon that is making fools of you all," said Madelon, in a hard, quiet voice.

"Did Burr Gordon say he didn't stab him?" cried her father.

"No; he wouldn't own it. He is trying to shield me."

"He did it himself, and he'll hang for it."

"No, he won't hang for what I did while I draw the breath of life. I've got the strength of ten in me. You don't know me, if I am your daughter." Madelon freed her bridle with a quick movement, and the mare flew forward into the barn.

David Hautville stood looking after her in utter fury and bewilderment. Her last words rang in his ears and seemed true to him. He felt as if he did not know his own daughter. This awakening and lashing into action, by the terrible pressure of circumstances, of strange ancestral traits which he had himself transmitted was beyond his simple comprehension. He shook his head with a fierce helplessness and went into the barn.

"Go in and get the supper," he ordered, "and I'll take care of the mare."

As Madelon came out of the stall he grasped her roughly by the arm and peered sharply into her face. The thought seized him that she must surely not be in her right mind — that Burr's treatment of her and his danger had turned her brain. "Be you crazy, Madelon?" he asked, in his straightforward simplicity, and there was an accent of doubt and pity in his voice.

"No, father," she replied, "I am not crazy. Let me go."

She broke away from him and was out of the barn door, but suddenly she turned and came running back. The sudden softness in his voice had stirred the woman in her to weakness. She went close to her father, and threw up her arms around his great neck, and clung to him, and sobbed as if she would sob her soul away, and pleaded with him as for her life.

"Father!" she cried — "father, help me! Believe me! Tell them I did it! Tell them it is true! Don't let them hang Burr. Help me to save him, father! Don't let them! Save him! Oh, you will save him, father? You will? Tell me, father — tell me, tell me!" Madelon's voice rose into a wild shriek.

A sudden conviction of his solution of the matter and of his own astuteness came over David Hautville's primitive masculine intelligence. His daughter was wellnigh distraught with her lover's faithlessness and his awful crime and danger. She was to be watched and guarded lest she make a further spectacle of herself; but treated softly as might be, for she was naught but a woman, and liable to mischievous ailments of nerve and brain. David pressed his daughter's dark head with his hard, tender hand against his shoulder, then forced her gently away from him.

"It'll be all right," said he, soothingly — "it'll be all right. Don't you worry."

"Father, you will?"

"I'll fix it all right. Don't you worry."

"Father, you promise?"

"I'll do everything I can. Don't you worry, Madelon. You'd better go in and get supper now. I'll go along to the house with you and get the lantern. It's getting too dark to do the work here."

David drew his daughter along, out of the barn, across the snowy yard to the house, she pleading frantically all the way, he soothing her with his sudden wisdom of assent and evasion.

The hearth fire was blazing high when Madelon entered the kitchen. The red glare of it was on her white face, upturned to her father's with one last pleading of despair. She clutched his arm and shook his great frame to and fro.

"Father, promise me you'll go over to New Salem to-night and tell them to set him free and take me instead! Father!"

"We'll see about it, Madelon," answered David Hautville. There was a tone in his voice which she had never heard before. It might have come unconsciously to himself from some memory, so old that it was itself forgotten, of his dead wife's voice over the child in her cradle. Some echo of it might have yet lingered in the old father's soul, through something finer than his instinct for sweet sounds from human throat and viol — through his ear for love.

"Get the supper now, and we'll see about it," said David Hautville. He began fumbling with clumsy fingers, all unused to women's gear, at the string of this daughter's cloak; but she pulled herself away from him suddenly, and the old hard lines came into her face. "We'll say no more about it," said she. She lit a candle quickly at the hearth fire, and was out of the room to put away her cloak and hood. Her father lighted his lantern slowly and went back to the barn, plodding meditatively through the snowy track, with the melting mood still strong upon him. He was disposed to carry matters now with a high and tender hand with the girl to bring her to reason, and he brought all his crude diplomacy to bear upon the matter.

When he reached the barn his son Eugene stood in the doorway. He had just come from the woods, and the smell of wounded cedar-trees was strong about him. He stood leaning upon his axe as if it were a staff. "Who's been out with the mare?" he asked.

"Your sister."

"Where?"

"To New Salem."

"To see *him*?"

David nodded grimly. His lantern cast a pale circle of light on the snow about them.

"About — that?"

"To get him to own up she did it."

Eugene Hautville stared at his father, scowling his handsome dark brows. He was the most graceful mannered of all the Hautville sons, and by some accounted the best-looking.

"Is she crazy?" he said.

"No, she's a woman," returned his father, with a strange accent of contempt and toleration.

"Did the coward lay it to her when she gave him the chance?" demanded Eugene.

"No; she said he wouldn't, to shield her."

Eugene moved his axe suddenly; the lantern-light struck it, and there was a bright flash of sharp steel in their eyes. "Shield her!" he cried out, with an oath. "I wish I could meet him in the path once. I'd give him a taste before they put the rope 'round his neck, the lying murderer!"

David nodded his head in savage assent.

"What's going to be done with Madelon?" cried Eugene, fiercely.

"I've been thinking —" said his father, slowly.

"No sister of mine shall go about rolling herself in the dust at that fellow's feet if I can help it."

"I've been thinking — would you lock her in her chamber a spell?"

"Lock Madelon in her chamber! She'd get out or she'd beat her brains out against the wall."

"I don't know but she would," assented David, perplexedly. "You can't count on a woman when they rise up. She might go away a spell."

"Where?"

"We might send her somewhere."

Eugene laughed. The roan mare was pawing in her stall. Now and then she pounded the floor with a clattering thud like an iron flail.

"How far do you suppose that mare would go if you tried to send her anywhere?" he asked.

"Maybe Madelon wouldn't go."

"You'd have to halter the mare," said Eugene, "and drag her half the way and stand from under, or she'd trample you down the other." Eugene, although his words were strong, spoke quite softly, lowering his sweet tenor. From where they stood they could see Madelon moving to and fro behind the kitchen windows preparing supper.

"I don't know what to do," said David, after a pause.

"Watch her," returned Eugene, quietly.

"Watch her?"

"Yes. I've been under cover days before now watching for a pretty white fox or a deer I wanted." Eugene laughed pleasantly.

"Will you?"

"I'll stay by the house to-morrow. She sha'n't go about accusing herself of murder to save the man that's jilted her if I can help it." As he spoke Eugene's handsome face darkened again vindictively. He hated Burr Gordon for another reason of his own that nobody suspected.

Suddenly Abner Hautville came running into the yard. "Who is it there?" he called out. "Is that you, father? That you, Eugene? Hello!"

"Hello!" Eugene called back. "What's the matter?"

Abner come panting alongside. He had run from the village, and, vigorous as he was, breath came hard in the thin air. It was a very cold night.

"Where have they gone?" he demanded.

"Who?"

"Louis and Richard. Where have they gone?"

There was a ghastly look in Abner's face, in spite of the glowing red which the cold wind had brought to it. The other man seemed to catch it and reflect it in their own faces as they stared at him.

Eugene turned quickly to his father. "Aren't they in the house?" he asked.

"No, they ain't," returned David, with his eyes still on Abner's face.

"Sure they ain't up chamber?"

"No; I was home a good half-hour before Madelon came. There wasn't a soul in the house, and nobody could have come home since without my knowing it."

"They didn't come home this noon either," said Eugene.

"Thought you said they'd gone to see to their traps on West Mountain?" David rejoined.

"Thought they had when they didn't come." Eugene turned impatiently on Abner. "Where do you think they've gone — what do you mean by looking so?" he cried.

Abner dug his heel into the snow. "Don't know," he returned, in a surly voice.

"What do you suspect, then? Good God! can't you speak out?"

Abner's features were heavier than his brother's — his speech and manner slower. He paused a second, even then; then he turned towards the house, and spoke, with his face away from them, with a curious directness and taciturnity. "Didn't go to the traps on West Mountain," he said, then; "went there myself. They hadn't been there — no tracks; was home before father was to-night. Louis and Richard hadn't come. Went down to the village; hadn't been there."

"You don't mean Louis and Richard have run away?" demanded David.

"Both their guns and their powder-horns and shot-bags are gone," said Abner.

"They would have taken them anyway," said Louis.

"The chest in Louis's chamber is unlocked and the money he kept in the till is gone, and his fiddle is gone, and the cider-brandy and wormwood bottle to bathe his arm with, and two shoulders of pork out of the cellar, and a sack of potatoes, and the blankets off his and Richard's beds are gone too," said Abner. He began to move towards the house.

His father made a bound after him and grasped his arm. "What do you mean?" he cried out. "What do you think they've run away for?"

"Know as much as I do," replied Abner. He wrenched his arm away and strode on towards the house. Then David Hautville and his son Eugene stood looking at each other with a surmise of horror growing in their eyes.

"What does he mean?" David whispered, hoarsely.

Eugene shook his head.

Presently Eugene went into the barn and fell to feeding the roan mare, and David plunged heavily back to the house. He and Abner sat one on each side of the fire and furtively watched Madelon preparing supper.

She spoke never a word. Her red lips were a red line of resolution. Her despairing eyes were fixed upon her work without a glance for either of them.

However, when supper was set on the table, and she had blown the horn at the door and waited, and nobody else came, she turned with sudden life upon her father and her brothers, who had already begun to taste the smoking hasty-pudding. "Where are the others?" she cried out, shrilly. "Where are Louis and Richard?"

The men glanced at one another under sullen eyelids, but nobody answered. "Where are they?" she repeated.

"You know as much about it as we do," Eugene said, then, in his soft voice.

Madelon stood with wild eyes flashing from one to another. Then she gave a sudden spring out of the room, and they heard her swift feet on the chamber-stairs. The men ate their hasty-pudding, bending their brows over it as if it were a witches' mess instead of their ordinary home fare.

Madelon came back so rapidly that she seemed to fly over the stairs. They scarcely heard the separate taps of her feet. She burst into the room and faced them in a sort of fury. "They have gone!" she gasped out. "Louis and Richard have gone! Where are they?"

David Hautville slowly shook his head. Then he took another spoonful of pudding. The brothers bent with stern assiduity over their bowls.

"You have hid them away!" shrieked Madelon. "You have hid them away lest Louis own that he saw blood on my hand, and Richard that he gave me his knife! What have you done with them?"

Not one of the three men spoke. They swallowed their pudding.

"Father! Abner! Eugene!" said Madelon, "tell me what you have done with my brothers, who can testify that I killed Lot Gordon, and save Burr?"

David Hautville wiped his mouth on his sleeve, rose up, and took his daughter firmly by the arm.

"We know no more what has become of your brothers than you do," said he. "If they have gone away for the reason you say, your old father would be the first to bring them back, if you were guilty as you say, daughter of mine though you be. But we know well enough, wherever your brothers have gone, and for whatever cause they have gone, that you have done nothing worse then go daft, as women will, to shield a fellow that's used you ill. You shall put us to no more shame while I am your father and you under my roof. Abner, fill up a bowl with the pudding."

Madelon's face was deathly white and full of rebellion as she looked up in her father's, but she held herself still with a stern dignity and did not struggle. David Hautville's will was up. His hand on her soft arm was like a vise of steel. The memories of her childhood were strong upon her. She knew of old that there was no appeal, and was too proud to contend where she must yield.

"Take the bowl," said her father, when Abner extended it filled with the steaming pudding — "take the bowl, and go you to your chamber. Eat your supper, and get in to your bed and stay there till morning."

Madelon still looked at her father with that same look of speechless but unyielding rebellion. She did not stir to take the bowl or go to her chamber.

"Do as I bid ye!" ordered her father, in a great voice.

Madelon took the bowl from her brother's hand and went out of the room as she was bid; and yet as she went they all knew that there was no yielding in her.

CHAPTER VII

The next morning Madelon came down-stairs as usual and prepared breakfast. When it was ready the family sat up to the table and ate silently and swiftly. No one addressed a word to Madelon. After breakfast David and his son Abner put on their leather jackets and their fur caps, and set forth for the woods with their axes, but Eugene lounged gracefully over to the hearth and sat down on the settle, and began reading his Shakespeare book. Eugene was the only one of the Hautvilles who ever read books. He studied faithfully the few in the house — the Shakespeare, the *Pilgrim's Progress*, Milton, and *Gulliver's Travels*. The others wondered at him. They could not understand how any one who could handle a gun or a musical instrument could lay finger on a book. "Made-up things," said Abner once, with a scornful motion towards Shakespeare.

"No more made-up than fugue," retorted Eugene, hotly; but they all cried out on him.

This morning Madelon cast one quick glance at him as he sauntered over to the settle with his book. Then she did not look his way again. She worked quietly, setting the kitchen to rights.

The day was very cold; the light in the room was dim and white, the windows were coated so thickly with the hoar-frost. Eugene kept stirring the fire and adding sticks as he read.

Finally, Madelon had finished her work in the kitchen, and went up-stairs. Then Eugene arose reluctantly, went out into the cold entry, and stood by the door with his book in hand. Madelon, passing across the landing above, looked down and saw him standing there, and knew that what she suspected was true — that her brother was mounting guard over her lest she leave the house.

She finished her work in the chamber, and came down-stairs with some knitting-work in hand. She seated herself quietly in her own cushioned rocking-chair, and fell to work with yarn and clicking needles, like any peaceful housewife. She knitted and Eugene read, bending his handsome dark face, smiling with pleasure, over his Shakespeare book. This fierce winter day he was reading "A Midsummer-Night's Dream," and letting his fancy revel with Shakespeare's fairies in an enchanted summer wood. He was, however, alert as a watch-dog. He could at an instant's warning leave that delicate and dainty crew and those flowery shores, and intercept his sister, should she attempt to pass him and escape from the house.

Still, his alertness all came to naught, for Madelon, like some fleeing fox, took a sudden turn which no canny hunter could have anticipated. She sat somewhat away from the hearth and well at Eugene's back. He would have asked her why she did not draw nearer the fire and if she were not cold had he not feared to encounter a sulky humor. He could not see the lengths of linen cloth, which she herself had spun and woven, lying in a great heap on the floor, half at her back, half under her petticoats. However, could he have seen it he would have thought of it merely as some mysterious domestic and feminine proceeding about which he neither knew nor cared to know anything.

Madelon, as she knitted, ever measured the distance between her brother and herself with her great black eyes, training her nerves and muscles for what she had to do as she would have trained a bow and arrow.

Eugene turned a leaf in his Shakespeare book. Madelon made a leap, so soft and swift that it seemed like an onslaught of Silence itself, and he was smothered and wound about and entangled in folds of linen as if it had been in truth his winding-sheet. He struggled as best he might against his linen bands, and cried out as angrily as he could for the linen that bound his mouth and his eyes, but he could not release himself. Eugene was strong and lithe, but Madelon was nearly as strong as he at any time; and now the great tension of her nerves seemed to inform all her muscles with the strength of steel wire.

Eugene sat bound hard and fast to the settle, with his face swathed like a mummy's, with only enough space clear for breath. "Let me go, or I'll —" he threatened, in his smothered tone.

Madelon made no reply. She watched him struggle to be sure that he could not free himself. Then she went out of the room. Eugene called after her in a choke of fury, but she spoke not a word.

Up-stairs she hastened to her own chamber, and put on her red cloak and hood, and was down the stairs again, out the door, and hurrying up the road to the village. From time to time she glanced behind her to be sure that her brother had not freed himself, and was not in pursuit; then she sped on faster. The road was glare with ice, but she did not slow her pace for that. She was as sure-footed as a hare. She kept her arms close to her sides under her red cloak, and did not pause until she came out on the village street where the houses were thick. Then she went at a rapid walk, still glancing sharply behind her to see if she were followed, until she came to Parson Fair's house. She went up the front walk, between the rows of ice-coated box, and up the stone steps under the stately columned porch, and raised the knocker and let it fall with sharp impetus. The door opened speedily a little way, and Parson Fair himself stood there, his pale, stern old face framed in the dark aperture. He bowed with gentle courtesy and bade her good-morning, and Madelon courtesied hurriedly and spoke out her errand with no preface.

"Can I see your daughter, sir?" said she.

Parson Fair looked at Madelon's white face, touched on the cheeks and lips with feverish red, at her set mouth and desperate eyes. The story of her connection with the Gordon tragedy had not penetrated to his study, neither did he know how Burr had forsaken her for his Dorothy; but he saw something was amiss with her, although he was not well versed in the signs of a woman's face. Parson Fair, moreover, felt somewhat of interest in this Madelon Hautville, for he had a decorously restrained passion for sweet sounds which she had often gratified. Many a Sabbath day had he sat in his beetling pulpit and striven to keep his mind fixed upon the spirit of the hymn alone, in spite of his leaping pulses, when Madelon's great voice filled the meeting-house. It was probable that he also, notwithstanding his Christian grace, shared somewhat the popular sentiments towards these musical and Bohemian Hautvilles; yet he looked with a dignified kindness at the girl."

"I trust you are not ill," he said, without answering her question as to whether she might see Dorothy.

Madelon did not act as if she heard what he said. "Can I see your daughter, sir?" she repeated. She cast an anxious glance over her shoulder for fear Eugene might appear in the road.

Parson Fair still eyed her with perplexity. "I believe Dorothy is ill in her chamber," he said, hesitatingly. "I do not know —"

Madelon gave a dry sob. "I beg you to let me see her for a minute, sir," she gasped out, "for the love of God. It is life and death!"

Parson Fair looked shocked and half alarmed. He had not had to do with women like this, who spoke with such fervor of passion. His womankind had swathed all their fiercer human emotions with shy decorum and stern modesty, as Turkish women swathe their faces with veils.

Madelon, still under the fear of Eugene, pressed inside the door as she spoke, and he stood aside half involuntarily. "I beg you to let me see her," she repeated. She looked at the stately wind of the stairs up to the second floor, as if she were minded to ascend without bidding to Dorothy's chamber.

"She is ill in her chamber," the Parson said again, with a kind of forbidding helplessness.

"I would see her only for a minute. I beg you to let me, sir. It is life and death, I tell you — it is life and death!"

Whether Parson Fair motioned her to ascend, or whether he simply stood aside to allow her to pass, he never knew, but Madelon was up the winding stairs with a swirl of her cloak, as if the wind had caught it. Parson Fair followed her, and motioned her to the south front chamber, and was about to rap on the door when it was flung open violently, and the great black princess stood there, scowling at them.

"I have a guest here for your mistress," said Parson Fair; but the black woman blocked his way, speaking fast in her wrathful gibberish.

However, at a stately gesture from her master she stood aside, and he held the door open, and Madelon entered. "You had better not remain long, to tire her," said the parson, and closed the door. Immediately the uncouth savage voice was raised high again, and quelled by the parson's calm tone. Then there was a great settling of a heavy body close to the threshold. The black woman had thrown herself at the sill of her darling's door, to keep watch, like a faithful dog.

Madelon Hautville, when she entered Dorothy Fair's room, had her mind not been fixed upon its one end, which was above all such petty details of existence, might well have looked about her. No such dainty maiden bower was there in the whole village as this. Madelon's own chamber, carpetless and freezing cold, with its sparse furniture and scanty sweep of white curtains across the furred windows which filled the room with the blue-white light of frost, was desolation to it.

A great fire blazed on Dorothy Fair's chamber hearth. The red glow of it was over the whole room, and the frost on the windows was melting. Curtains of a soft blue-and-white stuff, said to have been brought from overseas, hung at Dorothy's windows and between the high posts of her bed. She had also her little rocking-chair and footstool frilled and cushioned with it. There was a fine white matting on her floor, and a thick rug with a basket of flowers wrought on it beside her bed. The high white panel-work around Dorothy's mantel was carved with curving garlands and festoons of ribbon and flowers, and on the shelf stood tall china vases and bright candlesticks. Dorothy's dressing-table had a petticoat of finest dimity, trimmed with tiny tassels. Above it hung her fine oval mirror, in a carved gilt frame. Upon the table were scattered silver and ivory things and glass bottles, the like of which Madelon had never seen. The room was full of that mingled perfume of roses and lavender which was always about Dorothy herself.

The counterpane on Dorothy's bed was all white and blue, and quilted in a curious fashion, and her pillows were edged with lace. In the midst of this white-and-blue nest, her slender little body half buried in her great feather-bed, her lovely yellow locks spreading over her pillow, lay Dorothy Fair when Madelon entered. She half raised herself, and stared at her with blue, dilated eyes, and shrank back with a little whimper of terror when she came impetuously to her bedside.

"You don't believe it," Madelon said, with no preface.

Dorothy stared at her, trembling. "You mean —"

"I mean you don't believe he killed him! You don't believe Burr Gordon killed his cousin Lot!"

Dorothy sank weakly back on her pillows. Great tears welled up in her blue eyes and rolled down her soft cheeks. "They *saw* him there," she sobbed out, "and they found his knife. Oh, I didn't think he was so wicked!"

Madelon caught her by one slender arm hard, as if she would have shaken her. "*You* believe it!" she cried out. "You believe that Burr did it — *you*!"

"They — saw — him — there," moaned Dorothy, with a terrified roll of her tearful eyes at Madelon's face.

"*Saw* him there! What if they did see him there? What if the whole town saw him? What if you saw him? What if you saw him strike the blow with your own eyes? Wouldn't you tear them out of your own head before you believed it? Wouldn't you cut your own tongue out before you'd bear witness against him?"

Dorothy sobbed convulsively.

"I would," said Madelon.

Dorothy hid her face away from her in the pillow.

Madelon laid her hand on her fair head, and turned it with no gentle hand. "Listen to me now," she said. "You've got to listen. You've got to hear what I say. You ought to believe without being told, without knowing anything about it, that he's innocent, if you're a woman and love him; but I'm going to tell you. Burr Gordon didn't kill his cousin Lot. I did!"

Dorothy gave a faint scream and shrank away from her.

"I did!" repeated Madelon. "Now do you believe he's innocent, when somebody else has told you?"

Dorothy's face was white as her pillows, her eyes big with terror. There was a soft thud against her door. The black woman was keeping arduous watch.

"You couldn't!" Dorothy gasped out.

"I could! Look at my hands; they are as strong as a man's."

"You — couldn't!"

"I could, and I did."

Dorothy shook her head in hysterical doubt.

"Listen," said Madelon — "listen. I'll tell you why I did it, Dorothy Fair. Burr Gordon had been with me a little before he went with you. Perhaps you knew it. If you did, I am not blaming you — he's got taking ways, you couldn't help it; and I am not blaming him — he's a man, and you're fairer complexioned than I am. But I was fool enough to be mad without any good reason — you understand I am not saying anything against him, Dorothy Fair — when I saw him with you at the ball. He had a right to take anybody to the ball that he chose. It was naught to me, but I was mad. I have a quick temper. And I started home when that young man from Kingston offered to fiddle for the dancing after you and Burr went out; and my brother Richard made me take his knife for fear I might meet stragglers, and I had it open under my cloak. And when I got to that lonely part of the road, after the turn, I saw somebody coming, and I thought it was Burr. He walked like him. And I looked away — I did not want to see his face; and when I came up to him the first thing I knew he threw his arm around me and kissed me, and — something seemed to leap up in me and I struck with Richard's knife. And — then he fell down, and I looked and it was not Burr — it was his cousin Lot. And — then Burr came, and we heard whistling, and others were coming, and he made me run, and the others came up and found him; and now they say he did it and not I. It was I who stabbed Lot Gordon, Dorothy Fair!"

"It was Burr's knife, with his initials cut in the handle, that they found," said Dorothy, with a kind of piteous doggedness. There was in this fair little maiden the same power of adherence to a mental attitude which her father had shown in his religious tenets. Wherever the men and women of this family stood they were fixed beyond their own capability of motion.

Madelon gave a bewildered sigh. "I know not how that was," said she, "unless —" a red flush mounted over her whole face. "No, he would not have done that for me," she said, as if to herself.

A red flush on Dorothy's face seemed to respond to that on Madelon's. "You think he put his knife there to take suspicion from you?" she cried out, quickly.

Madelon shook her head. "I don't know about the knife," she said, "but I know I stabbed Lot Gordon."

"He would not have done that," said Dorothy, with troubled, angry blue eyes on her face. "He would have thought of — others. He never changed the knife, Madelon Hautville!"

"I know nothing about the knife," repeated Madelon, "but Burr Gordon did not kill his cousin."

"He was there, and it was his knife," said Dorothy. There was now a curious indignation in her manner. It was almost as if she preferred to believe her lover guilty of murder rather than unduly solicitous for her rival.

Madelon Hautville turned upon her with a kind of fierce solemnity. "Dorothy Fair," said she, "look at me!" and the soft, blue-eyed face, full of that gentle unyielding which is the firmest of all, looked up at her from the pillows — "Dorothy Fair, did that man, who's locked up over there in jail in New Salem, for a crime he's innocent of, ever kiss you?"

Madelon's face seemed to wax stiff and white. She looked like one who bared her breast for a mortal hurt as she spoke. Dorothy went pink to the roots of her yellow hair and the frill on her night-gown. She made an angry shamed motion of her head, which might have signified anything.

"And you can believe this thing of him after that!" said Madelon, with a look of despairing scorn. "He has kissed you, Dorothy Fair, and you can think he has committed a murder!"

Dorothy gasped. "They said —" she began again.

"*They* said! Are you a woman, Dorothy Fair, and don't you know that the man you love enough to let him kiss you should do no wrong in your eyes, or else it's a shame to you, and you should kill him to wipe it out?" Dorothy shrank away from her in the bed, her frightened blue eyes staring at her over her shoulder. "My God! don't you know," said Madelon, "the man you love is yourself? When you believe in his guilt you believe in your own; when you strike him for it you strike yourself. Don't you know that, Dorothy Fair?"

Dorothy looked at her, all white and trembling. She gave a half-sob. Suddenly Madelon's tone changed. "Don't be afraid," said she. "I'm different from you. I don't wonder he liked you better. It's no blame to him. I know you care about him. You don't believe he did it."

"I don't know," sobbed Dorothy. The door opened a crack, and the black woman's watchful eyes appeared.

"Oh, you do know, you do know! I tell you, I did it — I! Can't you believe me? I'm a wicked woman, and I love anybody I love in a different way from any that a woman as good as you are can. I did it, Dorothy, and not Burr! He mustn't suffer for it. We must see him, you and I together! Don't you believe me?"

"I don't — know," sobbed Dorothy. The dark face appeared quite fully in the door. Madelon cast a quick glance about the room. Dorothy's pretty Bible, with a blue-silk-ribbon marker hanging from it, lay on her dimity dressing-table. Madelon sprang across and got it. The black woman stood in the doorway, muttering to herself. She looked all ready to spring to Dorothy's defence. Madelon did not notice her at all. She went close to Dorothy, put the Bible on the bed, and laid her right hand upon it.

"I swear upon this Holy Book," said she, "that this hand of mine is the one that stabbed Lot Gordon. I swear, and I call God to witness, and may I be struck dead as I speak if what I say is not true. Now do you believe what I say, Dorothy Fair?"

Dorothy looked at her and the Bible in bewildered terror. She nodded.

CHAPTER VIII

Something like joy came into Madelon's face. "Then we will save him, you and I!" she cried out. "We will save him together! He shall not be hung! He shall be set free! They shall let him out of jail to-day, and put me there instead. We will save him! He would not own that I was guilty and he innocent; Lot would not own it, nor my brother Richard, but now — we will save him — now!"

"How?" asked Dorothy, feebly.

"He will own it to you. Burr will own it to you if you go and plead with him. He can't help owning it to you. And then you shall go to Lot, and when you ask him for your sake, that you may marry Burr, if he knows Burr has told you, and does not care about me, he will speak. He will be sure to speak for you. Come!"

Dorothy raised herself on one elbow and stared at Madelon, her yellow hair falling about her fair startled face. "Where?" said she.

"With me to New Salem."

"To New Salem?"

"Yes, to New Salem — to see Burr."

"But I am ill, and the doctor has bid me stay in bed. I have been ill ever since the ball with a headache and fever."

"You talk about headache and fever when Burr is there in prison! I tell you if my two feet were cut off I would walk to him on the stumps to set him free!"

"How can I go?" said Dorothy. Her blue eyes kindled a little under Madelon's fiery zeal.

"We will take your father's horse and sleigh."

"But the horse is gone lame, and has not been used for a month."

"I will get one from Dexter Beers at the tavern," said Madelon, promptly. "I will lead him over here and harness him into the sleigh."

"My father will not let me go," said Dorothy.

"He is a minister of the gospel — he will let his daughter go to save a life."

"I tell you he will not," said Dorothy. "I know my father better than you. He will not let me go out when I am ill. It is freezing cold, too. If I go I must go without his knowledge and consent."

"I am going without my father's," said Madelon, shortly, "and I go at a greater cost than that, too."

"It's the second time I have deceived and disobeyed my father in a week's time," Dorothy said.

"You talk about your father when it is Burr — Burr — that's at stake!" Madelon cried out. "What is your father to Burr if you love him? That ought to go before anything else. It says so in your Bible

— it says so in your Bible, Dorothy Fair!"

Dorothy, with her innocent, frightened eyes fixed upon the other girl's passionate face, as if she were being led by her into unknown paths, put back the coverlet and thrust one little white foot out of bed. Then swiftly the black woman, who had entered the room, backed against the door as stiffly as a sentinel, darted forward, and would have thrust her mistress into bed again, making uncouth protests the while, had not Dorothy motioned her away with a gentle dignity, which was hers for use when she chose.

"Go down-stairs, if you please," said she, "and see if my father is in his study. If he is in there, and busy over his sermon, go to the barn, and drag out the sleigh for us."

Dorothy, white and fair as an angel, in her straight linen nightgown, stood out on the floor, in front of her great black guardian, who made again as though she would seize her and force her back, and pleaded with her in a thick drone, like an anxious bee, not to go.

"Do as I bid you!" said Dorothy, and glided past her to her dimity dressing-table, and began combing out her yellow hair.

The black woman went out, muttering.

"If my father is in his study on the north side of the house, and busy over his sermon, we can get away; otherwise we cannot," said Dorothy, combing the thick tress over her shoulder.

Madelon went to a south window of the room and looked out. She could see the barn, and across the road, farther down, the tavern. She watched while Dorothy bound up her hair, and soon she saw the black woman run, with a low crouch of her great body like a stealthy animal, across the yard.

"Your father is in his study," Madelon said, quickly. "I will go over to the tavern for a horse if yours is too lame."

"He can scarce stand," said Dorothy. Her soft voice trembled; she trembled all over — then was still with nervous rigors. Bright pink spots were on her cheeks. A certain girlish daring was there in this gentle maiden for youthful love and pleasure, else she had not stolen away that night to the ball, but very little for tragic enterprise. And, moreover, her fine sense of decorum and womanly pride had always served her mainly in the place of courage, which she lacked.

Sorely afraid was Dorothy Fair, if the truth were told, to go with this passionate girl, who had declared to her face she had done murder, to visit a man who she still half believed, with her helpless tenacity of thought, was a murderer also. The love she had hitherto felt for him was eclipsed by terror at the new image of him which her fearful fancy had conjured up and could not yet dismiss, in spite of Madelon's assurances. She was, too, really ill, and her delicate nerves were still awry from the shock they had received the night of the ball. Parson Fair had been sternly indignant, and his daughter had quailed before him, and then had come the news concerning Burr. Sage tea, and hot foot-baths, and the doctor's nostrums had not cured her yet. Her very spirit trembled and fluttered at this undertaking; but she could not withstand this fierce and ardent girl who upbraided her with the cowardice and distrust of her love. Instinctively she tried to raise her sentiment to the standard of the other's and believe in Burr.

Madelon paused a second as she went out, and gave a strange, scrutinizing glance at her.

"Why do you not wear your blue-silk quilted hood with the swan's-down trimming?" said she. "It becomes you, and it is warm over your ears."

"Yes, I will," said Dorothy, looking at her wonderingly.

Madelon went softly out of the house, and ran across and down the road to the tavern. Dexter Beers, the landlord, was just going around the wide sweep of drive to the stable with a meal-sack over his shoulder. No one else was in sight; it was so cold there were no loafers about. Madelon ran after him, and overtook him before he reached the stable door.

"Can you let me take a horse?" said she, abruptly.

Dexter Beers looked slowly around at her with a quick roll of a black eye in a massive face. He had an enormous bulk, which he moved about with painful sidewise motions. His voice was husky.

"What d'ye want a horse for?" said he.

"I want it to put in Parson Fair's sleigh."

"What for?"

"To take Dorothy to ride."

"Parson's horse lame yet?"

Madelon nodded.

"Where's yours?"

"I can't have him."

Dexter Beers still moved on with curious lateral twirls of his shoulders and heaves of his great chest, with its row of shining waistcoat buttons.

"Pooty cold day for a sleigh-ride," he observed, with a great steam of breath.

"I'll pay you well for the horse," said Madelon, in a hard voice. She followed him into the stable. He heaved the meal-sack from his shoulder to the floor with a grunt. Another man came forward with a peck measure in his hand. He was young, with a frosty yellow mustache. He had gone to school with Madelon and knew her well, but he looked at her with uncouth shyness without speaking. Then he began unfastening the mouth of the sack.

Madelon stepped forward impatiently towards the horse-stalls. There were the relay of coach-horses, great grays and bays, champing their feed, getting ready for their sure-footed rushes over the mountain roads when the coaches came in. She passed them by with sharp glances.

A man whose face was purplish red with cold was out in the rear of the stable, rubbing down a restive bay with loud "whoas," and now and then a stronger word and a hard twitch at the halter. He looked curiously at Madelon as she walked up to one of the stalls.

"Better look out for them heels!" he called out, as she drew nearer. She paid no heed, but went straight into the stall, untied the horse, and began to back him out. "Hi, there!" the man shouted, and Dexter Beers and the young man came hurrying up. "Better look out for that gal — I believe she's gone crazy!" he called out. "I can't leave this darned beast — she'll get kicked to death if she don't look out. That old white won't stan' a woman in the stall. Whoa, there! whoa, darn ye! Stan' still!"

"Hullo, what ye doin' of?" demanded Dexter Beers, coming up.

Madelon calmly backed the horse out of his stall. "I want to hire this horse," said she, holding his halter with a firm hand.

"That horse?"

"Yes. I'll pay you whatever you ask."

Dexter Beers stared at her and the horse dubiously. "Jest as soon set a woman to drivin' the devil as that old white," volunteered the man who was cleaning the bay. The young man stood gaping with wonder.

"Can I have this horse or not?" demanded Madelon. Her black eyes flashed imperiously at Dexter Beers. Her small brown hand held the halter of the old white with a grasp like steel.

"Dunno 'bout your drivin' that horse," said Dexter Beers. "'Fraid you'll get run away with. Better take another."

"Isn't this horse the fastest you've got on a short stretch?"

"S'pose he is, but I dunno 'bout a woman's drivin' of him."

Madelon looked as if she were half minded to spring upon the back of the old white and settle the matter summarily. She fairly quivered with impatience.

"A woman who can drive David Hautville's roan can drive this horse, and you know it," said she. She moved forward as she spoke, leading the high-stepping old white, and Dexter Beers stood aside.

"Well, David Hautville's roan is nigh a match for this one," he grunted, hesitatingly, "but then ye know your own better. Hadn't ye better —"

But the old white was out of the stable at a trot, with Madelon running alongside.

"Don't ye want a man to hitch him up?" Dexter Beers called after her; but she was out of hearing.

"If the gal's ekal to drivin' that horse, she's ekal to hitchin' of him up," said the man who was cleaning the bay. "If a gal wants to drive, let her hitch. Ye'd better let a woman go the whole figger when she gits started, just as ye'd better give an ugly cuss of a horse his head up hill an' down. It takes the mischief out of 'em quicker'n anything. Let her go it, Dexter — don't ye fret."

"I don't want her breakin' any of the parson's daughter's bones with none of my horses," said Dexter Beers, uneasily. "Wonder where the parson is?"

"Let 'em go it! They won't git smashed up, I guess," said the other. "I've seen that gal of Hautville's with that mare of his'n. She kin drive most anythin' short of the devil, an' old white's got sense enough to know when he's well driv, ugly's he is. He wa'n't on the track for nothin'. He ain't no wuss, if he's as bad, as that roan mare. Let 'em *go* it!"

"Wonder what's to pay?" said the young man, who had not spoken before.

"Dunno," said Dexter Beers. "Somethin's to pay — that girl acted queer."

"S'pose she takes it hard 'bout Burr Gordon. He used to fool 'round her, I've heerd, afore he went courtin' the parson's gal."

"Dunno — queer she's so thick with the parson's gal all of a sudden."

"Lord, I wouldn't tech a gal that could git the upperhand of a horse like that roan mare with a ten-foot pole," half soliloquized the man at work over the bay. "Wouldn't have her if she owned half the township, an' went down on her knees to me — darned if I would. Don't want no woman that kin make horse-flesh like that knuckle under. Guess a man wouldn't have much show; hev to take his porridge 'bout the way she wanted to make it. Whoa, there! stan' still, can't ye? Darned if I want nothin' to do with sech woman folks or sech horses as ye be."

Dexter Beers moved laboriously out to the stable door and peered after Madelon, but she had disappeared in Parson Fair's yard. The white horse had gone up the road at a brisk trot, but she had easily kept pace with him. She also harnessed him into the sleigh with no difficulty. The animal seemed docile, and as if he were to belie his hard reputation. There was, however, a proud and nervous cant to his old white head, and he set his jaw stiffly against his bit.

Dorothy came out in her quilted silk pelisse and her blue hood edged with swan's-down, and got into the sleigh. The black woman was keeping watch at the parson's study door the while, but he never swerved from his hard application of the doctrines.

The sleigh slipped noiselessly out of the yard and up the road, for Madelon had not put on the bells. The old white went rather stiffly and steadily for the first quarter-mile; then he made a leap forward with a great lift of his lean white flanks, and they flew.

Dorothy gave a terrified gasp. "Don't be frightened," Madelon said. "It's the horse that used to beat everything in the county. He's old now, but when he gets warmed up he's the fastest horse around for a short stretch. He can't hold out long, but while he does he goes; and I want to get a good start. I want to strike the New Salem road as soon as I can."

Madelon had a growing fear lest Eugene might have freed himself, and might ride the roan across by a shorter cut, and so intercept her at the turn into the New Salem road. He might easily suspect her of attempting to see Burr again. If she passed the turn first she could probably escape him if her horse held out; and, indeed, he might not think she had gone that way if he did not see her.

Dorothy held fast to the side of the sleigh, which seemed to rise from the track as they sped on. "Don't be frightened," Madelon said again. "This is the only horse in town that can beat my father's on a short stretch, and I don't know that he can always, but I don't think he has been used, and father's was ridden hard yesterday. I can manage this one in harness better than I can father's. Don't be frightened." But Dorothy's face grew pale as the swan's-down around it, and her great blue eyes were fixed fearfully upon the bounding heels and flanks of the old white race-horse.

Madelon strained her eyes ahead as they neared the turn of the New Salem road. There was nobody in sight. Then she glanced across the fields at the right. Suddenly she swung out the reins over the back of the old white, and hallooed, and stood up in the sleigh.

Dorothy screamed faintly. "Sit still and hold on!" Madelon shouted. Dorothy shut her eyes. It seemed to her she was being hurled through space. Her slender body swung to and fro against the sleigh as she clung frantically to it.

Eugene Hautville, on the roan, was coming at a mad run across the open field on the right towards the turn of the road. It seemed for a second as if Madelon would reach it before he did; but they met there, and the roan reared to a stop in the narrow road directly in front of the old white, who plunged furiously.

"Look out there!" shouted Eugene, as the sleigh tilted on the snow-crust. The old white's temper was up at this sudden check, but the woman behind him had a stronger will than he. She brought him to a straining halt, and then she spoke to her brother.

"You let us pass!" she said, sternly.

"Where are you going?" he demanded. He looked uneasily at Dorothy as he spoke. It was easy enough to see that she was a restraint upon him, and that fair, timid face in its blue hood held his indignation well in check.

"We are going to New Salem," replied Madelon. "Let us pass."

"I want to know what you are going for," said Eugene; and he tried to speak with fire, but he still looked furtively at Dorothy.

Nobody had ever suspected how that lovely face of hers had been in his dreams, unless it had been for a time Dorothy herself. Nobody had noticed in meeting, of a Sabbath day long since, when Dorothy had first returned from her Boston school, sundry glances which had passed between a pair of soft blue eyes in the parson's pew and a pair of fiery black ones in the singing-seats.

Dorothy, half guiltily in those days, had arranged her curls and tied on her Sunday bonnets with a view to Eugene Hautville's eyes; and always, when she returned from meeting, had gone straight to her looking-glass, to be sure that she had looked fair in them. But nobody had ever known, and scarcely she herself.

She had come to think later that she had perhaps been mistaken, for never had Eugene made other advances to her than by those ardent glances; and Burr had come, and she had turned to him, and thought of Eugene Hautville only when he crossed her way, and then with a mixture of pique and shame. Never by any chance did her eyes meet his nowadays of a Sabbath day, and she listened coldly to his sweet tenor in the hymns. Now, suddenly, she looked straight up in his face and met his eyes, and a pink flush came into her white cheeks.

"Please to let us pass," she said, in her gentle tone, which had yet a tincture of command in it. Any woman as fair as she, who has a right understanding of her looking-glass, has, however soft she may be, the instincts of a queen within her. She felt a proud resentment for her own old folly and for Eugene's old slighting of her, and indignation at his present attitude as she looked up at him with sudden daring.

Eugene threw back his head haughtily. "She wants to see Burr Gordon," he thought, and would have died rather than let her think he would stand in the way of it. He jerked the roan aside, and seemed as if he would have been flung into the way-side bushes with her curving plunge.

"Pass, if you wish," he said, with a graceful bend in his saddle, and was past them, riding the other way towards the village.

CHAPTER IX

When they reached the county buildings, the court-house and the jail, in New Salem, the old race-horse was still not nearly spent, although he breathed somewhat hard. When Madelon sprang out to blanket and tie him he seemed to vibrate to her touch like electric steel, and showed that the old fire had not yet died out of his nerves and muscles.

Poor Dorothy Fair's knees were weak under her as she got out of the sleigh. Her pretty face was pitiful, her sweet mouth drooping at the corners like a troubled child's.

Madelon looked at her sharply when they stood before the jail door waiting for admittance. "I have seen you wear a curl each side of your face outside your hood," said she.

"I didn't think of it to-day," Dorothy replied, with forlorn surprise.

Madelon went close to the other girl peremptorily, as if she had been her mother, pulled forward two soft curls from under her hood, and arranged them becomingly against the pale cheeks; and Dorothy submitted.

Alvin Mead opened the jail door, and his great face took on a forbidding scowl when he saw Madelon Hautville.

"Can't let ye in," he said, gruffly. "Ain't a visitin' day." He would have shut the door in their faces had not Madelon made a quick spring against it.

"I don't want to come in!" she cried. "I don't want to see him to-day. It's this lady who wants to see him."

"Can't see nobody," said Alvin Mead, filling up the door like a surly living wedge.

"You must let us see him," persisted Madelon. "She's Parson Fair's daughter. She is going to marry Burr Gordon — she must see him."

Alvin Mead shook his head stubbornly. Then Dorothy spoke, thrusting her fair face forward, and looking up at him with terrified, innocent pleading, like a child, and yet speaking with a gentle lady's authority. "I beg you to let me come in, only for a few moments," said she. "I will not make you any trouble. I will come out directly when you bid me to."

Alvin Mead looked at her a second, then at Madelon with rough inquiry. "Who did ye say she was?" he growled.

"Parson Fair's daughter, the lady that's going to marry Burr Gordon."

"I can't let but one of ye see him, and she can't stay more'n ten minutes," said Alvin Mead, and moved aside, and Madelon and Dorothy entered.

They followed Alvin Mead down the icy, dark corridor to

Burr's cell door. He unlocked it, and bade Dorothy enter. He cast a forbidding look at Madelon. "I will stand here," she said with a strange meekness, almost as if her heart were broken; but when the jailer prepared to follow Dorothy into Burr's cell she caught him by the arm and tried to force him back, and cried out sharply that he should let her see him alone. "She is the girl he is going to marry, I tell you!" she said. "Let them see each other alone. You cannot come between two like that when they are in such trouble."

Alvin Mead looked at her a second irresolutely. Then he stepped back in the corridor and locked the cell door. "That the gal? Thought ye was the one," he said, with a half-chuckle, with coarse, sharp eyes upon her face.

"He is going to marry her," Madelon repeated. She stood stiff and straight like a statue, and waited. Once, when Alvin made an impatient motion as though to open the door, she restrained him with such despairing eagerness that he drew back and looked at her wonderingly, and stood in surly silence awhile longer.

"She's got to come out now," he said, at last. "I've got other things to tend to. Can't stay here no longer, nohow. He unlocked the door and threw it open with a jerk. "Time's up!" he shouted, and Dorothy came out directly, almost as if she were running away. Alvin Mead clapped to the door with a great jar and locked it. Madelon, had she tried, could not have got a glimpse of Burr; but she did not try. She sprang at Dorothy Fair, and took her by the shoulders, and looked into her scared face with agonized questioning.

"Did — he confess?" she gasped out. "Did — he tell you, did he — tell you, Dorothy Fair?"

Dorothy shook her head in a mute terror that was almost horror. It seemed as if she would sink to the floor under Madelon's heavy hands. Alvin Mead stood staring at them.

"Didn't he — tell you — I was the one who — stabbed Lot? Didn't he — tell you?"

"She's at it again," muttered Alvin Mead.

Dorothy shook her head. "He wouldn't speak," she said, faintly. "He would say nothing about it."

Madelon fairly shook her. "Couldn't you make him speak? You!"

"I couldn't, I couldn't, Madelon!"

"Did you tell him your heart would break if he didn't — that you couldn't marry him if he didn't?"

"Yes — don't, don't — look at me so, Madelon."

Alvin Mead stepped forward. "Look at here — you're scarin' of that gal to death," he interfered. "You'd better take your hands off her."

Then Madelon turned to him, and grasped at the keys in his hands, as if she would wrest them from him. "Unlock the door and let me in, and let Burr Gordon out!" she demanded, wildly.

The jailer wrested his keys away with a contemptuous jerk, and took the skin from Madelon's hands with them. "You're crazy," he said.

"I am not crazy! You've got an innocent man locked up in there, and I, who am guilty and tell you so, you will not arrest. It is you who are crazy. Let me in!"

Alvin Mead laid a rough hand on Madelon's shoulder. "Now you look at here, gal," said he. "I've had about all this darned nonsense I'm a-goin' to stan'. That chap is in jail for murder, an' in jail he's a-goin' to stay till I git orders from somebody besides you to let him out. An' what's more, don't you come here on no sich tomfool arrant agin. If you do you won't git in. I ain't no objection to gals he was goin' to marry ef he hadn't broke the laws comin' to see him a leetle spell, if they'll go away peaceable when they're bid, but as for havin' sech highstericky work as this, I'll be darned if I will. Now I can't stan' here foolin' no longer; you'd better be gittin' right along home, an' don't you break this other gal's neck with that old stepper you've got out there."

Madelon Hautville said not another word. She went out of the jail quickly, and she and Dorothy were soon in the sleigh and flying down the road. The old racer was not so old nor so weary that the impetus of the homeward stretch failed to stir him — for a mile or so, at least. After that his pace slackened, and then Madelon turned to the other girl, who looked up at her with a kind of piteous defiance. "What did you say to him?" she demanded.

"I — begged him — if he — did not kill Lot to — say so," replied Dorothy, faintly; then she shrank and quivered before the other girl, who started wrathfully, half as if she would fling her from the sleigh.

"*If* he did not kill Lot to say so!" repeated Madelon. "*If* he did not! You know he did not."

"He would not tell me so," said Dorothy, with her stubbornness of meekness, and her blue eyes met Madelon's, although there were tears welling up in them.

"Tell you so!" cried Madelon. "What are you made of, Dorothy Fair?"

"He would not," repeated Dorothy. "If he *was* innocent, why should he not have told me if he loved me?"

Madelon looked at her. "You don't love him!" she cried out, sharply. "You don't love him, and that's why. You don't love him, Dorothy Fair!"

Dorothy flushed red and drew herself up with gentle stiffness.

"You cannot expect me to unveil my heart to you," said she.

"You have betrayed it," persisted Madelon. "You don't love him, Dorothy Fair! Shame on you, after all!"

"What right have you to say that?" demanded Dorothy, and this time with some show of anger.

"The right of another woman who does love him, and would save his life," Madelon answered, fiercely. "The right of a woman who can love more in an hour than such as you in a lifetime!"

"You — don't know —"

"I do know. You don't love him or you would not have distrusted him. You would have made him tell you the truth. You would have flung your arms around him, and you would not have let him go until he told you. Did you do that? Answer me: did you do that?"

A great wave of red crept over Dorothy's face, but she replied, with cold dignity: "I throw my arms around no man unbidden!"

"Unbidden!" repeated Madelon, and scorn seemed to sound in her voice like the lash of a whip. She flung out the reins over the horse's back, and they slipped along swiftly over the icy crust, and not another word did she speak to Dorothy Fair all the way home.

CHAPTER X

When they entered Parson Fair's south yard there was a swift disappearance of a dark face from a window, and the door was flung open, and the grimly faithful servant-woman came forth and lifted Dorothy out of the sleigh, crooning the while in tender and angry gutturals. Poor Dorothy Fair shook like a white flower in a wind, for beside the rigor of the cold, which seemed to pierce her very soul, the chill of fever was still upon her. She chattered helplessly when she tried to speak, and there were sobs in her throat. The black woman half carried her into the house, and up-stairs to her own chamber, where the hearth-fire was blazing bright. She covered her up warm in bed, with a hot brick at her feet, and dosed her with warm herb drinks, and coddled her, until, after some piteous weeping, she fell asleep.

But for Madelon Hautville there was no rest and no sleep. She felt not the cold, and if she had fever in her veins the fierce disregard of her straining spirit was beyond it. No knowledge of her body at all had Madelon Hautville, no knowledge of anything on earth except her one aim — to save her lover's life. She was nothing but a purpose concentrated upon one end; there was in her that great impetus of the human will which is above all the swift forces of the world when once it is aroused.

She unharnessed the horse quickly from the parson's sleigh, and led him, restive again at the near prospect of his stall and feed, back to the tavern stable, paid for him, and struck out on the homeward road, straight and swift as one of her Indian ancestors. A group of men in the stable door stood aside with curious alacrity to let her pass; they stared after her, then at each other.

"I swan!" said one.

"Wouldn't like to be in the way when that gal was headed anywheres," said another.

"If that gal belonged to me I'd get her some stronger bits," said the man who had been cleaning the bay horse when Madelon came for the white.

"I believe she's lost her mind," said the tavern-keeper. "It's the last time I'll ever let her have a horse, and I told her so." There came a blast of northwest wind which buffeted them about their faces and chests like an icy flail, and they scattered before it, some to their duties in the stable, some into the warm tavern for a mug of something hot to do away with the chill. It was too cold a day to gossip in a doorway. It was not long past noon, but the cold had seemed to strengthen as the sun rode higher. The wind blew from the icy northwest more frequently in fiercer gusts. Madelon Hautville sped along before it, her red cloak flying out like a flag, and took no thought of it at all. She was, while still in the flesh and upon the earth, so intensified in spirit that there existed for her consciousness neither heat nor cold. She reached the old road, the short-cut, stretched down through the stiff white woods to her own home; she hastened along it a little way, then she stopped and faced back and stood irresolute. The icy wind stiffened her face, but she did not note it. She looked back at the road with its blue snow-furrows stretching between the desolate woods, at the spires and roofs of the village beyond. If one followed that road to the village and took the first one upon the right, and travelled ten miles, one would come to the town of Kingston.

Madelon began moving along on the road to the village, vaguely at first, as if half in a dream, then with gathering purpose. Back she went, in her tracks, straight to the village and the tavern stable, and asked of Dexter Beers another horse to drive to Kingston. But he refused her, standing before her, blocking the stable door, looking aside with a kind of timid doggedness. "Can't let ye have another horse to-day nohow," said he; "too cold to let 'em out."

"I'll pay you well," said Madelon.

"Pay ain't no object. Can't let none of 'em out but the stage-horses in no sech weather as this." Still Dexter Beers did not look at Madelon's stern and angry eyes; he gazed intently at a post in an icy slant of snow in the yard on the left.

He had the usual masculine dread of an angry woman, and, moreover, he had a sharp-tongued wife, but he had also the masculine tenacity of a position. He stared at the post as if his spirit held fast to it, and braced itself against the torrent of feminine wrath which he expected; but it did not come. Madelon Hautville set her mouth hard, wrapped her red cloak around her with a firm gesture, as if she were a soldier about to start on a long march, and walked out of the yard and up the road without another word.

"I swan!" said Dexter Beers.

The red-faced hostler approached with a pail in each hand bound for the well; he was watering the coach-horses for the next relay. "What's up?" he inquired, pushing past him.

"I'll be darned if I don't believe that gal of Hautville's has started to walk to Kingston, 'cause I wouldn't let her have another horse!"

"Let her go it," droned the red-faced man, with a short chuckle.

"Hope she won't freeze her feet nor nothin'," said Dexter Beers, uneasily.

"Let her *go* it!" said the red-faced man, swinging across the yard with his pails.

Madelon Hautville walked on steadily. She reached the right-hand turn, and then she was on the direct Kingston road, with a ten-mile stretch before her. It was past one o'clock, and she could not reach her journey's end much before dark.

About two miles after the turn of the road the more thickly set habitations ceased, and there were only isolated farm-houses, with long, sloping reaches of woods and pasture-lands between. The pasture-lands were hummocked with ice-coated rocks and hooped with frozen vines; they seemed to flow down in glittering waves, like glaciers, over the hill-sides. The woods stood white and petrified, as woods might have done in a glacial era. There was no sound in them except now and then the crack of a bough under the weight of ice, and slow, painful responses, like the twangs of rusty harp-strings, to the harder gusts of wind. The cold was so intense that the ice did not melt in the noonday sun, and there were no soft droppings and gurglings to modify this rigor of white light and sound. Occasionally a rabbit crossed Madelon's path, silent as a little gray scudding shadow, and so swiftly that he did not reach one's consciousness until he was out of sight. There was seldom a winter bird, even, in sight. The ice on the trees and the pastures had locked and sealed their larders. Their little beaks could not pierce it for seeds and grubs, and so they were forced to repair to kitchen doors and barnyards in quest of stray crumbs from the provender of men and cattle.

The rabbits, and an ox-team drawing a sled laden with cedar logs, slipping with shrill, long squeaks over the white road, driven by a man with a red face in an ambush of frozen beard, were all the living things she met for the first four miles. The man clambered stiffly down from his sled just before he met her, and began walking, stamping, rubbing his ears, and swinging his arms violently the while. He stared hard at Madelon, and gave a sort of grunt as he passed. It was an instinctive note of comradeship with another in a situation hard for their common humanity. The man, toiling painfully along that hard road, on that bitter day, with hands and feet half frost-bitten, and face smarting as if with fire, his aching lungs straining with the icy air, felt that he and the woman struggling over the same road had common cause for wrath against this stress of nature, and so made that half-surly, half-sympathetic grunt as he passed her. But she did not respond. She did not even glance at him as she went along. Her face glowed all over, red as a rose with the freezing wind; she wrapped her cloak instinctively tight around her, and walked a little stiffly, as if her feet might be somewhat numb; but there was in her fixed dark eyes no recognition of anything but some end she had in view beyond his ken.

The man stopped and looked seriously after her, and past her down the road. "Wonder what she's up to!" he muttered. Then he struggled on after his oxen, who plodded along with goat's-beards of their frozen breath hanging from their jaws.

Two miles farther on there was a sudden loud blast of a horn, and following upon it a great jangle of bells and the tramp of hoofs, and Madelon knew the Ware and Kingston stage was coming. Presently the top of the coach and the leaders' heads appeared above the rise of the road, and Madelon stood well aside to meet it, pressing in among the crackling icy bushes.

There was another blast of the horn, then a wild rush of sure-footed horses down the hill, and the coach was past, going towards Ware. Madelon had caught only a glimpse of the frost-white driver on the box, a man beside him shrugged up miserably in great-coat and comforter, with back rounded and head bent against the cold, and some chilled faces in the windows. Some of the passengers had come from Wolverton, ten miles past Kingston, and one might freeze to death on a long stage journey a day like that. There was, perhaps, less danger in a walk, but there was danger in that should the cold increase, and it did increase hourly. Madelon's feet grew more and more numb. She stamped them from time to time, but more from instinct than from any real appreciation of the discomfort they gave her. So wrought up was she with zeal that it seemed she might have set out to walk through a fiery furnace as soon as through this frozen waste, and perhaps have had her flesh consumed to ashes, with her soul still intent upon its one purpose. All thought of her own self, save as an instrument to save the life of the man she loved, was gone out of the girl. Jealousy was purged out of her; all resentment for faithlessness, all longing for possession were gone. She bore in her heart the greatest love of her life as she sped along down the frozen road to Kingston.

The last two miles of the way poor Madelon struggled hard to cover. She drew short, gasping breaths, as if she were on a high mountain-top. The cold strengthened as the daylight waned. The very air seemed frozen and resolved into a cutting diamond-dust of frost. Suddenly Madelon awoke to the fear that she could not walk much farther. She had eaten nothing since morning; the cold and fatigue were consuming her life as the flame consumes the wick of the lamp when the oil is lacking.

"I must get there!" she said to herself. She stamped her numb feet desperately. She beat herself pitilessly with her stiff hands. She set forth on a run towards Kingston, and quickened her blood a little in that way, although she panted and fairly gasped for breath.

She drew a sigh of relief when she gained the last rise in the road, and the town of Kingston lay before her a mile in the valley. It was growing dark and the village lights were coming out when she had passed the straggling farms and come into the little centre of the town where the stores, the meeting-houses, and the tavern were grouped.

The village main street looked almost deserted. There was only one sleigh in sight, drawn up in front of the store. The horse was well covered with a buffalo-skin and an old bed-quilt in addition, which his master's wife had doubtless provided on account of the terrible cold.

As Madelon reached the store a man came out with a molasses-jug in hand and arms clasping parcels, which he began stowing away under the seat of the sleigh. Madelon went up to him. "Can you tell me where Mr. Otis lives?" said she. She could scarcely enunciate. Her very tongue seemed stiff with the cold.

The man turned and stared at her with sharp blue eyes under red brows frost-white between his cap and twice-wound red tippet. "Hey?" he said, in a muffled voice.

"Can you tell me where Mr. Otis lives?"

"Otis?"

"Yes, sir."

"Which Otis d'ye mean? There's two Otises. D'ye mean Calvin Otis or Jim Otis?"

"He has a son that plays the fiddle," answered Madelon, faintly.

"Then it's Jim ye mean. He died last year. He had a son Jim that plays the fiddle. Lives down the road on the left-hand side, five houses below the meeting-house. House with three popple-trees in front — sets close to the road."

Madelon started, but the man's voice arrested her. "You look most froze," said he. "Hadn't ye better go in there an' warm up?" He pointed towards the store-windows with a rosy glow of light and warmth transfusing their thick layers of frost. "It's pipin' hot in there — warm ye all through in a minute. It's a terrible cold night. Old man in there, lived 'round these parts risin' eighty years, says he never knew sech a night. Better just step in there."

Madelon shook her head and started on.

"Where did ye come from?" called the man.

"Ware Centre," Madelon gasped out, as the freezing wind struck her.

"Good Lord! you don't mean to say you've walked risin' ten mile from Ware Centre a day like this!"

Madelon was gone, bending before the wind, without another word.

"Good Lord!" said the man, "a woman walkin' from Ware Centre this weather!" He stood staring after the girls' retreating figure; then he started to unblanket his horse. But he stopped and stared again, and finally went into the store to tell the news.

Madelon kept on as fast as she was able, but she was nearly spent. Her exultation of spirit might indeed survive fleshly exhaustion and perhaps in a measure overcome it, but it could not prevent it altogether. When she reached the fifth house below the white meeting-house, the house set close to the road, with three poplar-trees in front, she had just strength enough to stagger to the door and raise the knocker. Then she leaned against the door-post, and it was only with a fierce effort that she kept her grasp upon her consciousness. She did not seem to feel her body at all.

CHAPTER XI

Presently a bolt was shot and the door pushed open with an effort. It was little used, and there was ice against it. Then a man's face peered out irresolutely into the dusk. A knock upon the front door, upon a night like this, seemed so unlikely that he doubted if he had heard rightly.

"Anybody here?" he said. Then he saw the woman's figure propped stiffly against the door-post. "Who is it?" he asked, in a startled voice. "Is it you, Mrs. Lane?"

Madelon aroused herself. "I want to see Mr. Otis's son a minute if I can," she said, with a great effort. Then she raised her piteous eyes to the face before her, and realized dimly that it was the face of the young man who had taken her place at the ball, and sent her homeward to work all this misery on that dreadful night.

"I am Mr. Otis's son," returned the young man, wonderingly. "What" — then he gave a cry — "why, it is you!"

"I want — to — see you — a minute," said Madelon, and her voice sounded far away in her own ears.

The young man started. "Why, you're half frozen," he cried out, "and here I am keeping you standing out here! Come in."

Madelon shrank back. "No," she faltered, "I — only want to ask —"

But Jim Otis took her by the arm with gentle force, and she was so spent that she could but let him have his way, and lead her into the house and the warm living-room, staggering under his supporting clasp.

"Mother," called Jim Otis — "mother, come here, quick!" He placed Madelon tenderly on the settle, and his mother came hurriedly out of the pantry.

"What is it?" she asked. "What is the matter, Jim? Who was it knocked? Why, who's that?"

Madelon leaned back helplessly in the corner of the settle, her head hanging half unconsciously. The young man stooped over her and unfastened her cloak and hood. "Come here, quick, mother!" he cried, and his voice was as sweet with pity as a woman's. "This poor girl is half dead with the cold."

Mrs. Otis, large and fair-faced, with her soft, massive curves swathed in purple thibet, stared for a second in speechless wonder. "Who is it? How did she get here?" she whispered.

"Hush — I don't know. She's from Ware Centre. Her name's Hautville."

"Seems to me I've heard of her. What has she come here for, Jim?"

"Hush — I don't know. She'll hear you. Go and get something hot for her to drink. I saw her at the ball the other night. Go quick, mother."

"I'll get her some brandy cordial," said Mrs. Otis, with sudden alacrity. She needed time always to get her mental bearing thoroughly in any emergency, but action was prompt afterwards. She made a quick motion towards the cupboard, but Madelon aroused herself suddenly. Her senses had lapsed for a few minutes upon coming into the warm room. "Where am I?" she asked, in a bewildered way.

"In our house," replied Mrs. Otis, promptly. "Jim just brought you in, and it's lucky you come just as you did, for I don't know but you'd froze to death if you'd been out much longer. Now, I'll get you some of my brandy cordial, and that'll warm you right up. Did you come way over from Ware Centre this dreadful night?"

"Yes, ma'am," replied Madelon, with the dazed look still in her eyes. Mrs. Otis looked back on her way to the cupboard.

"Rode way over from Ware Centre in an open sleigh?" she said.

"No, ma'am; I walked."

Mrs. Otis stopped and looked at Madelon with a gasp, then at her son. "She's out of her head, I'm afraid," said she.

"You didn't really walk over from Ware Centre?" questioned Jim.

"Yes, I did," replied Madelon. She stood up with sudden decision. "I want to see you a minute," she said to Jim. Then she turned to Mrs. Otis. "I don't need anything to take," said she. "I was only a little dizzy for a minute when I came into this warm room. I feel better now. I only want to ask your son a question, then I must go home —"

Before Mrs. Otis could speak she asked the question with no preface.

"Didn't you see him give me the knife?" she cried out, with fiercely imploring eyes upon Jim Otis's face.

The young man turned deadly white. He looked at her and did not answer.

"Didn't you?" she repeated.

"What knife?" asked Jim Otis, slowly.

"You know what knife! The knife that my brother handed me when I started home from the ball — the knife that I stabbed Lot Gordon with. Tell me that you saw it, that you saw me take it, here before your mother, and then you must go to New Salem and testify, and set Burr Gordon free! He is in prison for murder, and I am guilty, and they will not believe it. You must tell them, and they will. You saw my brother give me that knife."

Still Jim Otis, with his white face, stood looking at her, and answered not a word. His mother, continually opening her mouth to speak, then shutting it, looked first at one, then at the other, with round, dilated eyes, turning her head and quivering all over her soft bulk, like some great agitated and softly feathered bird.

"Why don't you speak?" demanded Madelon.

"What is it you want me to say?" said Jim Otis, then, hesitatingly.

"Say? Say that you saw my brother Richard give me the knife that I did the deed with."

Jim Otis stood silent, with his pale, handsome face bent doggedly towards the floor.

"Say so! You saw it!"

Still Jim Otis did not speak, and Madelon pressed close to him, and thrust her agonized face before his. "Have mercy upon me and speak!" she groaned.

"Jim, what does she mean?" asked his mother, in a frightened whisper. "Is she out of her head?"

"No; hush, mother," replied Jim. Then he turned to the girl. "No," he said, with stern, defiant eyes upon her face, "I did not see your brother give you the knife."

"You did! I know you did!"

"I *did not!*"

"You did see him! You were looking at us when I went out!"

"I was tightening a string in the fiddle when you went out," said Jim Otis.

"You must have seen."

"I tell you I did not."

Madelon looked at him as if she would penetrate his soul, and he met her eyes fully.

"I did not see your brother give you the knife," he replied, with a steady, unflinching look at her; but a long shudder went over him as he spoke. The first deliberate lie of his whole life was Jim Otis telling, for he had seen Richard Hautville give his sister the knife.

Madelon believed his lie at last, and turned away. What with her sore exhaustion of body and this last disappointment her heart almost failed her. She went back to the settle for her cloak and her hood, and tied them on, while the others stood watching her, seemingly in a maze. She made for the door, but Jim Otis stopped her.

"You cannot go back to Ware Centre to-night," he said.

Madelon looked at him with proud determination, although she could scarce stand. "I must go," said she, and would have pressed past him, but he took hold of her arm.

"Mother," he said, "tell her she cannot go. There has been no such night as this for forty years, and it is dark now. To-morrow morning I will carry her home; but to-night, as she is, it is out of the question. Tell her so, mother."

Mrs. Otis gathered herself together then, and came forward and laid hold of Madelon's arm, and strove to pull her back towards the settle. "Come," said she, as if Madelon were a child — "come, that's a good girl. You stay with us till morning, and then my son shall hitch up and carry you home. I shouldn't dare to have him go way over to Ware Centre to-night, cold as 'tis. He ain't very tough. You stay here with us to-night, and don't worry anything about it. I don't know what you're talkin' about, an' I guess you don't — you are all wore out, poor child; but I guess there didn't nobody have any knife, and I guess he'll git out of prison pretty soon. You just take off your things, and I'll get some pillows out of the bedroom, and you lay down on the settle by the fire while I get some supper. The kettle's on now. And then I'll heat the warming-pan and get the spare-room bed as warm as toast, and mix you up a tumbler of hot brandy cordial, and then you drink it all down and get right into bed, and I'll tuck you up, and I guess you'll feel better in the morning, and things will look different."

"Let me go," Madelon said to Jim Otis.

"She mustn't go, mother," he said, never looking at Madelon at all, although he still held fast to her straining arm.

"Well," said Mrs. Otis, "You ain't no daughter of mine, and if you set out to go I suppose I ain't any right to hinder you. But there's one thing maybe you ain't thought of — I can't let my son take you 'way over to Ware Centre a night like this, nohow. He's all I've got now, and I can't have anything happen to him. He can't go with you, and there ain't any stable here, and there ain't a neighbor round here that will hitch up and carry you there to-night, and — I suppose you know, if you've got common-sense, that if you set out to walk there, the way you are, you don't stand much chance of gettin' there alive."

Madelon stared at her.

"I don't really know myself what you and my son have been talkin' about," continued Mrs. Otis, "but near's I can make out you think you've done something wrong, and somebody's in prison you want to get out. I suppose you've got sense enough to know that if you freeze to death going home to-night you can't do anything more to get him out. Then there's another thing — it's night. You can't do much to get him out anyway before morning. I don't believe they ever let folks out at night, and my son shall carry you over just as soon as it's fit in the morning, and you'll do just as much good as if you went to-night."

Still Madelon stood staring at her. Then presently she began unfastening her hood and cloak. "If you can keep me till morning I shall be obliged," she said, with a kind of stern gratitude.

"Stay just as well as not!" cried Mrs. Otis. "Jim, just take her things and lay 'em in the bedroom. Then you have her set right down close to the hearth, and get all warmed through, while I get supper."

Handsome young Jim Otis stood by with his brows knit moodily while Madelon Hautville removed her wraps, then took them over his arm, and conducted her to the warm seat in the hearth-corner which his mother designated.

In his heart he judged this girl whom he was defending to be guilty, yet was full of intensest admiration, and was sorely torn between the two and his own remorse over his false witnessing. "If I'm called into court and sworn on the Bible, I won't own up that I saw her take that knife," he muttered to himself, as he laid the red cloak and hood on the high feather-bed in his mother's room.

This handsome, stalwart young man, who had hitherto been considered full of a gay audacity where womenfolk were concerned, able to make almost any pretty girl flutter at his smile, was strangely abashed before this beautiful Madelon Hautville, stained, in his eyes, with crime. He brought in wood and mended the hearth fire; he moved about doing such household tasks as were allotted to his masculine hands, and scarcely let his eyes rest once upon the girl in the chimney-corner. He dreaded the sight of that beautiful face which gave him such a shock of pity and admiration and horror. Jim Otis's mind could not compass this new revelation of a woman, but he would not betray her even for her own pleading if he went down perjured to his grave. So valiant was he in her defence that he withstood her against her own self.

Madelon's mother had died when she was a little girl. She could not fairly remember that ever in her whole life she had been so tended and petted as she was that night by Jim Otis's mother. Kind indeed her father and her brothers had always been to her. They had watched over her with jealous fondness, and had taken all rougher tasks upon themselves, but the devotion of woman, which extends to all the minor details of life, she had never known.

She had never had a supper-table set out for her own especial pleasure with this and that dish to tempt her appetite, as Mrs. Otis set out hers that night. A dish of a fine and sublimated porridge did Mrs. Otis make for her — a porridge mixed with cream and sprinkled with nutmeg and fat plums. "I thought some hot porridge would do you good," said Mrs. Otis, when she sat the smoking bowl before Madelon. Then she whispered low, that her son, who was putting another stick on the fire before coming to table, might not hear, "It's the same kind of porridge I had after my son was born — with cream and plums in it. I used to think there never was anything so good." This porridge might well have possessed a flavor of the sweetest memories of motherhood to the older woman, but to the girl, wild with longing to be gone and carry out her purpose, manna from heaven would not have yielded its full measure of sweetness.

She would scarcely have eaten at all had not Jim Otis's mother remarked, as she watched her reluctant sips of the good porridge, "As I said just now, you ain't any daughter of mine, and I ain't any right to dictate, but if you want to get that man, whoever he is, out of prison, you'll have to eat enough to get some strength to do it."

Simply placid as Mrs. Otis looked, she had often wisdom enough to gain her ends by means of that shrewd finesse of government which appeals to the reason of others as applied to the furthering of their own desires.

Madelon after that swallowed her porridge almost greedily, and when supper was over went up-stairs to bed, following Mrs. Otis as readily as any meek young daughter of her own might have done. The spirit of resistance was laid for the time in this poor Madelon Hautville, but it had yielded, after all, more to the will of her own reason than to Jim Otis's mother or the weariness of her own flesh.

When Mrs. Otis came down-stairs she was flushed with pleasant motherly victory. "She's drunk all that hot cordial," she said to her son, "every drop of it, and I've tucked her into bed with the extra comfortables over her, an' she eat quite a good supper, an' I told her to go right to sleep, and I guess she will."

"If she don't she'll be down sick," said Jim, sternly. He sat by the fire, tuning his fiddle.

"She can't hear your fiddle so it'll keep her awake, can she?" asked Mrs. Otis, anxiously.

"Of course she can't, up in the front chamber, with all the doors shut. Wouldn't have touched it if she could."

"Well, I don't s'pose she can. Jim —"

Jim twanged a string. "What is it, mother?"

"I don't want to have you think I'm interferin', Jim. I know you're grown-up now, and I know there's things a young man might not want to tell his mother till he gets ready, but I do kind of want to know one thing, Jim."

Jim tightened the G string. He bent his face low over his violin. "I don't know as I've ever kept much back from you, mother," he said, soberly.

"No, I know you ain't, Jim; you've always told more to your mother than most boys. But I didn't just know but this might be something you hadn't got ready to speak about."

"What is it you want to know, mother?"

"Jim, is that your *girl?*"

Jim laughed a little, although his eyes were grave; he raise the fiddle to his shoulder. "Lord, no, mother. I wouldn't get a girl without asking you."

"I didn't know but you might have seen her over to Ware when you've been there to parties, and not said anything."

"I never saw her but that once, mother." Jim struck up "Kinloch of Kinloch," but he played softly, lest by any chance Madelon, aloft in her chamber, might hear.

"She's handsome as a picture," said his mother. "Who is it that's in prison, Jim?"

"A young man by the name of Gordon."

"What for?"

"They think he stabbed his cousin."

"My sakes! Do you s'pose he did, Jim?"

"I don't know, mother. I wasn't there."

"I s'pose the young man that did it is this girl's beau, and that's why she's so crazy to get him out."

Jim played the merry measure softly, and made no reply.

His mother stood before him quivering with curiosity, which she restrained lest it defeat its own ends. She had learned early that too impetuous feminine questioning is apt to strike a dead-wall in the masculine mind.

"I didn't quite understand what she meant about a knife," she ventured, with an eager glance at her son. He played a little louder, as if he did not hear.

"I s'pose she come here, walked all that way from Ware Centre, this dreadful night, 'cause she thought you could help to get her young man out of prison."

Jim nodded as he fiddled.

"But I can't see how your seein' her brother give her a knife could do any good. Of course that sweet, pretty girl didn't do it herself. But you didn't see her brother give her the knife, Jim?"

"Didn't you hear me say I didn't?" replied Jim, with sudden force. "Don't let's talk any more about it, mother. It's a dreadful piece of work, anyway. I don't half know what it means myself. That poor girl is 'most crazy because that fellow is in prison. That's why she came on this wild-goose chase after me. You can't tell anything by what she says."

"Wasn't he a nice kind of a fellow before this happened, Jim?"

"No, he was a scamp," said Jim Otis, angrily. He struck into the "Fisher's Hornpipe" with fury, regardless of the girl up-stairs.

"Land sakes, Jim, don't fiddle quite so loud as that — I'm dreadful afraid she'll hear," said his mother. "I shouldn't thought a girl that looks as sweet as she does would ever have taken up with a scamp."

"The sweetest girls are the worst fools," answered Jim, bitterly, but he obeyed his mother and played less loudly. The shadows of the winter night might have footed it to the soft measures of the hornpipe which Jim Otis played on his fiddle. His mother could scarcely hear it in the pantry when she went in there to set away the supper dishes. She shut the door every time, lest her son should feel the icy air from the fireless closet. She had always a belief that Jim was delicate, and took a certain pride in it, although she could not have told why.

Everything that was in the least likely to freeze to its injury had to be removed from the cold pantry and set on the hearth that bitter night. It was quite a while before her soft, heavy pattering, which jarred the house when she stepped on certain parts of the floor, ceased, and she took her knitting-work and sat down in her rocking-chair opposite her son.

Jim continued to fiddle, touching the strings as if his fingers were muffled with down. The wind whistled more loudly than his fiddle; it had increased, and the cold with it. Some of Mrs. Otis's crocks froze on the hearth that night. No such cold had been known in Vermont for years. The frost on the window-panes thickened — the light of the full moon could not penetrate them; all over the house were heard sounds like those on a straining ship at sea. The old timbers cracked now and then with a report like a pistol. "It's a dreadful night," said Mrs. Otis, and as she spoke the returning wind struck the house, and she gasped as if it had in truth taken her breath away.

A few minutes before nine o'clock Mrs. Otis put away her knitting-work and got the great Bible off the desk. "Stop fiddling now, Jim," she said, solemnly. Mrs. Otis spoke with more direct authority in religious matters than in others. She felt herself well backed by the spiritual law. Jim finished the tune he was playing and lowered his fiddle from his shoulder. His mother found the place in the Bible, and the holy words were on her tongue when there was a sharp clash of sleigh-bells close under the window.

"Somebody's drove into the yard!" cried Mrs. Otis. "Who do you s'pose 'tis this time of night?"

"Hullo!" shouted a man's voice, hoarsely, and Jim shouted "Hullo!" in response, and started towards the door.

"Ask who's there before you open the door," said the mother, anxiously. She stood listening a moment after Jim had gone; then she caught her shawl from a peg, put it over her head, and followed him — she was so afraid some harm would come to her son.

The outer door was open, and before it was drawn up a sleigh and a great, high-shouldered, snorting and pawing horse. In the sleigh was a man muffled in furs like an Eskimo, leaning out and questioning Jim.

"When did she come?" asked the man.

"About five o'clock," answered Jim.

Then Mrs. Otis understood that they were talking about the girl in her spare-chamber, and she interposed, standing in the doorway. "She was just about tuckered out, what with the cold and that awful tramp," said she. "She most ought to have rode over." Mrs. Otis's voice was soft and conciliatory.

"We didn't know she was coming," replied the man in the sleigh, courteously, "or we should not have let her walk so far on such a day."

"Be you her brother?" questioned Mrs. Otis.

"Yes. I'm her brother Eugene."

"And you drove over to see where she was?"

"Yes; we've been very anxious."

"Well, you can be easy about her for to-night," said Mrs. Otis. "She's tucked up nice and warm in my spare-chamber bed, and I give her a tumbler of my brandy cordial, and I guess she's sound asleep."

"He wants to take her home to-night, mother," said Jim, and there was a curious appeal in his tone.

Mrs. Otis, standing there on the door-step in the freezing moonlight, turned quickly upon the man in the sleigh, and all the soft conciliation was gone from her voice. "You ain't plannin' to take that girl way home to Ware Centre to-night?" said she.

"Father sent me for her," replied Eugene Hautville.

"Well, she ain't goin' a step!"

"Her father will expect me to bring her," said Eugene, with his unfailing courtesy. "He has been very anxious. I had hard work to find where she was. My father won't be satisfied if I come home without her."

"That girl ain't going out of this house to-night!"

"I've got a bearskin here to wrap her up in. She is used to being out in all weathers," persisted Eugene, gently.

"She can't go. Pull her out of a warm bed such a night as this! If you try to take that poor child out to-night I'll stand in my spare-chamber door, and you'll have to walk over me to do it — and my son won't see his mother hurt, I guess!"

Jim Otis stepped closer to the sleigh and spoke to Eugene Hautville in a low voice.

"Well," said Eugene, slowly, "maybe you're right, Otis. I don't know what father will say, but if she was as used up as you tell for, I don't know as 'tis safe. It is an awful night."

"I guess it ain't safe, and she ain't going," maintained Mrs. Otis from the door-step.

Then Eugene Hautville bent well out of his sleigh and asked a question in the other man's ear.

"Yes, she did," replied Jim Otis.

"The poor girl is crazy over it," said Eugene. He and Jim talked for a few moments, but Mrs. Otis, straining her ears on the door-step, could not hear.

Suddenly Jim said, quite distinctly, "She wanted to know if I saw him give her the knife."

There was a pause; then Eugene Hautville asked, in a voice with which he might have addressed a judge of his life and death, "Did you?"

"No," said Jim Otis.

CHAPTER XII

The next morning there took place in a few hours a great change in the temperature. It moderated rapidly. The frost on the windows and the ice-ridges in the roads did not soften yet, since the sun was overcast by heavy clouds, but the terrible rigor and tension of the cold was relaxed, and men could breathe without constraint. At eight o'clock, when Jim Otis and Madelon started for Ware Centre, there was a white film of fallen snow over the distant hills and scattering flakes drove in advance of the storm.

A mile out of Kingston it snowed hard. "Hadn't you better have that extra shawl mother put in over your shoulders?" Jim Otis suggested.

But Madelon shook her head. "The snow won't hurt me," she said. She sat up straight in the sleigh, and there was a look in her eyes, fixed ahead on the white drive of the storm, as if her spirit were out-speeding her body. She had her strength again that morning. She had slept and eaten. She had submitted to the exigencies of life that she might gain power to resist them again.

Jim Otis drove a stout little mare with a good wind for speed, but she had not the stride of David Hautville's great roan. Moreover, after the first stretch, she slacked on the hills and fell into walks in the lonely reaches, almost as if she had learned it in a lesson. Many a pretty girl, flushing sweetly under Jim Otis's gay smile, and perhaps under his caressing arm, had ridden behind that little canny mare, who learned well the meaning of the careless rein along the woodland roads.

However, to-day there was no careless rein. At the first slack Madelon herself had reached the whip and touched the gently ambling neck. "She has more speed in her than this," said she, shortly.

"She hasn't been driven for two days, either," asserted Jim Otis. "Wake up, Molly!" He took the whip himself and flourished it with a quick little snap over her back. In truth, Jim Otis was as anxious to be at this journey's end as Madelon, for he feared every minute lest she should ask him again if he had seen her take the knife, and that he would again have to oppose falsehood to her frantic pleading. But Madelon had believed him. She did not beg him again for his evidence. She sat still at his side with a strained look in her black eyes, and they rode in silence, with the storm heaping its white flakes on their shoulders, until they reached Ware Centre.

Then Madelon turned quickly to Jim Otis. "Don't drive to my home," said she; "I would rather not go home yet. Drive to Burr Gordon's house, please. I want to see his mother. Don't turn — keep straight on."

"Yes, I know where he lives," said Jim, soberly. He drove very slowly. They were drawing near the turn in the road. "See here," he said, suddenly, "don't you think you'd better go home now?" He spoke with nothing of the half-gay, half-caressing authority with which he was wont to turn a pretty girl to his mind, but timidly rather, and kept his eyes fixed on the mare's nodding head, hooded with snow.

"No, I must see Burr's mother," replied Madelon.

"But your folks will be expecting you, won't they?" persisted Jim Otis. He felt that he had a duty of loyalty towards this desperate girl's father and brothers as well as to herself. He had promised Eugene Hautville to bring her home this morning, and who could tell where she might wander and when she might return if he left her now?

He still did not look at Madelon as he spoke, but he felt her turn and fasten her eyes upon his face, and somehow they compelled his. He raised them and saw her beautiful face full of a scorn of passion which he might die and never know in himself.

"What do you think that is to me," said she, "when I've got to save his life? If you do not wish to carry me farther, go back. I will walk."

"I will take you wherever you wish," returned Jim Otis, and touched up the mare, and neither spoke again until they reached Burr Gordon's house, high on its three terraces, with Lot Gordon's opposite. Then Jim halted his mare in the road before it, and would have alighted to assist Madelon, but she sprang out before him. "I am much obliged to you and your mother for what you have done for me," said she, and turned with a swing of her red cloak, and was skimming up the terraces like a red-winged bird.

As for Jim Otis, he slewed his sleigh about recklessly, and shook the whip over the little mare, and drove up the road. When he reached the turn which he knew led to the Hautville house he drew rein, and sat pondering in his sleigh for a few minutes. He was in doubt whether he should inform Eugene Hautville of his sister's whereabouts or not. Finally he spoke to the mare, and continued on his way to Kingston.

The terraces which Madelon mounted were all covered with the gathering snow. When she reached the last the door was opened, and Burr Gordon's mother, Elvira, stood there. "I am sorry there's so much snow for you to wade through," said she, in a sweet, quiet voice.

"I don't mind it, thank you," replied Madelon, harshly. She felt incensed with this mother of Burr's, who came to the door and greeted her as if she were an ordinary caller, and her son were not in prison.

"You had better shake it off your skirts or you'll take cold," said Mrs. Gordon.

"I am not afraid," returned Madelon. She gave her skirts a careless flirt and entered the door with the snow still clinging to her.

"If you will wait a moment," said Mrs. Gordon, "I will get a broom and brush the snow from you before it melts. Then you won't take cold."

"I don't care to have you, thank you," said Madelon. Mrs. Gordon said no more, but led the way to the sitting-room. She was a tall, slender woman with the face of a saint, long and pale, and full of gentle melancholy, with large, meek-lidded blue eyes and patiently compressed lips. She had a habit of folding her long hands always before her, whether she walked or sat, and she moved with sinuous wavings of her widow-bombazine.

The room into which she ushered Madelon was accounted the grandest sitting-room in the village. When Burr's father had built his fine new house he had made the furnishings correspond. He had eschewed the spindle-legged tables and fiddle-backed chairs of the former generations, and taken to solid masses of red mahogany, which were impressive to the village folk. The carpet was a tapestry of great crimson roses with the like of which no other floor in town was covered, and, moreover, there was a glossy black stove instead of a hearth fire.

"Please be seated," said Mrs. Gordon. She indicated the best chair in the room. When her guest had taken it, she sat down herself in the middle of her great haircloth sofa, and folded her long hands in her lap. Mrs. Gordon had the extremest manners of the old New England gentlewoman — so punctiliously polite that they called attention to themselves. She had married late in life, having been previously a preceptress in a young ladies' school. She was still the example of her own precepts — all outward decorum if not inward composure.

Madelon Hautville, opposite her, in her snow-powdered cloak, with her face like a flash of white fire in her snow-powdered silk hood, seemed in comparison a female of another and an older race. She might well, from the look of her, have come a nearer and straighter road from the inmost heart of things, from the unpruned tangle of woods and undammed course of streams, from all primitive and untempered love and passion and religion, than this gentlewoman formed upon the models of creeds and scholars.

Madelon looked at the other woman a second with fierce questioning. Then she sprang up out of the chair where she had been placed, and stood before her on her sofa, and cried out, abruptly, "I have come to tell you about your son. He is not guilty.

I, myself, stabbed Lot Gordon!"

"Please be seated," said Elvira Gordon, and her folded hands in her lap never stirred.

"Seated!" cried Madelon, "seated! How can *you* be seated, how can you rest a moment — you, his mother? Why do you not set out to New Salem now — now? Why do you not walk there, every step, in the snow? Why do you not crawl there on your hands and knees, if your feet fail you, and plead with him to confess that I speak the truth, and tell them to set him free?"

"I beg of you not to so agitate yourself," said Elvira Gordon. "You will be ill. Pray be seated."

Madelon bent towards her with a sudden motion, as if she would seize her by the shoulders.

"Are you his mother," she cried — "his mother — and sit here, like this, and speak like this? Why do you not move? Why do you not start this instant for New Salem — this instant?"

"I beg you to calm yourself," replied Elvira Gordon. "I have been to New Salem to visit my son. I have prayed with him in his prison."

"Prayed with him! Don't you know that he is innocent, and in prison for murder — your own son? You stop to pray with him; why don't you act to save him?"

"You will make yourself ill, my dear."

"Don't you believe that your son is innocent?" demanded Madelon. "Don't you believe it?"

Her eyes blazed; she clinched her hands. She felt as if she could spring at this other woman with her gentle murmurings and soft foldings, and shake her into her own meaning of life. If her impulse had had the power of deed, Elvira Gordon's little cap of fine needle-work would have been a fiercely crumpled rag upon her decorous head, her sober bands of gray hair would have streamed like the locks of a fury, the quiet clasp of her long fingers would have been stirred with some response of indignant defence if nothing else. Madelon, with her, realized that worst balk in the world — the balk of a passive nature in the path of an active one — and all her fiery zeal seemed to flow back into herself and fairly madden her.

"I hope," said Elvira Gordon, "that my son will be proved innocent and set free."

"*Proved* innocent! Don't you know your own son is innocent?"

"I pray without ceasing that he may be acquitted of the crime for which he is imprisoned," replied Elvira Gordon, over her folded hands.

Madelon looked at her. "You are a good woman," said she, with fierce scorn. "You are a member of Parson Fair's church, and you keep to the commandments and all the creed. You are a good woman, and you believe in the eternal wrath of God and the guilt of your own son. You believe in that, in spite of what I tell you. But I tell you again that I, and not your son, am guilty, and I will save him yet!"

Madelon Hautville gathered her red cloak about her, and Mrs. Gordon arose as she would have done when any caller was about to take leave. It would scarcely have seemed out of keeping with her manner had she politely invited Madelon to call again. However, her quiet voice was somewhat unsteady and hoarse when she spoke to Madelon on the threshold of the outer door, although the words were still gently formal. "I am grateful to you for the interest you take in my son," she said; "I hope you will not excite yourself so much that you will be ill."

"I will die if that can save him," answered Madelon Hautville, and went down the snowy steps over the terraces.

Elvira Gordon, when she had closed the door, drew the bolt softly. Truth was, she thought the girl had gone mad through grief and love for her son. Believing, as she did, that the love was all unsought and unreturned, and being also shocked in all her delicate decorum by such unmaidenly violence and self-betrayal, she regarded Madelon with a strange mixture of scorn and sympathy and fear.

Moreover, not one word did she believe of Madelon's assertion that she herself was guilty. "She is accusing herself to save my son," thought Elvira Gordon, and her heart seemed to leap after the girl with half-shamed gratitude, in spite of her astonishment and terror, as she watched her go out of the yard and across the road to Lot Gordon's house. Mrs. Gordon stood at one of the narrow lights beside her front door and watched until Madelon entered the opposite house; then she went hastily through her fine sitting-room to her own bedroom, and there went down on her knees, and all her icy constraint melted into a very passion of weeping and prayer. Those placidly folded hands of hers clutched at the poor mother-bosom in the fury of her grief; those placid-lidded eyes welled over with scalding tears; that calmly set mouth was convulsed like a wailing child's, and all the rigorous lines of her whole body were relaxed into overborne curves of agony. "Oh, my son, my son, my son!" lamented Elvira Gordon. "Have mercy, have mercy, O Father in heaven! Let him be proved innocent! Let Lot Gordon live! Oh, my son!"

Elvira Gordon had the stern pride of justice of a Brutus. She would not without proof discover even to the passionate pleading of her own heart that she believed her son innocent, but believe it she did. Every breath she drew was a prayer that Lot Gordon might yet speak and clear Burr. This morning she had some slight hope that that might come to pass, for the sick man had passed a comfortable night except for his old enemy, the cough.

"It's my belief," Margaret Bean had told Elvira, when she had sped across the road in the early morning to inquire, "that it's his old trouble that's going to kill him when he does die instead of anything else."

"Has he spoken yet?" asked Elvira, eagerly.

"No, he ain't; but there's none so still as them that won't speak." Margaret Bean nodded shrewdly at Elvira. Her voice was weak and hoarse as if from a cold or much calling, but there was sharp emphasis in it. She gave a curious impression of spirit subdued and tearfully rasped, like her face, yet never lacking.

"You — think he — could?" whispered Elvira Gordon.

"'Tain't for me to say," replied Margaret Bean. "He lays there — looks most as if he was dead." She wiped her eyes hard, with a handkerchief so stiff that it looked on that cold morning frozen as with old tears. Margaret Bean was famous for her fine starching in the village; it was her chief domestic talent, and she was faithful in its application in all possible directions.

"I wish he would speak if he could," said Mrs. Gordon.

"I do, if it's for the best," returned Margaret Bean. She hesitated; there were red rings around her tearful eyes, like a bird's. "I can't believe your son did it, nohow, Mis' Gordon," said she.

"I hope if my son is innocent he will be proved so," returned Elvira Gordon. She was too proudly just herself not to use the word *if*, and yet she could have slain the other woman for the sly doubt and pity in her tone.

"It's harder for you than 'tis for him, layin' there," said Margaret Bean, nodding towards the house. There was an odd gratulation of pity in her tone. She rubbed her eyes again.

"We all have our own burdens," replied Elvira, with a dignified motion, as if she straightened herself under hers. "I hope he will be able to speak — soon."

"I hope so, if it's for the best," said Margaret Bean.

CHAPTER XIII

Elvira Gordon had gone home hoping that Lot might yet speak. She had heard his rattling cough as she picked her way out of the icy yard, and Madelon also heard it when she entered it. She knocked at the side door, and Margaret Bean opened it. She had a gruel cup in her hand.

"I want to see him," said Madelon.

Margaret Bean looked at her. Her starched calico apron flared out widely over her lank knees across the doorway.

"I'm afraid he ain't able to see nobody this morning," said she, and the asperity in her tone was less veiled than usual. Her voice was not so hoarse. She was mindful of this girl's former conduct at her master's bedside, and herself half believed her mad or guilty. A suspicious imagination had Margaret Bean, and Madelon would have found in her a much readier belief than in others.

"I've got to see him, whether he's able or not," said Madelon.

"The doctor said —"

"I'm going to see him!"

Madelon pushed roughly in past the smooth apron and ran through the entry to Lot's room, with the housekeeper staring after her in a helpless ruffle of indignation.

"She's gone in there," she told her husband, who appeared in the kitchen door, dish-towel in hand. Margaret Bean's husband always washed the dishes and performed all the irresponsible domestic duties of the establishment. He was commonly adjudged not as smart as his wife, and little store was set by his counsels. Indeed, at times the only dignity of his man's estate which seemed left to this obediently pottering old body was the masculine pronoun which necessarily expressed him still. However, even in that the undisturbed use was not allowed. "Margaret Bean's husband" was usually substituted for "He," and nothing left of him but the superior feminine element feebly qualified by masculinity.

Margaret Bean's husband's name was Zenas, but scarcely anybody knew it, and he had almost forgotten it himself through never being addressed by it. Margaret herself spoke of her husband as "Him," but she never called him anything, except sometimes "You." However, he always knew when she meant him, and there was no need of specification.

Now he half thought she was appealing to his masculine authority from her bewildered air. He stiffened his meek old back. "Want me to go in there and order her out?"

"*You!* Go back in there and finish them dishes."

Margaret Bean's husband went back into the kitchen, and Margaret followed Madelon with a sly, determined air, to Lot's room.

The great square northwest room was warm, but the frost had not yet melted from the window-panes. The room looked full of hard white lines of frost, and starched curtains, and high wainscoting; but the hardest white lines of all were in Lot Gordon's face, sunken sharply in his pillows, showing between the stiff dimity slants of his bed-hangings as in a tent door. He looked already like a dead man, except for his eyes. It seemed as if the life in them could never die when they saw Madelon. She bent over him, darkening the light.

"Speak now!" said she.

Lot Gordon looked up at her.

"I tell you, speak! I will not bear this any longer. I am at the end."

Still Lot Gordon looked up at her silently.

Then Madelon made a quick motion in the folds of her skirt, and there was the long gleam of a hunting-knife above the man in the bed. Margaret Bean, standing by the door, shrieked faintly, but she did not stir.

"I have tried everything," said Madelon. "This is the last. Speak, or I will make your speaking of no avail. I will strike again, and this time they shall find me beside you and not Burr. My new guilt shall prove my old, and they will hang me and not him. Speak, or, before God, I will strike!"

Then Lot Gordon spoke. "I love you, Madelon," said he.

"Say what I bid you, Lot Gordon; not that."

"All your bidding is in that."

"Will you?"

"I will clear — Burr."

Madelon slipped her knife away, and stood back. Margaret Bean slunk farther around past the bedpost. Neither of them could see her.

"On one condition," said Lot Gordon.

"What?"

"That you marry me."

Madelon gasped. "You?"

Lot laughed faintly, stretching his ghastly mouth. "You think it is an offer of wedlock from a churchyard knight," he said.

"What are you talking about, Lot Gordon?"

"Marry me!"

"Marry you? I am going to prison to-day for stabbing you. If you die, I die for your murder. Marriage between us? You are mad, Lot Gordon."

Lot Gordon opened his mouth to speak, but he coughed instead. He half raised himself feebly, and his cough shook the bed. Madelon waited until he lay back, gasping.

"You are mad to talk so," she said again, but her voice was softer.

"No madder — than — my ancestors made me," Lot stammered, feebly. Great drops of sweat stood on his forehead.

Madelon stood looking at him. He lay still, breathing hard, for a little; then he spoke again. "Say you will marry me, and I will clear him," he said, "or else — strike as you will. But all will believe that Burr struck the first blow and you the second for love of him, and though he be not hung, the mark of the noose will be round his neck in folks' fancies so long as he draws the breath of life."

"I will marry you," said Madelon.

"Don't cheat yourself," Lot went on, in his disjointed sentences, broken with the rise of the cough in his throat. "This wound may not be — mortal — after all, and a man lives — long, sometimes, when he's sore put to it for breath. The spark of life dies hard, and you may fan it into a blaze again. All the doctor's nostrums may not stir my poor dying flesh — but give the spirit — what it craves — and 'tis sometimes — strong enough — to gallop the flesh where it will. Lord, I've seen a tree blossom in the fall, when 'twas warm enough. It may be a long life we'll — live together, Madelon. Don't — cheat — yourself into — thinking you'll be my widow, instead of — my wife. My wife you may be, and — the mother of my children."

Madelon moved towards him with a curious, pushing motion, as if she thrust out of her way her own will. She bent over him her white face, holding her body aloof. "I will marry you, come what will. Now, set him free."

Great tears stood in Lot's eyes. "Oh," he whispered, "you think only of him. I love you better than he does, Madelon."

"Set him free," said she, in a hard voice.

Lot heaved a great sigh, and rolled his eyes feebly about towards the door.

"Find — Margaret Bean," he began; and with that Margaret Bean, who had kept the door ajar, slid out softly, "and tell her — to send her husband to — Parson Fair, and — Jonas Hapgood, and she — must go the other way for — the doctor. Tell them to come at once."

With that Lot fell to coughing again, but Madelon went out quickly, and found Margaret Bean in the kitchen mixing gruel.

"Mr. Gordon wishes your husband to go at once for Parson Fair and Jonas Hapgood, and you for the doctor," said she.

"Is he took worse?" asked Margaret Bean, innocently, with a quick sniff of apprehension.

"No, he is no worse, but he wishes to see them. He said to go at once."

Margaret Bean cast an injured eye at the window, all blurred with the clinging shreds of the storm. "I don't see how I can get out in this awful storm nohow," she said. "I've got rheumatism now. Why can't *he* go to see 'em all, I'd like to know?"

"The doctor lives a quarter of a mile the other way. It will save time."

Margaret Bean looked at the gruel. "I've got to make this gruel for him."

"I will make it. Get your shawl, quick."

"It ain't b'iled."

"I tell you I will make it."

"Why can't *he* go to both places?"

"I will go myself!" Madelon cried, suddenly. She had been bewildered, or that would have occurred to her before. She had never been one to send where she could go, but for the time Lot Gordon's will had overcome hers. "Tell your husband to go to the parson's and the sheriff's, quick, and I will go for the doctor," said she, and was flashing out of the yard in her red cloak before Margaret Bean had time to turn herself about from the prospect of her own going. Then she ordered her husband imperiously into his boots and great-coat and tippet, and sent him forth.

She finished the gruel, and took it in to the sick man, and fed him with hard thrusts of the spoon. Lot looked about feebly for Madelon, and Margaret Bean replied to the look, in her husky voice, "She's gone, instead of me. I've got rheumatism too bad to venture out in such a storm and get my petticoats bedraggled." She spoke with a little whine of defiant crying, but Lot took no notice. He was exhausted. After he had eaten the gruel, he pointed to the chimney-cupboard.

"What is it ye want?" said she.

Lot pointed.

"How do I know what ye want when ye jest p'int like that?"

But there came then a look into Lot Gordon's eyes as expressive as a word, and Margaret Bean crossed over to the chimney-cupboard, and got out the brandy-flask and a wine-glass and some loaf-sugar. She mixed a little dose of the brandy and sugar, and would have fed it to the sick man as she had the gruel, but he motioned her aside, raised himself with an effort, and drank it down eagerly. Then he lay still, and soon a faint flush came into his face. Margaret Bean went back into the kitchen and mixed some bread, with her eye upon the window.

Presently there was a wild gallop and great clash of bells past the window, and a shout at the door. Margaret Bean put on her little blue shawl and opened it when the shout had been twice repeated. Old David Hautville sat there in his sleigh, keeping a tight rein on his tugging roan. "My daughter here?" he shouted. "Whoa, there!"

"There's sick folks here," said Margaret Bean, shivering in the doorway. "You hadn't ought to holler so." Her tearful eyes were more frankly hostile than usual. She had always looked down from her own slight eminence of life upon these Hautvilles, and now was full of scorn that her master was to marry one of them.

"I want to know if my daughter is here," said David Hautville, and he did not lower his voice. It sounded like a hoarse bellow of wrath, coming out of the white whirl of snow. His fur coat was all crusted with snow, his great mustache heavy with it; the roan plunged in a rising cloud of it.

"No, she ain't here," replied Margaret Bean, and her weak voice seemed by its very antithesis to express the utmost scorn and disgust at the brutality of the other.

"Has she been here?"

"Yes, she's been here." Margaret made as though to shut the door, but David Hautville stopped her.

"Did she start for home?"

"You'd better ask somebody that knows more about it."

"Where did she go?"

"You'd better ask somebody that knows about it!" repeated Margaret Bean, in her malicious meekness. Then she shut the door.

David Hautville, with a great "whoa!" leaped out of the sleigh. He led up the roan with a fierce pull to the fence, and tied her there. Then he strode into the house, and through the entry to Lot's room, with no ceremony.

"Where is my daughter?" he demanded, standing at Lot's bedside in his great fur coat, all bristling with points of snow.

"She'll be back presently," answered Lot. His voice was a little stronger; there were two red spots on his cheeks.

"Where's she gone?"

"For the doctor."

All at once David Hautville gave a great start. "Why, you're talking!" he cried out. "You couldn't speak."

Lot nodded vaguely.

"You're better, then?" cried the other, with a sharp look at him.

Lot nodded again.

"When did she come here?"

"Just now."

"Same damned nonsense, I suppose. She's gone mad. If the law don't finish that fellow, I will!"

Lot motioned towards a chair. "Sit down," he whispered.

"She coming back with the doctor?"

"Yes," Lot coughed.

David Hautville settled into a chair with a surly grunt. He

watched Lot cough, holding to his straining chest, and thought that he must be worse, else he would not have sent for the doctor. He resolved to wait and take his daughter home with him, by force if necessary, but with no more disturbance of this man, who might be sick unto death. Seeing Lot cast his eyes about as if looking for something, and make a motion towards the table at his side, he rose up quickly and got him a spoonful of the cough mixture in a bottle thereon, and administered it to him gently.

"Don't you touch my wet coat," said David Hautville, "or yo'll get a chill," and he held himself carefully away from the sick man.

When Lot lay back, panting, he returned to his chair and did not speak again. The two remained in silence until there came the jingle of bells, the tramp of horses' feet, and the voice of men out in the yard.

Lot lay still, with his eyes closed. David Hautville raised his head and looked at the window, thick with frost. Presently the door was opened softly, and the doctor came in, with Parson Fair and Jonas Hapgood. Madelon, in her snow-powdered red cloak, came last. David started up fiercely when he saw her; then he stood back and waited. The doctor bent over Lot and began counting his pulse. He eyed him sharply.

"The pendulum still swings," said Lot.

The doctor started. "You can speak, then!" he cried out, brusquely.

Lot smiled.

The doctor was old, and his long struggle with birth and death had begun to tell upon him. He had already visited Lot that morning, after a hard night with a patient, back in the hills. His face was haggard under its sharp gray bristle of beard; his eyes fierce, like an old dog's, with fatigue and hunger. He had just reached home and sat down to his breakfast when this new call came. He had thought Lot was dying from Madelon's imperative summons, and she had not undeceived him. She was growing cunning in her desperate efforts to save Burr Gordon.

"What in thunder did ye send for me again for?" he snapped. This old country doctor was never chary of plain speaking, and his brusqueness had increased his popularity. Many of his patients were simple countrywomen, who had greater belief in that which they feared. They repeated his half-savage speeches to each other, and added, "He's a good doctor, if he does speak out."

Lot only smiled that covert smile of his, which seemed to imply some wisdom of humor beyond the ken of others. "I ought to be dying," he said, with grim apology. "I ought not — to have disturbed you all for a less reason than to witness my final exit, but I want you to witness something else." Lot Gordon spoke quite strongly and connectedly.

"What?" asked the doctor, irritably.

"I want to make a statement," said Lot Gordon.

There was a pause. Jonas Hapgood, with his look of heavy facetiousness, slightly tempered now with curiosity, stood lounging into his great snowy boots at the foot of the bed. Parson Fair, the consolation for the dying which he had thought to administer still in his mind, which could not swerve easily, his slender height in his black surtout inclined towards the sick man with gentle courtesy, waited. Margaret Bean peered around the bed-curtain. Madelon stood near the doctor, her face white as if she were dead, and a look of awful listening upon it. In the background David Hautville, wrathful and wondering, towered over them all.

"I wish to declare in the presence of these witnesses," said Lot Gordon, "the doctor here testifying that I am in my right mind" — the doctor gave a surly grunt of assent — "that it is my firm belief that all mortal ills come to man through his own agency, and this last ill of mine is no exception. I declare solemnly before you all that my cousin Burr Gordon is not guilty of administering this wound which I bear in my side."

The sheriff started forward. "Who did do it, then?" he cried out.

"I myself," replied Lot Gordon.

CHAPTER XIV

There was a gasp of astonishment from the company. Jonas Hapgood began to speak, but Madelon's soprano drowned out his thick bass.

"How dare you," she cried out, "swear to that lie? Liar! You are a liar, Lot Gordon!"

Then, before Lot could reply, David Hautville came forward with a mighty plunge, and grasped his daughter by the arm, and forced her to the door.

"Get ye out of this," growled David Hautville; but Madelon turned her face back in the doorway for one last word. "Don't you know," she shrieked back to Lot Gordon, in her pitiless despair — "don't you know that I would rather have seen the inside of my prison-cell to-night and the gallows to-morrow than this, Lot Gordon?"

"Quit your talk!" shouted David Hautville; and she followed his fierce leading out of the house into the yard.

"Get ye into this sleigh," ordered her father; and she obeyed. Suddenly the fire of passion and revolt seemed to die out in her; it was like a lull in a spiritual storm. She rode home with her father, and neither spoke. David Hautville now considered the matter as past any words of reasoning. He was convinced that his daughter's fair wits were shaken, and that nothing but summary dealing, as with a child, could avail anything. When they reached home he bade her, with a kind of stern forbearance, to get into the house at once and see to her work there, and she obeyed again.

All that day, and many days after that, poor Madelon Hautville, who had been striving like any warrior against the powers and principalities of human wills and passions, and had grounded her arms after a victory which had left her wounded almost to death, carried her bleeding heart and walked her woman's treadmill. She scoured faithfully the pewter dishes and the iron pots. She swept the hearth clean and baked and brewed and spun and sewed. Her lot would have been easier had her woe befallen her generations before, and she could, instead, have backed her heavy load of tenting through the snow on wild hunting-parties, and broken the ice on the river for fish, and perchance taken a hand at the defence when the males of her tribe were hard pressed. Civilization bowed cruelly this girl, who felt in greater measure than the gently staid female descendants of the Puritan stock around her the fire of savage or primitive passions; but she now submitted to it with the taciturnity of one of her ancestresses to the torture. Week after week she went about the house, and neither spoke nor smiled. Burr Gordon was set free, fully acquitted of the charge against him; Madelon's denial of

Lot's false confession had gone for nothing. Half the village considered her hysterical and irresponsible, and Lot Gordon, it was agreed, was just the man to lay violent hands upon his own life, steal and use his cousin's knife, and keep mute to fasten the guilt upon him, as he had confessed.

A week after Burr's release Louis and Richard Hautville came home. They had been trapping on Green Mountain, they said, camping in the little lodge they had built there. When they came in laden with stark white rabbits and limp-necked birds, and one of them with a haunch of venison on his back, Madelon faced them with sudden fierceness, as if to speak. Then she turned away to her work, without a word of greeting. The boy Richard stared at her with a quiver, as of coming tears on his handsome face. He whispered to Eugene, when she went into the pantry.

"Best let her alone," said Eugene. "She's been so ever since."

Not one of them knew of her promise to marry Lot Gordon, and Lot had bound Margaret Bean over to secrecy. All the village was as yet ignorant of that, but there was enough besides to afford a choice bone of gossip to folk sunken in the monotony and isolation of a Vermont country winter. The women put their heads together over it at their quilting-bees, and the men in their lounging-places in the store and tavern. This mystery, which endured as well as their hard-packed snows, and kept their imaginations always upon the stretch, was a great acquisition to them. Plenty of mental activity was there in Ware Centre that winter, and the brains of many were smartly at work upon some of those problems whose conditions, being all unknown quantities of character and circumstance and fate, are beyond all rules of solution.

Would Burr Gordon marry Dorothy Fair, or would he, after all, turn again to his old love, who had shown such devotion to him that it had almost turned her brain? Unless, indeed — for there is room in gossip for all suspicion, and surmise can never be quite laid at rest — her brain had not been turned, and she had struck the blow, as she said. But, in that case, why had Lot taken her guilt upon himself? Why had he cleared Burr at his own expense, and saved her? If he had done it for love of Madelon, he had also set his rival free to woo her, and had established her innocence in his eyes.

Lot still lived. Would he die, finally, of his wound or of his disease? Would he recover and come out of his house alive again? Time went on, and the people knew no more than they knew at first; but they continued to watch, crossing the gleams of all the neighboring window-panes with sharp lines of attention, hushing conversation in the store if a Hautville or a Gordon entered, and rolling keen eyes over shoulders after meeting one of them upon the country roads. But especially they were alert in the meeting-house upon Sabbath days. Their eyes were slyly keen upon Dorothy Fair, softly wrapped in her blue wadded silk and swan's-down, holding up her head with gentle state in the parson's pew; upon Burr Gordon, somewhat pale and moody in his smart Sunday coat; and Madelon, up in the singing-seats. They never, in those days, saw Madelon elsewhere. She went to meeting every Sabbath day and sang as usual, but between the hymns she sat with her beautiful face as irresponsive to all around her as a painted portrait, and more so, for the eyes of a portrait will often seem to follow an ardent gazer. Madelon's father and brothers, except Richard and Louis, who kept their own counsel, were much bewildered among themselves at her strange mood, and were inclined to hold the opinion that her wits were a little shaken, and, moreover, to keep it quiet and secret from everybody until she should be quite restored. They said little to her, treating her with a kind of forbearing compassion; but the indignation of them all was fierce, although held well in check, against Burr Gordon. Him they held accountable for all.

Burr Gordon might well have been quit of any charge of cowardice had he shrunk from facing the male Hautvilles on those days. They passed him in the road with the looks of surly dogs in leash. None of them except Eugene gave him a nod of recognition. Eugene bowed always, with his unfailing grace of courtesy, but he hated him more than all the others, for he was jealous on his own account as well as his sister's. It was said that Burr Gordon, since his acquittal, was courting Dorothy Fair steadily, although they had not been seen out together.

Burr had been to the Hautville house twice since his return from New Salem, but had not been admitted. Once when he called Madelon had been alone in the house, and caught a glimpse of her old lover coming into the yard. She had sprung up, letting her needle-work slide to the floor, and fled with her face as white as death and her heart beating hard into the freezing best room, and stood back in a corner out of range of the windows, and listened to the taps of the knocker and finally to Burr's retreating steps. Then she crept across to a window and peered around the curtain, and watched him out of sight as if her soul would follow him; then she stole out the door and looked up and down to see if anybody was in sight; and then she flung herself down upon her knees and kissed her lover's cold footprint in the snow.

The second time Burr came was on an evening, when her father and all her brothers except Richard were at the singing-school. She knew Burr's step when he drew near the door, and bade Richard shortly to answer the knock, and say she was busy and could see nobody, which he did with all the emphasis which his fiery young blood could put into words of dismissal. The boy, of all the others, alone knew a reason why he should be more lenient with Burr; and yet this very reason seemed to swell his wrath and hold him more deeply responsible for a deeper disgrace. When he had shut the door hard upon Burr, he turned to his sister. "I would have killed him rather than let him in," said he.

Madelon took another stitch in her work. Her face looked as if it were carved in marble. Richard stood staring at her a second; then he flung out of the room, and the doors closing behind him shook the house. Richard's manner towards his sister was sometimes full of a fierce sympathy and partisanship, sometimes of wild anger and aversion. He looked ten years older in a few weeks. Both he and Louis appeared to avoid the other members of the family, and kept much together, and yet even in their close companionship they also seemed to have a curious avoidance of each other; one was seldom seen to look in his brother's face, or address him directly.

One morning, a month after Burr's release, Margaret Bean came to the Hautville door. She was well wrapped against the cold, her head especially being swathed about with lengths of knitted scarf over her silk hood; there was only a thin sharp gleam of face out of it, like a very lance of intelligence. Margaret held out the stiff white corner of a letter from the folds of her shawl. "He sent it," she said to Madelon, who came to the door.

Madelon opened the letter and read it. "I can't come," she said, shortly. "I'm busy. Tell him he must write what he wants to tell me."

Margaret Bean's eyes were sharp as steel points. She had not known what was in the letter. "Hey?" said she, pretending that she had not heard, in order to make Madelon repeat and perhaps reveal more.

"I can't come," said Madelon. "He can write what he wants to tell me."

Suddenly a great red flush spread over her pale face and her neck. She lowered her eyes before the other woman as if in utter degradation of shame, and shrank back into the house and closed the door in Margaret Bean's face.

Margaret Bean stood for a moment, a silent, shapeless figure in the cold air. "Pretty actions, I call it," said she then, quite loudly, and went out of the yard with a curious tilting motion on slender ankles, as of a balancing bale of wool.

Madelon slipped her letter into her pocket as she entered the kitchen. Her father and all her brothers were there. It was shortly after breakfast, and they had not yet gone out.

"Who was it at the door?" her father asked. He sat by the fire in his great boots.

"Margaret Bean."

"What did she want?"

"Lot Gordon sent for me to come over there."

"What for?"

"He wanted — to — tell me something."

"You ain't going a step. I can tell ye that."

"I — told her I couldn't go," said Madelon. Her voice was almost breathless, and still that red of shame was over her face. She bent her head and turned her back to them all, and went out of the room. The male Hautvilles looked at one another. "What's come over the girl now?" said Abner, in his surly bass growl.

"She's a woman," said his father, and he stamped his booted feet on the floor with a great clamp.

Madelon meantime fled up-stairs to her chamber, with her first love-letter from Lot Gordon in her pocket. Until this the reality of all that had happened had not fully come home to her. Without acknowledging it to herself she had entertained a half-hope that Lot might not have been entirely in earnest — that he might not hold her to her promise. And then there had been the uncertainty as to his recovery. But here was this letter, in which Lot Gordon called her — her, Madelon Hautville — his sweetheart, and begged her to come to him, as he had something of importance to say to her! He used, moreover, terms of endearment which thrilled her with the stinging shame of lashes upon her bare shoulders at the public whipping-post. She lit the candle on her table, snatched the letter out of her pocket, crumpled it fiercely as if it were some live thing that she would crush the life out of, and then held it to the candle-flame until it burned away, and the last flashes of it scorched her fingers. Then she caught a sight of her own miserable, shamed face in her looking-glass, and flushed redder and struck herself in her face angrily, and then fell to walking up and down her little room.

Her father and brothers down below heard her, and looked at each other.

"There was that Emmeline Littlefield that went mad, and fell to walking all the time," said Abner.

The others listened to the footsteps overhead with a gloomy assent of silence.

"They had to keep her in a room with an iron grate on the window," said Abner, further, with a pale scowl.

Then David Hautville took down his leather jacket from its peg with a jerk, and thrust his arm into it. "I tell ye, she's a *woman*," he said, in a shout, as if to drown out those hurrying steps; and then he went out of the room and the house, and disappeared with axe on shoulder across the snowy reach of fields; and presently all his sons except Eugene followed him. Eugene remained to keep watch over his sister.

CHAPTER XV

After his father and brothers were gone, Eugene got Louis's fiddle out of the chimney-cupboard and fell to playing with an imperfect touch, picking out a tune slowly, with halts between the strains, as if he spelled a word with stammering syllables. Eugene's musical expression was in his throat alone; his fingers were almost powerless to bring out the meaning of sweet sounds. A drunken crew on a rolling vessel might have danced to the tune that Eugene Hautville fingered on his brother's fiddle that morning while his sister walked back and forth overhead, running the gantlet, as it were, of an agony which his masculine imagination could not compass, well tutored as it was by the lessons of his Shakespeare book.

When Margaret Bean came to the door the second time she heard the squeak of the fiddle, and clanged the knocker loud to overcome it. Madelon and Eugene reached the door at the same time, and Margaret Bean extended another letter. "Here's another," said she, shortly, to Madelon. She tucked the hand which had held the letter under her shawl and hugged herself with a shiver, ostentatiously. "I'm most froze, traipsin' back and forth, I know that much," she muttered.

Eugene stood aside with a flourish and a graceful, beckoning wave of his hand. "Won't you come in and warm yourself?" he said, and he smiled in her face as if she and no other were the love of his heart.

But Margaret Bean had a shrewd understanding which no grace of flattery could dazzle, and felt truly that nowadays her principal claim to masculine admiration lay in her fine starching specialty of housewifery; and of that she gave no show, bundled up against the cold in her shapeless wools. So she put aside the young man's smiling courtesy scornfully, as not belonging to her, and spoke in a voice as sharp as an edge of her own well-stiffened linens. "no, sir," said Margaret Bean; "I've got bread in the oven and I can't stop, and I ain't coming in for two or three minutes and set with my things on, and get all chilled through when I go out. I'll stand here while your sister reads that letter. He said the answer would be just 'yes' or 'no,' and I shouldn't have to wait long. 'She ain't one to teeter long on a decision,' says he; 'she finds her footin' one side or the other.' He talks queer, queerer'n ever sence he was hurt. I pity anybody that gets him."

"Tell him 'yes,'" said Madelon, abruptly; and then she wheeled about and went into the house.

"Well," said Margaret Bean, harshly. The door closed before her; Eugene had forgotten his courtesy, and followed his sister into the house without a good-day to the guest.

Margaret Bean stood for a minute looking at the house, with its yawn of blank windows in her face; then she went out of the yard, bearing her message to Lot Gordon.

Eugene Hautville was startled at the look on Madelon's face when she went into the house. "Madelon, what is it?" he said, softly. But she did not answer him a word; she ran across the room and thrust Lot Gordon's letter into the fire. Eugene followed her and turned her about gently, and looked keenly in her white face.

"What was in that latter?" said he.

Madelon shook her head dumbly.

"Madelon?"

"Wait. You will know soon. I can't tell you," she gasped out then.

"Was it from Lot Gordon?"

She nodded.

"What is he writing to you about? You are my sister, and I have a right to know."

"Wait," she gasped again. "Oh, Eugene, wait. I — can't —"

Suddenly Madelon hung heavy on her brother's arm. "Madelon," he cried out loudly to her, as if she were deaf — "Madelon, don't! You needn't tell me. Madelon!"

Eugene almost lifted his sister into the rocking-chair on the hearth, and hastened to get her a cup of water; but when he returned with it she motioned it away, and was sitting up, stern and straight and white, but quite conscious.

"Hadn't you better drink it, Madelon?" pleaded Eugene.

"No. What do I want it for? I am quite well," said she.

"You almost fainted away."

"I don't want it."

Eugene set the cup on the dresser; then he came back to Madelon, and stood over her, looking at her, his dark face as pitiful as a woman's. "Madelon, why can't you tell me what new thing is making you act like this?" he said. Madelon made an impatient motion and started up, and would have gone out of the room, but Eugene flung an arm around her and held her firmly. "What is it, poor girl?" he whispered in her ear.

Madelon had soft woman's blood in her veins, after all. Suddenly she shook convulsively, and would have kept her face firm, but she could not. She put her head on her brother's shoulder, and sobbed and wept as he had never seen her do, even when she was a child, for she had never been one to cry when she was hurt. Eugene sat down in the rocking-chair with his sister on his knee, and smoothed her dark hair as gently as her mother might have done. "Poor girl! poor girl!" he kept whispering; but, softly caressing as his voice was, his eyes, staring over his sister's head at the fire, got a fierce and fiercer look; for he was thinking of Burr

Gordon and cursing him in his heart for all this. "Good Lord, Madelon, can't you put that fellow out of your head?" he cried out, sharply, all at once.

Then Madelon hushed her sobs, with a stern grip of her will upon her quivering nerves, and raised herself up and away from him. "That has nothing to do with this," she said, coldly. "Let me go now, Eugene."

But Eugene held her strongly with a hand on either arm, and scanned her keenly with his indignant eyes. "He is at the root of the whole matter," said he, "and you know it. I wish —"

"I tell you Burr Gordon has nothing to do with this last. He knows nothing of it. Let me go, Eugene."

But Eugene still held her and looked at her. "Madelon —"

"What? I can sit here no longer. I have work to do. There is nothing the matter with me. I have nothing to complain of. What I do I do of my own free will."

"Madelon," whispered Eugene, with a red flush stealing over his dark face, his eyes dropping a little before her, "you don't — think she will — marry him?"

"Who? Dorothy?"

Eugene nodded.

"Of course she will — marry him, Eugene Hautville."

Eugene set his sister down suddenly and got up. "All I've got to say is, then," he cried, with a movement of his right arm like a blow, "it's a damned shame that the child can't be taken care of among us all."

"What do you mean, Eugene Hautville?"

"I mean that she had better lie down in her grave than marry that —"

"Take care what you say, Eugene."

"I say she had —"

"Better lie down in her grave than marry him — than marry Burr Gordon? What do you mean? Who are you, that you talk in this way? He is better than you all; not one of you is fit to tie his shoe."

"Madelon, are you mad? He is a lying villain, and you know it, and — God knows it's only on her account I speak. Some one ought to tell her."

"Tell her, tell her! What do you think I would tell her if I were to speak? If she were to come to me and ask me if Burr ever courted me and played me false for her, I would tell her, no, no, no! If she were to ask me if Burr ever kissed me, or said a fond word to me, or gave me a fond look, I would tell her, and this last is the truth, that he never gave me more than a passing thought, and 'twas only my own short-sightedness and conceit that made me think 'twas more than that, shame to me! Isn't he a man, and shouldn't a man look well about him among us to be sure his heart is set? I'd tell her 'twas something for her to hold up her head for among other women all the days of her life, because he chose her. That's what I'd tell her."

"Madelon!"

"Dorothy Fair shall not cheat Burr now, when he has set his heart upon her. It would be worse than all that has gone before. I tell you I won't bear that. He shall have her if he wants her. He has suffered enough."

"But you — you," gasped Eugene. "I thought you — I thought you wanted him yourself, Madelon."

"I've gone past myself. All I think of now is what he wants," said she, shortly. She turned to go out of the room; then she stopped and spoke to him over her shoulder: "There's no need of talking any more about it." She added: "I know what I've set out to do, and I can go through with it." Then the door shut after her, and Eugene sat down with his Shakespeare book. But he could not read; he sat moodily puzzling over his sister, whose unfulfilled drama of life held his mind better than them all.

But puzzle as he might, he never once dreamed of the truth — that his sister Madelon had promised to marry Lot Gordon in a month's time, and sent her "yes" by word of mouth of Margaret Bean that morning. Somehow, even with the ashes of the letter of proposal before his eyes on the hearth, and his sister's "yes" ringing in his ears, knowing as he did that Lot as well as Burr had lost his heart to her, he could not conceive of such a possibility. He was too well acquainted with Madelon's attitude towards Lot, and she had never been one to walk whither she did not list for any man. He could not imagine the possibility, well versed as he was, through his Shakespeare lessons, in the feminine heart, of his sister's yielding her proud maiden will to any man. He would as soon have thought of a wild-cat which he had trailed in the woods, which knew him as his mortal enemy, whose eyes had followed him with stealthy fury out of a way-side bush, to unbend from the crouch of its spring and walk purring tamely into his house at call, and fall to lapping milk out of a saucer on the hearth. But no man can estimate the possibilities of character under the lever of circumstances, and there is power enough abroad to tame the savage in all nature. Madelon Hautville had yielded to a stress of which her brother knew nothing, and he therefore scouted the idea, if it crossed his mind like a wild fancy, of her yielding at all. He rather came to the conclusion that the letter had announced Burr's engagement to Dorothy Fair, and that Madelon's "yes" had signified proud approval of it. He leaned to this conclusion the sooner because of the miserable tendency which a jealous heart has to force all suspicions to open its own sore. "He's going to marry

Dorothy Fair," Eugene told himself. "It was like Lot to tell Madelon, and ask her if she was pleased with it. And that was why she acted so. Her heart broke at first and she cried, and then she stood up and hid it. He's going to marry Dorothy Fair!"

Eugene had a strong imagination, whereby he could suffer a thousandfold, if he would, every woe of his life. Sitting now by his hearth fire, with his Shakespeare book, full of the joys and sorrows of immortal lovers, disregarded upon his knees, he let his fancy show him many a picture which tore his heart, although look upon it he would. He saw Dorothy Fair in her wedding-gown; he saw her blush like a rose through her bridal lace; he saw her following Burr up the meeting-house aisle the Sabbath after her marriage with a soft rustling of silken finery, and a toss of white bridal plumes over her fair locks. He saw those glances, which he swore to himself boldly enough then had first been his, turned upon his rival; he imagined sweet words and caresses which he had never tasted, and were perchance the sweeter for that, bestowed upon Burr.

Suddenly he started up and flung down his book upon the settle, and put on his fur cap and was out of the house. "The first turn of her heart was towards me, and I was the first man she coupled with love in her thoughts, and nothing can undo it," he said, aloud, fiercely to himself as he went up the lonely snowy road; and he believed it then. Those soft blue glances of Dorothy's came back to him so vividly that he seemed to see them anew whenever his eyes fell upon the way-side bushes, or the cloud-shadowed slopes of white fields, or the dark gaps of solitude between the forest pines.

For the first time a fierce insistence of his rights of love was upon him. Straight to the village he went, and to Parson Fair's house. But he did not enter; his madness was not great enough for that. He did not enter, but he went past with a bold, searching look at all the windows and no pretence of indifference, and up the road a little way. Then he returned and passed the house again, and looked again; and this time Dorothy's face showed between the dimity sweeps of her chamber curtains. He half stopped, and then came another glance of blue eyes which verified those that had gone before, straight into his, which replied with a dark flash of ardor, and then Dorothy's face went red all of a sudden, and there was a vanishing curve of blushing cheek and a flirt aside of fair curls, and the space between the dimity curtains was clear.

Eugene stood still beneath the window for a few minutes. There were watchful eyes in the neighboring windows. In the tavern-yard, farther down the street, Dexter Beers and old Luke Basset stood, also fixedly staring at Parson Fair's house.

"Wonder if he thinks there's any trouble — fire or anything," said Dexter Beers.

"Don't see no smoke," said old Luke.

Eugene Hautville, rapt in that abstraction of love which is the completest in the world, and makes indeed a world of its own across eternal spaces, knew nothing and thought nothing of outside observers. He was half minded for a minute to enter Parson Fair's house. Had Dorothy appeared outside, the impulse to seize her and bear her away with him and fight for her possession against all odds, like any male of his old savage tribe when love stirred his veins, would have been strong within him. But she did not come, nor appear again in the window. She stood well around the curtain and peeped; but he did not know that, and presently he went away.

When he passed the tavern Dexter Beers hailed him. "Say, anythin' wrong to the parson's?"

"No," returned Eugene, sharply, and strode on.

"Didn't know but you see smoke, you were lookin' up at the house so stiddy," called Beers, conciliatingly; but Eugene swung down the road without another look. All his grace of manner was forgot in the stir of passion within him. What had Dorothy Fair meant by that look? Was she betrothed to Burr Gordon? Was she playing with him for her own amusement? And what was he to do, what could he do, for the sake of his love, with honor?

Eugene left the road after he had cleared the village, and struck off across the fields for a long tramp through snowy solitudes as well known to him as, and better suited to him for perplexed thoughts than, any place in his home. In a way, out-doors was the truest home of all these Hautvilles, with the strain of wild nomadic blood in their veins.

The sight of the little fireless dwellings of woodland things, the empty nests revealed on the naked trees, the scattered berries on leafless bushes, the winter larders of birds, the tiny track of a wild hare or a partridge in the snow, disturbed less the current of their inmost life, as being more the wonted surroundings of their existence, than all the sounds and sights and savors within four domestic walls.

Eugene tramped on for miles over paths well known to him, which were hidden now beneath the snow, pondering upon himself and Dorothy Fair, and never gave his sister, whose guardian he had been, another thought.

CHAPTER XVI

Madelon, half an hour after Eugene had left, put on her cloak and hood, and went down the road to Lot Gordon's. "I want to see him a minute," she said to Margaret Bean when the woman answered her knock, and went in with no more ado. Her face was white and stern in the shadow of her hood.

Margaret Bean recoiled a little when she looked at her. "He's up," said she, backing before her, half as if she were afraid. "I guess you can walk right in."

Madelon went into the sitting-room, and Lot's face confronted her at once, white and peaked, with hollow blue eyes lit, as of old, with a mocking intelligence of life.

He was sunken amid multifold wrappings in a great chair before the fire, with a great leathern-bound book on his knees. Beside him was a little stand with writing-paper thereon, and sealing-wax and a candle, a quill pen and an inkstand. All the room was lined with books, and was full of the musty smell of them.

Madelon went straight up to Lot and spoke out with no word of greeting. "I have sent your answer," said she. "I will keep my promise, but have you thought well of what you do, Lot Gordon?"

Lot looked up at her and smiled, and the smile gave a curiously gentle look to his face, in spite of the sharp light in his eyes.

"The thought has been my meat and my drink, my medicine and my breath of life," said he.

"If I were a man I would rather — take a snake to my breast than a woman who held me as one —"

"Two parallel lines can sooner meet than a woman know the heart of a man. What do I care so I hold you to mine?"

Madelon stood farther away from him, but her eyes did not fall before his.

"Why did you lie" said she. "You knew I stabbed you, and not yourself. You are a liar, Lot Gordon."

But Lot still smiled as he answered her. "However it may be with other men, no happening has come to me since I set foot upon this earth that I brought not upon myself by my own deeds. The hand that set the knife in my side was my own, and I have not lied."

"You have lied. Tell them the truth."

"I have told the truth that lies at the bottom of the well."

"Call them all in now, and tell them — I — did it, I —"

Lot Gordon raised himself a little, and looked at her with the mocking expression gone suddenly from his face. "What good do you think it would do if I did, Madelon?" he said, with a strange sadness in his voice.

She looked at him.

"I shall not die of the wound. You can't escape me by prison or a disgraceful death, and as for me, do you think it would make any difference to me if all the village pointed at you, Madelon?"

Madelon looked at him as if she were frozen.

"All the way to be set loose from your promise is by your own breaking it," said Lot.

"I will keep my promise," said Madelon, shutting her lips hard upon her words. She turned away.

"Madelon," said Lot.

She went towards the door as if she did not hear.

"Madelon."

She turned her white face slightly towards him and paused.

"Won't you come here to me a moment?"

"I cannot until I am driven to it!" she cried out, passion leaping into her voice like fire. "I cannot go near you, Lot Gordon!"

She opened the door, and then she heard a sob. She hesitated a second, then looked around; and Lot Gordon's thin body was curled about in his chair and quivering with sobs like any child's.

Madelon closed the door, and went back and stood over him. She looked at him with a curious expression of pity struggling with loathing, as she might have looked at some wounded reptile.

"Well, I am here," she said, in a harsh voice.

"All my life my heart has had nothing, and now what it has it has not," moaned Lot, as if it had been to his mother. He looked up at her with his hollow blue eyes swimming in tears. He seemed for a minute like a little ailing boy appealing for sympathy, and the latent motherhood in the girl responded to that.

"You know I cannot help that, Lot," she said. "You know how you forced me into this to save the one I do love."

"Oh, Madelon, can't you love me?"

She shrank away from him and shook her head, but still her dark eyes were soft upon his face.

"Does not love for you count anything? I love you more than he — I do, Madelon."

"It is no use talking, I can never love you, Lot," she said, but gently.

"It ought to count. Love ought to count, dear. It is the best thing in the world we have to give. And I have given it to you; oh, God, how have I given it to you, Madelon!"

"Lot, don't — it's no use."

"Listen — you must listen, dear. You must hear it once. It can't turn you more against me. You don't know how I have loved you — you don't know. Listen. Never a morning have I waked but the knowledge of you came before the consciousness of myself.

Never a night I fell asleep but 'twas you, you I lost last, and not myself. When I have been sick the sting of my longing for you has dulled all my pain of body. If I die I see not how that can die with me, for it is of my soul. I see not why I must not bear it forever."

"Lot, I must go!"

"Listen, Madelon; you must listen. When I have taken my solitary walks in the woods and pried into the secrets of the little wild things that live there in order to turn my mind from my own musing, I found always, always, that you were in them — I cannot tell you how, but you were, Madelon. There was a meaning of you in every bird-call and flutter of wings and race of wild four-footed things across the open. Every white alder-bush in the spring raised you up anew before me to madden me with vain longing, and every red sumach in the fall. When I have sat here alone every book I have opened has had in it a meaning of you which the writer knew not of. You are in all my forethoughts and my memories and my imaginations. The future has your face, and the past. My whole world is made up of you and my vain hunger. Oh, love, and not toil, is the curse of man!"

"You knew about Burr," Madelon said, in a quiet, agitated voice. "Why — did you?"

Lot gave a sharp cry, as if he had been wounded anew. "Oh," he cried, "you are blind, blind, blind — a woman is born blind to love! If I had had the face and the body of him it would have been me you would have turned to, Madelon. Don't you know? can't you see? He has been false to you, he cares no more for you. But if he had? In the end it is love and love alone that sweetens life, and what could his love be to mine?"

Madelon turned away again. "I can't stand here any longer, Lot," she said, and moved towards the door.

But Lot called her piteously: "Madelon, come back! If you have any mercy, come back!"

She stood irresolute, frowning; then she went back. "What is it?" she asked, impatiently.

"Madelon, kiss me once."

"I can't — I can't! Don't ask that of me, Lot."

"Madelon, once!"

Madelon bent over him, keeping her body stiffly aloof, and kissed him on his hollow forehead. Lot closed his eyes and smiled like a contented child; then suddenly he opened them upon Madelon, and the look in them was not a child's. She shrank away with a strong shudder, flushing with anger and shame, and made resolutely for the door again. She looked back and spoke out sharply to him, with her hand on the latch: "Mind you do not say one word about — what I said I'd do, until the last." Then she went out, flinging to the door quickly lest she hear Lot's voice again.

When she got home there was no one there. Eugene had not returned. She went about preparing dinner as usual; it was on the table when the men, all except Eugene, came home, and none of them dreamed she had left the house. They inquired where Eugene was, and she replied that she did not know. They did not suspect that she had taken advantage of this lack of guardianship, and yet there was something unwonted in her manner which led them to look at each other furtively when they first noticed it. The perfect poise of decision at which she had arrived affected their minds in some subtle fashion. Eugene, when he returned late in the afternoon, noticed the change in her, in spite of his own perturbation. He looked hard at her staid face, fixed into a sort of unquestioning and dignified acquiescence with misery, but he said nothing. Madelon, in this state, was not to be questioned even by her father. He simply muttered to himself, as he strode out of the room, that she was a woman.

Madelon's manner was the same as the days went on. There ceased to be any question as to her sanity among her father and brothers. She no longer paced overhead like a wild thing. She no longer made fierce outbreaks of despairing appeal. They no longer kept watch over her lest she commit some folly, and became easier in their minds about her.

They made no objections when, three weeks later, she asked for the sleigh and the roan to go to New Salem and make some purchases for herself. She went early in the afternoon, and returned in good season with her parcels. They did not dream that she had been in a strange spirit of bitterness and shameful misery and feminine pride to purchase her wedding-gown for her marriage with Lot Gordon.

Her frantic and unreasoning impulse of concealment was still strong. It was almost as if the whole horror of it were not so plainly thrust upon her if none but she knew it; then there was the agony of shame which made her fain to turn her back and deafen her ears to her own self, let alone all these others.

They rather wondered, the next morning, when they saw Madelon seated at work upon some shining lengths of silk, at the magnificence of her purchase in New Salem; but they knew that she had a little private fund of her own, which they had never questioned her right to spend.

"Guess she's been saving her egg-and-butter money," Abner said, when she went out for something.

His father nodded. "Glad she's got a new gown. Guess she'll show folks she ain't quite done for on account of that fellow," he said.

When Madelon was seated at her work again, and he passed

her to leave the room, he laid a heavy, caressing hand on her black head. "Glad ye've got ye a handsome gown," said he. "It's money well spent."

That day there was a great snow-storm — the last of the season. There had been many such that winter. Snow fell upon snow, and the bare ground was never seen. This time the storm lasted two days. On the morning of the third the sun came out and the wind blew. There was a northern gale all day. The new snow arose like a white spirit from its downfall, and was again all abroad in the air. It moved across the fields in great diamond-glittering shafts; it crested itself over the brows of hills in flashing waves; it lengthened its sharp slants of white light from hour to hour against the windward sides of the fences and houses.

On the morning of the next day everything was still. The snow lay transfixed in blue whirlpools around the trees; the fields were full of frozen eddies, and the hill-tops curled with white wave-crests which never broke. There was a dead calm, and the mercury was fourteen degrees below zero. Everything seemed in the white region of death after the delirium of storm. That morning Madelon Hautville, after her household tasks were done, sat down again to sew her wedding-dress. The silk was of changeable tints, and flashed in patches of green and gold as it lay over her knee and swept around her to the floor.

All the others had gone, but presently, as she sewed, Richard came in with some parcels. He had been on an errand to the store. He tossed the packages on the dresser, then he went and stood directly in front of his sister, looking at her.

"I want to know if it's true," said he.

Then Madelon knew that he had heard. "Yes," said she.

"And that is —" Richard pointed at the silk.

"Yes."

Richard continued to look at his sister and the gorgeous silk. There was consternation in his look, and withal a certain relief. Boy as he was, he reasoned it out astutely. If Madelon married Lot Gordon the merest shadow of suspicion that her confession had been true would not cling to her, and Richard hated Burr, and was fiercely triumphant that he should not think his sister dying for love of him; and then Burr would lose the Gordon money.

All at once Madelon rose up, let her silk breadths slip rustling to the floor, and took Richard by the shoulder. "Richard," she said, "why could you not have told the truth about the knife, and not forced me to this? Why could you not?"

The boy looked aside from her doggedly. "I don't know what you mean about a knife," said he, but his voice shook.

"Yes, you do know, Richard! It is all over now. I must marry Lot. I have promised. I shall not try to escape it — I shall not try again to make people believe it was I. If you were to tell the truth now it would do no good. But you must tell me this, Richard. How came Burr Gordon's knife there instead of yours?"

The boy hesitated.

"Richard, you know you can trust me."

"Well," said Richard, slowly, in a low voice, "I came right up behind Burr before you were hardly out of sight. I'd got uneasy about your going home alone, and I'd thought I'd follow you unbeknown to you, and turn 'round and go back when you were safe in sight of home. Burr pulled my knife out of the wound quick and wiped it on the snow. 'Take it quick,' says he, and I knew what he meant, and put it in my pocket, and slid out of sight in the bushes; and then he whipped out his knife and laid it in the pool of blood, and the others came up, and 'twas all done in a second. That's how."

"He did it to save me," said Madelon, and her voice was fuller of exultant sweetness than it had ever been in a song.

"He's a rascal, that's what he is!" said Richard. "If he hadn't treated you so, it wouldn't ever have happened."

"He did it to save me," said Madelon, as if to herself; "it's worth all I'm going to do to save him." She sat down again, and took up her wedding-dress, and resumed sewing. Richard stood looking at her a minute; then he got his gun off the hooks where he kept it, put on his fur cap, and went out.

Madelon sat and sewed, in a broad slant of wintry sunshine, for an hour longer. Then a shadow passed suddenly athwart the floor, the door opened, and Burr Gordon was in the room. He came straight across to her, but she sat still and drew her needle through her wedding-silk.

"Madelon!" he cried out, "is this true that I have just heard? Madelon!" — Burr Gordon's handsome face was white as death, and he breathed hard, as if he had been running — "Madelon! tell me, for God's sake, is it — true?"

"Yes," said Madelon. She took another stitch. The self-restraint of her New England mother was upon her then. Burr Gordon, betrothed to Dorothy Fair, loving her not, yet still noble enough and kind enough to have perilled his life to save hers, should know nothing of the greater sacrifice she was making for him.

"You are going to marry — Lot?"

"Yes."

"Oh, my God!"

Burr Gordon stood a moment looking at the girl sewing the breadths of shining silk. Then he went over to the settle and sat down there and bent over, leaning his head on his hands. He knew no more at that moment of Madelon's mind than an utter stranger.

It well might be, he thought, that she no longer cared for him. It was not long since she had seemed to, but women, he had always heard, were fickle, and he had so treated her that it might have turned any woman's heart cold. And his cousin Lot had the family wealth, and if she married him she would inherit it, and not he. What could he say to her, sewing so calmly upon her wedding-dress, seemingly in utter acquiescence and content with her fate? Could he take another step without going deeper into the slough of shame and distress where it seemed to him he already stood? And there was Dorothy.

Madelon never glanced at him as she sewed. Presently he arose and went over to her again. "Madelon," he said, hesitatingly, coloring red, "tell me you do not have any hard feelings towards me? I know I deserve it."

"You deserve nothing; it is I," she said, in a low voice.

"You!"

"I know what you did to save my life," she said. Her voice gave out a rich thrill, like a musical tone, as she spoke. She bent lower over her work.

"That was nothing. Madelon" — he paused a moment; she was silent — "Madelon, tell me. Are you — are you satisfied — with this step you are going to take?"

"Yes."

"There is nothing I can do? You know I would do — anything to — You know if you wished — I would do whatever you said."

"You will marry Dorothy Fair," Madelon said, in such a tone of calm assertion that he quailed before it.

"Then you — are satisfied to — marry Lot — It is your wish?"

"Yes."

"Oh, my God!" said Burr, and went out, while Madelon took another stitch in her wedding-gown.

CHAPTER XVII

However the tale of Madelon's and Lot's engagement had found mouth — whether Margaret Bean had vented her knowledge when it grew too big for her or not — it was scarce one day before the whole village was agape with it. With that tendency of the human mind born of involuntary self-knowledge which leads it to suspect a selfish motive in all untoward actions, many gave unhesitatingly a reason for Madelon's choice.

The women nodded astutely at each other, and the men exchanged shrewd affirmative grunts. "She's goin' to marry Lot to pay off Burr," they all agreed. "She'll get all the money."

Madelon herself had never thought of that. She had never considered the fact that her marriage with Lot would rob Burr of his prospective wealth; and, if she had, she would have dismissed the thought as of no moment. Capacity for revenge of that sort was not in her; even the imagination of it was lacking. She would simply have resolved to give the property to Burr if she should outlive Lot, and she would have carried out her resolution. Consciously, perhaps, this consideration was no more evident to her father and her brothers than to herself. The Hautvilles were not mercenary, and retaliation, involving personal profit at the expense of an enemy, was not of their code. They did have, however, a consideration no less selfish, in a way, and no less acute when they heard the news. One and all thought, "Now Madelon will be cleared of all suspicion that she may have brought upon herself. Nobody will believe that Lot Gordon would marry a girl who attempted his life. Every hint of disgrace will be removed from her and us all by this marriage."

Louis, when he heard the news, gave an involuntary glance at his own hands at the thought of Madelon's crimsoned ones, to which he had tried to blind his memory. "Well, maybe it's the best thing that could happen," he said, grimly, but his wonder over it was great. He knew well enough, however he tried to hide the knowledge from himself, that Madelon's story had been true. He looked at his brother Richard, and Richard looked back at him; and one's knowledge for once faced the other's boldly in their utter astonishment. Then they nodded at each other in a stern understanding of assent. It was best their sister should cover her crime and avert the disgrace, which she had seemed to hang over all of them, in that way.

When the male Hautvilles came home to dinner, on the noon of the day after Burr called, Madelon knew at once that they had all heard. They sat down to the table and ate in silence. None of them spoke a word to Madelon on the subject, but she knew they had heard. After dinner they all went out again except her father.

He stood on the hearth, filling his pipe moodily, with an automatic motion of his fingers, his eyes aloof. Madelon moved about with quick, decided motions, clearing the dinner-table. David, when the tobacco was well packed in his pipe-bowl, turned his eyes mechanically upon the glowing coals on the hearth, but made no motion to light it. He looked slowly and furtively about presently at Madelon's wedding-silk, which lay heaped in a chair with a green and gold shimmer, as of leaves and flowers. All unmoved by, and oblivious of, the splendor of woman's gear was David Hautville usually, but this silk, radiant with the weaving of party-lights, affected him with a memory of old happiness, so vague that it was scarce more than a memory of a memory. In splendid silken raiment had Madelon's mother gone as a bride years ago. It had been in reality widely different from this gown of Madelon's, but still, looking at this, David Hautville's masculine eyes saw dimly beyond it another dapple of gorgeous tints, and heard a soft rustle of silken skirts out of the past. He would not have said that this bright mass of silk in the chair made him think of his wife's wedding-gown, but he knew by that thought it was Madelon's. He stared at it, scowling over his great mustache. Then he looked slowly around at his daughter. She was just coming out of the pantry, and faced him as he spoke.

"I suppose this is true I've heard," said he.

Madelon's face blazed red before his eyes, but her mouth was firm and hard, and her eyes unflinching. "Yes, sir," she replied; and she took a dish from the table and turned about, and went again into the pantry, carrying it.

David Hautville, rearing his great height before the fire, casting a long shadow over the room, stood, holding his unlighted pipe, and staring again at the wedding-silk, until his daughter returned. Then he brought his gaze to bear upon her again.

"I suppose you've thought over what you're going to do, and feel it's for the best," said he, with a kind of stern embarrassment. David Hautville felt no resentment because his daughter had not confided her engagement to him. From his very lack of understanding of the feminine character, and his bewilderment over it, he was disposed to give his daughter a wide latitude in a matter of this kind. Not comprehending the feminine gait to matrimony, but recognizing its inevitability, he was inclined to stand silently out of the road, unless his prejudices were too violently shocked. He had also a mild respect for, and understanding of, reticence concerning one's own affairs, and was, moreover, furtively satisfied with the match.

"Yes, I have," answered Madelon, calmly.

"How soon were you calculating —" asked her father, pressing the tobacco harder into the pipe-bowl, and casting a meditative eye at the coals.

"He said a month — that was three weeks ago Monday. To-day is Wednesday." Madelon Hautville spoke with her proud chin raised, and her eyes as compelling as a queen's; but in spite of her-self there came into her voice the tone of one who counts the days to death.

Her father looked at her sharply. She turned again towards her task at the table. "Well, Lot Gordon can give ye a good home," said he. "His health ain't very good, that's the most I see about it. But he may last a number of years yet — folks in consumption do sometimes; and I hear he's gettin' over that cut he give himself. I suppose he did that because he thought you wouldn't have him."

Madelon, moving about the table, did not say a word.

"It must have been that," said David Hautville. "I suppose he thought you favored —" he was about to speak Burr's name; then he stopped short. He was usually one to plunge upon dangerous ground, but this time something stopped him — perhaps a look in his daughter's face. He laid his pipe carefully on the mantel-shelf, went over to Madelon, and laid a heavily tender hand on her shoulder.

"D'ye want any money to buy your wedding-fixings with?" he said, in a half-whisper.

"I've got all I want," replied Madelon, wincing as if he had struck her.

"Because I've sold some skins, lately, and wood." David plunged a hand into his pocket, and began to pull out a leather pouch jingling with coins.

"I've got all the money I want, father," said Madelon, catching her breath a little, but keeping her face steady. Could her father have understood, if she had told him, the pretty maiden provi-dence, almost like one of the primal instincts, which had led her to save, year after year, little sums from her small earnings, towards her wedding-outfit? Could he, with his powerful masculine grasp of the large woes of life, have sensed this lesser one, and fairly known the piteous struggle it cost Madelon to spend her poor little wealth, which was to have furnished adornment for her bridal happiness with her lover, for such a purpose as this? Had she turned upon him then and there, and told him that she hated Lot Gordon, and would rather lie down in her grave than be his wife, he might have grasped that indeed, although not in her full sense of it, for the same sense of misery of that kind comes not to a man and a woman; but the other he would have puzzled over and solved it by his one sweeping solution of all feminine problems — by femininity itself.

However, he continued to stand beside his daughter, looking at her across that great gulf of original conceptions of things which love itself can never quite bridge. Tears came into his keen black eyes, and his voice was hoarse when he spoke again. "Well, Madelon," said David Hautville, with a firmer laying on of his heavy hand on his daughter's shoulder, "ye've been a good daughter and sister, and we're all of us glad you've got over this last foolishness, and we don't lay it up against ye, and — we'll all miss ye when ye're gone."

Madelon moved quietly away from her father's roughly tender hand. "I thought maybe the Widow Scoville would be willing to come here and live," said she. "She's a good cook and a good housekeeper. I'm going to see her about it."

"Well, we'll see," said David Hautville, huskily — "we'll see." He turned away, and looked irresolutely at the shelf whereon his pipe lay, at the wedding-silk on the chair, at his great boots in the corner at the outer door, then at his bass-viol leaning in the corner which the dresser formed against the wall, and a light of decision flashed into his eyes.

He drew his old arm-chair nearer the fire, carried the viol over to it, set it between his knees, flung an arm around its neck and began to play. His great chest heaved tenderly over it; its sweetly sonorous voice spoke to his soul. Here was the friend who vexed David Hautville with no problems of character or sex, but filled his simple understanding without appeal. These chords in which the viol spoke were from the foundations of things, like the spring-time and the harvest and the frosts; they abided eternally through all the vain speculations of life, and sounded above the grave. No imagination of a great artist had David Hautville, but his music was to him like his woodcraft. He traced out the chords and the harmonies with the same fervor that he followed the course of a stream or climbed a mountain-path. A great player was he, although the power of creation was not in him, for he fingered his viol with the ardor of a soul set in its favorite way of all others. As David Hautville played his great resonant viol he forgot all about his own perplexity and his daughter's love-troubles; but she, listening as she worked, did not forget.

Madelon, swept around with these sweet waves of sounds, never once had her memory of her own misery submerged. A strange double consciousness she had, as she listened, of her senses and her soul. All her nerves lapsed involuntarily into delight at the sounds they loved, and all her soul wept above all melodies and harmonies in her ears. The spirit of an artist had Madelon, and could, had she wished, have made the songs she sung; and for that very reason music could never carry her away from her own self.

She finished her household tasks and sat down again to sew upon her wedding-gown. After a while her father ceased playing, and leaned his viol tenderly back in its corner, pulled on his great boots, put on his leather jacket and his fur cap, lighted his pipe, shouldered his gun, and set out with his eyes full of the abstraction of one who follows alone a different path.

CHAPTER XVIII

Then Madelon sat alone, sewing, setting nice stitches in her green-and-gold silk. Like other women, heretofore when she had sewn a new gown she had builded for herself air-castles of innocent vanity and love when she should be dressed in it. Now she builded no more, but sat and sewed among the ruins of all her happy maiden fancies. She had given herself no care concerning any other arrangements for her wedding than this gown — she felt even no curiosity concerning it. She left all that to Lot, as a victim leaves the details of his death to the executioner. She supposed he would send for her and tell her before long. When she heard a scraping step at the door she knew instinctively that the message had come.

Margaret Bean's husband's simple old face confronted her when she opened the door. The weather was moderating fast that morning. The sun had the warmth of spring, and the old man stood in a shower of rainbow drops from the melting icicles on the eaves. He handed her a letter, backed clumsily and apologetically from under the drops, then retreated carefully down the slippery path, his clumsy old joints jolting.

Madelon, back in the kitchen, stood for a second looking at the letter. Then she opened it, and read the message written in Lot Gordon's strange poetic style:

"Madelon, — The rose waits in the garden for her lover, because he has wings and she has none. But had the rose wings and her lover none, then would she leave her garden and fly to him with her honey in her heart, for love must be found.
"Lot Gordon."

Enough strength of New England blood Madelon had to feel towards Lot a new impulse of scorn that he should write her thus, instead of bidding her come, simply, like a man, displaying his power over her that they both knew.

Small store of honey did she bear in her heart when she set out to obey Lot's call. She hurried along, indeed, with her cloak flying out at either side, like red wings in the south wind, but not from eagerness to see her lover. She was in constant dread lest she meet Burr on the road; but she gained Lot's house without seeing him or knowing that his miserable, jealous eyes watched her from an opposite window.

Burr was up in his chamber when Madelon went into his cousin's house. Presently he went down-stairs, where his mother was, with a face so full of the helpless appeal of agony that she looked at him as she used to do when he came in hurt from play.

"What is the matter, Burr, are you sick?" she said, in her quiet voice. She was sitting in a rocking-chair in the sun with her knitting-work. She swayed on gently as she spoke, and her long, delicate fingers still slipped the yarn over the needle.

"Yes, I am sick, mother; I am sick to death," Burr groaned out. Then he went down on the floor at his mother's feet, and hid his face in her lap, as he had used to do when he was a child in trouble. Mrs. Gordon's stern repose of manner had never seemed to repel any demonstration of her son's. Now she continued to knit above his head, but he apparently felt no lack of sympathy in her.

She asked no more questions, but waited for him to speak. "She's just gone in there," he half sobbed out, presently. "Oh, mother, what shall I do — what shall I do?"

"You'll have to get used to it," said his mother. "You'll have to make up your mind to it, Burr."

"Mother, I can't! Oh, God, I can't see her every day there with him. Mother, we've got to sell out and move away. You'll be willing to, won't you? Won't you, mother?"

"You forget Dorothy. She can't leave the town where her father is."

"I wish I could forget Dorothy in honor!" Burr cried out.

"You can't," said his mother, "and there's an end of it."

"I know it," said Burr. He got up and stood looking moodily out of the window.

"You know," said his mother, still knitting, "how I have felt from the very first about Madelon Hautville. I never approved of her for a wife for you; I approve of her still less now, after her violent conduct and her consent to marry Lot, whom she cannot care for. Still, since you feel as you do about it, I should be glad to have you marry her, if such a thing could be done with any show of honor; but it cannot. You know that as well as I. You must marry Dorothy Fair, and Madelon is going to marry Lot. Leaving everything else out of the question, it is out of your power to say anything on account of the money which you will lose by her marriage with him. You know what she might think."

"Curse the money!" Burr cried out. "Curse the money and the position and all the damned lot of bubbles that come between a man and what's worth more, and will last!"

"Burr, don't talk so!"

"I can't help it, mother. I mean it. Curse it, I say, and the infernal weakness that makes a man see double on women's faces when there's only one woman in his heart! Mother, why didn't you know about that last, so you could tell me when I was a boy?"

His mother colored a little. "I never taught you to be fickle," she said, with a kind of shamed bewilderment.

"I never have been fickle. This is something else worse." Burr looked at his mother again, with the old expression of his when he had come in hurt from play. No matter how long Burr Gordon might live, no matter what brave deeds he might do — and there was brave stuff in him, for he would have gone to the gallows rather than betray Madelon — there would always be in him the appeal of a child to the woman who loved him. "Mother, I don't know how to bear it," he said.

"You must bear it like a man."

"It is hard to bear the consequence of unmanly conduct like a man," said Burr, shortly; then he went out, as if the old comfort from his mother had failed him. As for her, she finished heeling her stocking, and then went out into the kitchen and made a pudding that her son loved for his dinner.

Burr went back up-stairs to his cold chamber, and watched for Madelon to come out of Lot's house. It seemed to him she was there an eternity, but in reality it was only a half-hour.

She had found Lot sitting as usual before the fire with a leather-covered volume on his knees. "I have come," she said, standing just inside the door; then she started at the look he gave her. There was a significance in it which she could not understand.

He did not say a word for full five minutes while she waited. He did not even ask her to be seated. "Do you know the date?" he asked then, harshly. There was no hint of roses and honey in his speech and manner to offend her like his letter.

"Yes, I do."

"You know the month is up on Monday?"

"I am not likely to forget."

"True," said Lot; "it is the last thing a girl will forget — the day set for her happy marriage." He laughed.

Madelon's face contracted. She set her mouth harder, and looked straight at Lot. "When you have done laughing," said she, "will you tell me what you want of me? I have to go home and get dinner."

Lot still looked at her with his mocking smile. "I wished to inquire if you are ready to become my bride on Monday," said he.

"Yes, I am ready. Is that all?"

"I wished also to inquire if you have any plans concerning the ceremony which you would like carried out."

"I have none."

"Then will it suit you to come here on Monday at two o'clock in the afternoon, since the doctor tells me I shall scarcely be able to go out myself, and be united to me by Parson Fair?"

"I am ready to carry out any plans you may make."

"Your father and your brothers and my cousin Burr and his mother will, of course, be present at our wedding," said Lot, with wary eyes upon her face.

Madelon looked at him as proudly as ever. "Very well," said

she. She waited a minute longer; then she laid her hand on the doorlatch.

"Wait a minute!" Lot cried. He looked at her hesitatingly. A flush crept over his white face. "Madelon," he began; then his cough interrupted him. He tried to force it back with fierce swallowings, but had to yield. He bent over double, and shook with rattling volleys. Madelon waited, her eyes averted, without a sign of pity. The near approach of her wedding-day caused a revolt of her whole maiden soul towards him so intense that it was as a contraction of the muscles. She was utterly hard to his suffering. At last he raised himself, panting, and cast a pale look around at her.

"Well, what do you want?" she said.

He motioned feebly towards is desk on the other side of the room. "Top drawer," he whispered, hoarsely; "left-hand corner — find — leather case — bring to me."

Madelon crossed the room to the desk, opened the drawer, found the leather case, and carried it to Lot. "Here," said she.

"Open it," Lot whispered.

Madelon pressed the spring in the case, and held it out open towards Lot without a glance at its contents.

"Look," he said.

Madelon glanced at the little gold watch, curled round with a long gold chain, which the case contained, and continued to hold it out towards Lot. "I've looked," said she. "Here, take it; I must go home."

"Oh, Madelon, it's for you."

"I don't want it."

"Take it — Madelon, won't you have it? I got it for you."

"No, I don't want it. Shall I put it back in the drawer?"

"Don't you think it's a pretty watch?"

"Yes. Shall I put it back?"

"You haven't any watch, Madelon."

"I don't want one." Madelon closed the case impatiently, and turned away.

"Oh, Madelon, won't you take it?" Lot begged, piteously.

"I told you no — I do not care for it." Madelon put the case back in the desk drawer. Then she drew her cloak together, and went to the door again.

"Oh," said Lot Gordon, weakly, in his hoarse voice, "the hardest thing in the whole world for Love to bruise himself against is the tender heart of a woman, when 'tis not inclined his way."

"Good-bye," said Madelon, and shut the door behind her fiercely. That last speech of Lot's, which, like many of his speeches, seemed to her no human vernacular, added terror to her aversion of him. "He's more like a book than a man," she had often thought, and the fancy seized her now that the great leather-bound book upon his knees, and all those leather-bound books against his walls, had somehow possessed him with an uncanny life of their own.

And she may have been in a measure right, for Lot Gordon, during his whole life, had dealt indirectly with human hearts through their translations in his beloved books rather than with the beating hearts of men and women around him. Still, although he spoke like one who learns a language from books instead of the familiar converse of people, and his thoughts clothed themselves in images which those about him disdained and threw off as impeding their hard race of life, poor Lot Gordon's heart beat in time with the hearts of his kind. But that Madelon could not know because hers was so set against it.

She hurried out of the house and the yard, dreading again lest she should encounter Burr. But her haste was of no avail, for he came straight down his opposite terraces, and met her when she reached the road.

She would have pushed past then, but he stood squarely before her. "Madelon, can't I speak with you a minute?" he pleaded. Madelon saw, without seeming to look, that Burr's handsome face was white as death and haggard.

"Are you sick?" she asked, suddenly. "Why do you look so? What is the matter with you?" and she put a half-bitter, half-anxiously compassionate weight upon the *you*.

"I believe I am going mad," Burr groaned, with the quick grasp of a man at the pity of the woman he loves. "Oh, Madelon!" He held out his hands towards her like a child, but she stood back from him, and looked straight at him with sharp questioning in her eyes.

"Do you mean —" she began; then stopped, and questioned him with her eyes again. She was seized with the belief, which filled her at once with agony and an impulse of fierce protection like that of a mother defending her young with her own wounded bosom, that Burr had had a falling out with Dorothy.

"Oh, Madelon!" Burr said again, and then he could say no more for very shame and honor. He had run out, indeed, in a half-frenzy.

"She *shall not* play you false!" Madelon cried out. "Dorothy Fair *shall* keep her word with you."

Burr looked at her, bewildered.

"Marry her at once," Madelon cried, with a quick rush of her words — "at once. Do you hear me, Burr Gordon? It's all the way to do with a girl like that. Do you hear me?"

"Yes, I hear you," Burr said, slowly, as if he were stunned.

"Dorothy Fair *shall* keep her promise to you — I will make her. She shall marry you whenever you say. I will go this very day and see her."

"There is no need for you to do that, Madelon. I will marry her at once, as you advise. I think she will be willing," Burr said, slowly and coldly. Then he left her without another word, and went up his terraces with his back bent like an old man's. He was holding hard to his heart the surety that Madelon no longer cared for him, for it is scarcely within the imagination of either man or woman that one can love and yet give away. But by the time he entered the house his spirit had awakened within him, and he made a proud resolve that since Madelon so advised and was herself to marry that he would marry Dorothy Fair as soon as she should be willing.

CHAPTER XIX

As for Madelon, she went home with her mind diverted from her own unhappiness by Burr's, and, in spite of his assurance, might have gone to visit her righteous anger upon Dorothy had she not heard that very night that Burr and Parson Fair's daughter were to be married in a month's time.

The next day Lot sent again for her, and she obeyed, with her proud sense of duty to her future husband, although every step she took towards him carried her farther away. His conduct began to puzzle her more than ever. Again he sent her to the desk drawer, and this time for a roll of precious rose-colored satin stuff, fit for a queen's gown; but she would have none of that either, although he pleaded with her to take it. When she started to go away he called her back, and called her back, and when she came had nothing to say, until she lost patience and went home.

And the day after that he sent again, and there was a great carved comb for her in the desk drawer, and some rose-colored satin shoes; but she thrust them back indignantly. "Understand once for all, Lot Gordon," said she, "you I will take, as I would take my death, because I have pledged my word; but your presents I will not take."

"I have been buying them and treasuring them, against the time you would have them, for years," pleaded Lot.

"I tell you I will not have them," said she.

That day, as the day before, he called her back again and again, and looked at her as if he had something on his mind which he would and could not say; and she went home at last resolved not to go again until she was obliged to for the marriage ceremony.

The next day was Sunday, and Madelon went to meeting and sang, as usual. Burr was not there, but pretty Dorothy was, and looked up at Madelon with a kind of wondering alarm when she sang. Madelon had the heart of one who sings her death-song, and there was something of it in her face that morning. Unconsciously people looked past her, when her voice rang out, to see some dead wall of horror at her back to account for the strange tones in it and the look in her face. She had never looked handsomer, however, than she did that day. Her cheeks had the bloom of roses, and her black eyes seemed to give out their own light, like stars.

She held up her head like a queen as she sang, and her wonderful voice sounded through and beyond the viols and violins, and all the other singing voices. The agony within her was great to penetrate the consciousness of others through this fair triumphant mask.

Madelon looked better than her rival that morning. Dorothy

sat, as usual, daintily clad in her Sabbath silks and swan's-downs, with a sweet atmosphere as of a flower around her; but her delicate color had faded, and her blue eyes looked as if she had been weeping and had not slept. She never glanced once at Eugene Hautville up in the singing-seats; but sometimes he looked at her, and then her face quivered under his eyes.

That noon Lot Gordon sent again for Madelon, but this time she refused to go. "Tell him I am busy and can't come," she told Margaret Bean's husband, who had brought the note. The old man went off, muttering over her message to himself lest he forget it. She heard him repeating it in a childish sing-song — "Tell him I'm busy and can't come; tell him I'm busy and can't come" — as he went out of the yard, slanting his old body before the south wind. The wind blew from the south that day in great gusts as warm as summer; the air was full of the sounds of running water, of sweet, interrupted tinkles and sudden gurgles and steady outpourings as from a thousand pitchers. The snow was going fast; here and there were bare patches that showed a green shimmer across the wind. Sometimes spring comes with a rush to New England on the 1st of April.

That afternoon Madelon went to meeting and sang again, and when she got home Margaret Bean was waiting for her, sitting, a motionless, swaddled figure, beside a window. The Hautvilles never locked their doors while away from home, and she had walked in and waited at her ease until Madelon should return.

Madelon came in alone; her father, Abner, and Eugene had stopped in the barn to look after the roan, who had gone somewhat lame in one foot, and Louis and Richard had lagged. Margaret Bean stood up when Madelon entered.

"You'd better come over," said she.

"Didn't I tell your husband I couldn't?" returned Madelon, harshly.

"You'd better, I guess."

"I've got my father's and brothers' supper to get, and other things to see to. Tell him he must leave me in peace to-day, or I'll never come." Madelon's voice rose high and strident. She unfastened her cloak as if it choked her. Margaret looked at her, her small black eyes peering out wrathfully from her swathing woollens. She was as much wrapped up on this mild day as she had been when the cold was intense. A certain dogged attitude towards the weather Margaret Bean always took. On Thanksgiving Day she donned her winter garments; on May Day she exchanged them for her summer ones, regardless of the temperature. She never made any compromises or concessions. She sweltered in her full regalia of wools on mild spring days; she weathered the early November blasts in her straw bonnet and silk shawl, without an extra kerchief around her stiff old neck. To-day she would not loosen her wraps as she sat waiting for Madelon in the warm room, but remained all securely pinned and tied as when she entered.

However, her discomfort, although she would not yield to it, aroused her temper. "You'd better come," said she, "or you'll be sorry."

Madelon made no reply.

"He's sick," said Margaret Bean; "he's took considerable worse." She nodded her head angrily at Madelon.

"Is his cough worse?"

"He can scarcely sit up," said Margaret Bean, with severe emphasis. She rose up stiffly, as if she had but one joint, so girt about was she. "If a woman's going to marry a man, I calculate it's her place to go to him when he's sick and wants her," she added.

"Is his cough worse?"

"Ain't his cough bad all the time? Well, I'm going. If folks 'ain't got any feelings, they 'ain't. I've got to make some porridge for him."

Madelon opened the door for her. "I'll come over after supper," said she; "you can tell him so."

After supper Madelon went over to Lot's in the early twilight. The tinkles and gurgles and plashes of water came mysteriously from all sides through the dusk. The hill-sides were flowing with shallow cascades, and the woods were threaded with brooks. The wind blew strongly as ever from the south; it had lost the warmth of the sun, but was still soft. The earth was full of a strange commotion and stir — of disorder changing into order, as if creation had come again. It might have been the very birthnight of the spring. Madelon, as she hurried along, felt that memory of old, joyous anticipation which enhances melancholy when the chance of realization is over. The spring might come, radiant as ever, with its fulfilment of love for flowers and birds and all living things, but the spring would never come in its full meaning, with its old prophecies, for her again.

Just before she reached Lot's home, Burr passed her swiftly with a muttered "good-evening." He was on his way to Dorothy Fair's.

"Good-evening," Madelon returned, quite clearly.

She found Lot sitting up, but she could see that he looked worse than usual. He was paler, and there was an odd, nervous contraction about his whole face, as if a frown of anxiety and perplexity had extended.

He held out his hand, but she took no notice of it.

"I have come," said she; "what is it?"

"Won't you shake hands, Madelon?"

Madelon held out her hand, with her face averted, but Lot did not take it, after all.

"My hand is too cold," he muttered; "never mind —" He continued to look at her, and the anxious lines on his face deepened.

"Are you feeling worse than usual?" Madelon asked; and a little kindness came into her voice, for Lot Gordon looked again like a sick child who had lost his way in the world.

Lot shook his head, with his wistful eyes still upon her face. A little light-stand, with his medicines and a candle, stood on his left. Presently he reached out and took a little box from off it, and extended it to Madelon. She shrank back.

"Take it, Madelon."

"No, I don't want it."

"Oh, Madelon, take it and open it at least, and let me see you."

Madelon took the box, with an impatient gesture, and opened it, and a ring set with a great pearl gleamed on its red velvet cushion. She closed the box and held it out towards Lot. "I want no presents, Lot," she said, but almost gently.

"Oh, Madelon, keep it!"

She reached across him, and laid the little box back on the table.

"There's another ring I've got for you you'll have to wear, Madelon."

"I will wear what I must, for the sake of my promise, when the time comes, but that is all I will do," returned Madelon; and she seemed to feel, as she spoke, the wedding-ring close around her finger like a snake.

"Can nothing I can give you please you, Madelon?"

"No, Lot," she said, but not ungently. She began to move away.

"Madelon," said Lot.

"Well?" Madelon waited, but Lot said not another word. She went on towards the door.

"Madelon," he whispered, and she stopped again; but this time also there was a long silence, which he did not break.

Madelon opened the door, and his piteous cry came for the third time, and she waited on the threshold; but again he said nothing more.

"Good-night," said she, shortly, and was out, and the door shut. Then she heard a cry from him, as if he were dying. "Madelon, Madelon!"

She opened the door with a jerk, and went back. "Lot," said she, sternly, "this is the last time I will come back. Once for all, what is it you want of me?"

Lot looked up at her, his face working. He strove to speak and could not. He strove again, and his voice was weak and gasping as if the breath of life had almost left him. "We — had better not be married — to-morrow," he said, with his piteous eyes upon Madelon's face.

She started, and stared at him as if she feared she did not hear rightly.

"I — have been — thinking it over," Lot went on, panting; "I am not as well — we had better wait — until — May. My cough — the doctor — we will wait — Madelon!" Lot's broken speech ended in a pitiful cry of her name.

"Why do you do this?" she asked, looking at him with her white, stern face, through which an expression of joy, which she tried to keep back, was struggling.

"I am not as well, Madelon," Lot answered, with sudden readiness and sad dignity. "If you do not object to the change of time we had best defer it."

Madelon looked away. "There is no need of any pretence between us," she said; "I am sorry you are not as well."

"But not sorry that our wedded bliss must be deferred?"

"No," said she. Then she went away, and that time Lot did not call her back. She heard him coughing hard as she went through the entry.

When she came out of the house into the tumultuous darkness of the spring night, and went down the road with the south wind smiting her with broadsides of soft air, and the living sounds of water ahead and on either hand of her, she was happy — in spite of Burr, in spite of everything — with the happiness of one to whom is granted a respite from death.

CHAPTER XX

When the mind has been strained up and held to the fur-thering of some painful end and then suddenly released, it sinks back for a time, alive to nothing but the consciousness of freedom and rest. Even the thought for the future, which is its one weapon against fate, is laid down. Madelon, for a few days after the post-ponement of her marriage, went about in a kind of negative hap-piness. There are few who have so much to bear that there is not left to them at least the joy of escape from another trial. Madelon had lost her lover indeed, but she was let loose for a while from a worse trouble than that.

When Madelon entered the house that Sunday night her face was so changed that it held her father's and her brothers' casual glances. Her cheeks were brilliant with the damp wind, her eyes gleaming, her mouth half smiling as she looked around. For the first time for weeks it seemed to Madelon that she had really come home, and the old familiar place did not look strange to her with the threatening light of her own future over it. She tossed off her hood and her red cloak, and proposed with her old manner that they have some music.

The men looked at her and each other. "She's a woman," old David muttered under his mustache, and got his viol.

Soon the grand chorus began, and Madelon sang and sang, with all her old fervor. The brothers kept glancing at her, half uneasily, but David wooed his viol as if it were his one love in the world, and paid no attention to aught besides.

The concert lasted late that night. It was midnight before they stopped singing and put their stringed instruments away.

Then Madelon turned to them all. "I am not going to be mar-ried to-morrow," she said, and her face flushed red. "I had better tell you. I am not going to be married for a month." She strove to control her voice, but in spite of herself it rang exultantly at the last.

Louis and Richard exchanged one look with a sudden turn of white faces. David stared hard and perplexedly at his daughter. "What's that ye say?" he asked, after a second's pause.

"I am not going to be married for another month."

"Why not?"

"Lot isn't as well as he was."

"What's the matter? That cut he got?"

"No, I guess not. I think it's his cough." Madelon paled and shivered, and turned away as she spoke, for the horror of her deed and the forced pity came over her again.

Her father caught her by the arm as she would have gone out of the room.

"Look ye here," he said, "is this the whole truth of it? We've got a right to know. Be ye going to marry him in a month's time?"

Madelon looked at him proudly. "I am going to marry him in a month's time, and I am not afraid to face all the truth in the world. Let me go, father."

When she was gone the father and sons stood staring at one another. There was on all their faces an under meaning to which not one would give tongue.

Richard jostled Louis's shoulder. "Suppose —" he whispered, looking at him with dismayed and suspicious eyes.

"Hush up!" returned Louis, roughly, and swung across to the shelf for his candle.

"If I thought —" began David, with force; then stopped, shaking his old head. The male Hautvilles went out, one after the other, their candles flaring up in their grimly silent faces. They were capable of concerted action without speech, and had evolved one purpose of going to bed with no more parley about Lot Gordon and Madelon that night. Brave as these men were, not one of them dared set foot squarely upon the dangerous ground which two of them knew, and three suspected, and look another in the face with the consciousness of his whereabouts in his eyes.

Truly afraid were they all, with that subtle cowardice which lurks sometimes in the bravest souls, of one another's knowledge and suspicions, as they filed up the creaking wooden stairs.

Richard looked at Louis in a terrified sidelong way when they were safe in their room with the door shut. "Hush up!" Louis whispered again, roughly, as if Richard had spoken. The two brothers were not to sleep much that night, each being tormented by anxiety lest Lot Gordon had resolved to stand by their sister no longer, and let disgrace fall upon her head; but neither would speak.

The candles flashed athwart the dark window-spaces of the Hautville chambers, and one by one went out. The house was dark and still, with all the sweet voices and stringed instruments at rest. Yet so full of sonorous harmony had it been not long since that one might well fancy that it would still, to an attentive ear, reverberate with sweet sounds in all its hollows, like a shell.

Madelon slept soundly that night, and when she woke on the morning of what was to have been her wedding-day felt as if she had a glimpse of her own self again, after a long dream in which she had been changed and lost. Richard went early to tell the woman who had been engaged to do the housework that she need not come for a month. After breakfast her father and brothers all went away, and she was alone in the house. She went about her work singing for the first time for weeks. She raised her voice high in a gay ditty which was then in vogue, entitled "The Knight

Errant":

> *"It was Dennis the young and brave*
> *Was bound for Palestine;*
> *But first he made his orisons*
> *Before Saint Mary's shrine.*

> *"'And grant, immortal Queen of Heaven,'*
> *Was still the soldier's prayer,*
> *'That I may prove the bravest knight*
> *And love the fairest fair.'"*

So sang Madelon, loud and sweet, as she tidied the kitchen. There were four verses, and she was on the last when the door opened stealthily and her granduncle, old Luke Basset, entered. Her back was towards him, and she did not see or hear him.

He waited, his old face fixed in a sly grin, standing unsteadily on his shaking old legs, and holding to the back of a chair for support, until Madelon sang at the close of the song,

> *"And honored be the bravest brave,*
> *Beloved the fairest fair,"*

and stopped. Then he spoke. "'Tain't so, then, I s'pose," said he, and his voice seemed to crack with sly suggestiveness.

Madelon faced around on him. "What isn't so?" she asked, coldly. "I didn't hear you come in."

Old Luke Basset shuffled stiffly to the hearth and settled into David's chair. "Well," said he, "I heerd in the store just now that your weddin' was put off, but I s'pose it ain't so, 'cause you seem to be in sech good sperits. A gal wouldn't be singin' if her weddin' was put off."

"Look here, Uncle Luke," said Madelon.

"Well?"

"My wedding is put off for a month; now that settles it. I don't want to say another word about it." Madelon went into the pantry.

Luke sent his old voice, shrill and penetrating as a baby's, after her. "They say 'tain't luck to have a weddin' put off. 'Ain't ye afeard he'll give ye the slip?"

Madelon made no reply. There was a rattle of dishes in the pantry.

Old Luke waited a moment; then raised his shrill, infantile voice again. "If this feller gives ye the slip, ye can jest hang up yer fiddle; ye won't git t'other one back. Parson Fair's gal's got 'nough fine feathers comin' from Boston to fit out the Queen of England, they say."

Madelon said nothing.

"D'ye hear?" called old Luke; but he got no reply. "Dexter Beers says a hull passel of stuff come up from Boston on the stage yesterday. Saturday," persisted old Luke, "Mis' Beers she see an eend of blue satin a-stickin' out of one of the bundles."

Old Luke waited again, with sharp eyes on the pantry. He could see therein a fold of Madelon's indigo-blue petticoat, and could hear the click of a spoon against a dish; that was all.

Old Luke tried his last prod of aggravation. "Folks air sayin' down to the store that mebbe there was some truth, arter all, in what you said 'bout the stabbin', an' mebbe that's the reason Lot is a puttin' off the weddin'," piped old Luke. He chuckled slyly to himself, but sobered suddenly, and cowered in his chair before Madelon.

She came out of the pantry with a rush, and stood before him, her eyes blazing. "There *was* truth in what I said, after all!" she cried. "The truth's the truth, whether there's folks to believe it or not, and I spoke it, and you can tell them so at the store."

Old Luke shrank before her. His old body seemed to cease to shape his clothes. He looked up at her with scared eyes.

"And the reason I have told for the wedding being postponed is the truth, too," continued Madelon. "I did stab Lot Gordon, and he knows I did, though he won't own it, and he's bound to stab me back my whole life. And we shall be married in a month fast enough — you needn't worry, Uncle Luke Basset."

Madelon stood over the old man a minute, quivering with impatience and utterly reckless anger and scorn, and he shrank before her with scared eyes, and yet a lurking of his malicious grin about his mouth. Then she made a contemptuous gesture, as if she would brush him out of her consciousness altogether, and went away out of the room without another word, and left him alone.

He turned his head slowly and looked cautiously around after the door was closed. He heard Madelon's quick tread up the stairs. "Gorry!" muttered old Luke under his breath, and scowled reflectively over his foxy eyes. Quite convinced in his own mind was old Luke Basset that his grandniece had spoken the truth, and had wounded Lot Gordon almost to death, and quite resolute was he also that he would, since she was his own kin, contend against the carping tongues of the village gossips with all the cunning in him.

Old Luke waited for some time. Then he got up stiffly and shuffled out on his tottering legs, scraping his feet for purchase on the floor, like some old claw-footed animal.

Out in the entry he paused a moment, with his head cocked shrewdly and warily towards the stairs. "Hey!" he called, but got no response. He opened the outer door, and, all ready to be gone should his niece appear, he called shrilly up the stairs, "Hey, Mad'lon — forgot to tell ye. Mis' Beers she said she see a bandbox 'mongst them things that come for the parson's gal; said 'twas most big 'nough to hold the bride, and she guessed 'twas the weddin'-bunnit."

Not a sound from above heard old Luke, and presently he gave it up and went out and down the road to the village, with occasional glances of a crafty old eye over his shoulder at Madelon's chamber window. Madelon had heard every word. She was folding up her own wedding-silk and putting it away in the cedar chest until she should want it. She put away her wedding-bonnet also, with its cream-colored plumes and its linings and strings of yellow satin, in the bandbox.

She set her mouth hard, and coupled bitterly her own poor wedding-finery with Dorothy Fair's grand outfit; and yet not for the reason that her Uncle Luke had striven to give her, for she would have held an old ragged blanket of one of her Indian grand-mothers like the bridal gown of a queen had Burr been her bride-groom.

Madelon heard the door shut, and knew her tormentor was gone; and after her fine attire was packed away she went down-stairs and about her tasks again. But she sang no more. The certainty of the future overcame her like the present, and her short-lived joy or respite was all gone. When her father and brothers came home at noon they found the old stern quiet in her face, and their suspicions that there had been a rupture with Lot ceased. They were relieved, but the boy Richard eyed her with furtive pity. That night he lingered behind the others when they dispersed for the night, and went up to Madelon and threw an arm around her, and laid his cheek against hers. "Oh, Madelon, I wish —" he began, and then he caught his breath, and his cheek against hers was wet, and Madelon turned and comforted him, as a woman will turn and comfort a man for even his pity for her sorrow.

"There is no need for you to fret," she said, with a sort of gentle authority, as if she had been his mother. "I've got my life to live, and I've got strength enough to live it. I shall do well enough."

Then she put him away from her softly, and went about set-ting bread to rise. But he followed beseechingly at her heels, with a little parcel which he had been hiding in a corner of the dresser. "I bought these for you, with some of my trap money, for a little present," the boy whispered, piteously; and Madelon smiled at him and took the parcel and opened it, and found therein a pair of fine red-satin shoes. Then he brightened at the delight which she showed, and went up-stairs to bed, feeling that after all it would be no such hard task for his sister to marry Lot Gordon, and cover her fault of mad temper and her disgrace. "He likes her so much he will treat her kindly, and she will have a fine house, and plenty of silk gowns, and feathers in her bonnets," reflected Richard, comfortably, with no more consciousness of his sister's outlook upon life than if his eyes were turned towards a scene in another world. Still he loved his sister with all his heart, although he never in his life had seen anything just as she saw it. He did not dream that Madelon's calm broke before his red-satin shoes, and that she was sitting alone before the kitchen fire with them in her lap, weeping bitterly. She was made of stern stuff to endure the worst of things; but, after all, the pitiful little accessories of grief and death are harder to bear without weakening, because all one's powers of defence are not enlisted against them. They are some-times the scouts that kill.

Poor Madelon looked at her brother's wedding-gift, the little red-satin shoes, in which she could never walk or dance with a merry heart, and her courage almost failed her. But it was only for a little while. She rose up and finished setting the bread to rise, and then she went to her chamber and packed away the shoes with the other things in the cedar chest.

Through the days that came now Madelon toiled as she had never toiled before, although she had always been an industrious girl. She had her own linen-chest, which she would take with her when she married, and now she bestirred herself to replenish the stores of the house she would leave, for the comfort of her father and brothers. Long before dawn the gentle hum of her spinning-wheel began, although the days were lengthening, and many a time she sat plying it on her solitary hearth until after midnight. She spent days at the great loom in the north chamber, marching back and forth before it, a straight, resolute figure of industry filling human needs, although with sweat of the brow and heart's blood. No happier was she for her hard toil, but it kept at least the spirit of fierce endurance alive within her, for no one succumbs entirely to misery with unfolded hands. Then, too, she was upheld somewhat by her pride in right-doing and providing for the inter-ests of her family. Enough of the New England conscience she had to give her a certain comfort in holding herself to duty, like a knife to a grindstone.

The third week of April had begun when one morning Dor-othy Fair came to the door. Madelon was out in the field beside the house, laying some lengths of cloth on the green sunny levels to whiten. The grass had turned quite green in places, and the sun was hot as midsummer. The buds on the trees opened before one's eyes, as if unfolded by warm fingers. People walked languidly, for the humid heat served to force nothing to life in them but dreams; but the birds lived on their wings and called out of all the distances.

Madelon, standing up from spreading her linen, caught sight of the swing of a blue petticoat, like the swing of a blue flower, beside the house door, and went towards it directly.

But when she reached the house the blue-clad visitor had disappeared within. Madelon entered and found Dorothy Fair in the north parlor. Eugene had been sitting in there with his Shakespeare book, and he had opened the door, bowing and wishing her good-day, with his courtly grace of manner, although his handsome face was pale.

Dorothy was pale, also, under her blue-ribboned bonnet. She courtesied on trembling knees, and spoke like a scared child, in spite of her training and genteel deportment. "Can I see your sister?" she said, in a half-whisper, and she did not raise her blue eyes to Eugene's face.

Eugene looked past her. "I see her coming now across the field," he said; "she has seen you and will be here presently."

Then he bade her enter, and made way for her, like a courtier for a princess, and seated her in the north parlor in the best rocking-chair, as if it were a throne. Then he sat down opposite her, with his Shakespeare book still on his knees. That morning he had been poring over "Romeo and Juliet." His imagination was afire with the sweet ardor of that other lover, and he would gladly have identified Dorothy, as she sat there, with Juliet; and so he adored her doubly.

Yet he saw only the tip of her little shoe below the blue hem of her gown, and dared not fairly glance at her face, although he bore himself with such calm ease that none could have suspected.

"It is a beautiful day," said Eugene.

"Yes," whispered Dorothy. Somehow for the moment Eugene forgot Dorothy's marriage, and Burr and his bitter jealousy, for suddenly a strange and unwarrantable sense of possession came over him. He looked fully at Dorothy, and scanned her drooping face, and smiled, and then Madelon came in.

Dorothy arose at once and greeted her with more of her usual manner. Then she fumbled uneasily with a little parcel she held, and glanced at Eugene, and then at Madelon. "I had an errand —" began Dorothy and stopped, and then Eugene said softly, still smiling, "I see you have some weighty matter to discuss," and bowed himself out with his Shakespeare book.

Then Dorothy, all trembling, and before he was fairly out of hearing across the entry in the other room, announced her errand. She had come to beg Madelon, whose rare skill in embroidering her own floral designs was celebrated in the village, to work for her the front breadth of one of her silken gowns with a garland of red roses. "I can work only from patterns which are marked out," said Dorothy; and then she held up a shining length of green silk upon which the garland already bloomed in her pretty feminine fancy. "I will pay you whatever you ask," said Dorothy, further. Then she started and shrank, for Madelon looked at her with such wrath and pride in her black eyes that she was frightened.

"What — have — I — done?" she faltered, piteously. And it was quite true that she did not know what she had done, for she reasoned always like a child, with premises of acts only and not of motives. She considered simply that Madelon had urged her to be true to Burr, and was herself to marry another man, and therefore could not be jealous, and that she wanted her gown embroidered.

Dorothy was not happy, and a nervous terror was always upon her which had caused her blue eyes to look out wistfully from delicate hollows and faded the soft pink on her cheeks; still she kept involuntarily to her feminine ways, and wanted her gowns embroidered.

"I want no pay!" Madelon cried, hoarsely.

"I meant no harm," Dorothy faltered, again. She remembered that Madelon Hautville had on divers occasions, for prospective brides, turned her marvellous skill in embroidery to financial profit, but she dared not say so for an excuse. "I could not do it myself," Dorothy said, further, trembling in every limb, "and — I thought maybe — you —"

Suddenly Madelon extended her hand. "Give me this silk," she said; "I will work the flowers on it for you, but never dare to speak to me of pay, Dorothy Fair."

Dorothy looked at her, made a motion as to give her the silk, then drew it back again.

"Give me the silk," said Madelon. Dorothy yielded up the silk hesitatingly, with a scared and apologetic murmur. Then she screamed faintly, for Eugene Hautville strode back into the room with a look on his face which she had never seen before. He snatched the silk out of Madelon's hand and thrust it roughly into Dorothy's.

"Take it home," he said. "My sister does no work on your wedding-clothes!"

Dorothy gasped and looked at him with wild terror in her blue eyes, and then he caught her in his arms, pressed her yellow head against his breast, and stroked it softly. "Don't be afraid," he said — and his voice had its wonderful gentle charm again. "Don't be afraid, dear child! I could not harm you if I tried — not a hard word shall be said to you, sweet!"

"*Eugene!*" cried Madelon, and her voice seemed to carry wrath like a trumpet. She laid hold of his shoulders, and forced him back, and Dorothy slipped out of his arms and stood aside, trembling and weeping, with a little worked apron which she wore thrown over her face. "Let me be!" Eugene cried, angrily, and would have gone to Dorothy again to comfort her, but Madelon in her wrath was as strong as he, and she thrust herself between them.

"You are no brother of mine, Eugene Hautville," she said, her face all white and fierce with anger. "You dare to touch her again, and you will find out that I can fight to keep her from you as well as Burr could if he were here. You *dare* to touch her again!" Then she turned to Dorothy. "Give me the silk," she said, in a hard voice. In her heart she blamed her more than her brother, although unnecessarily.

Dorothy shrank back. "No," she said, feebly, "I had better not."

"Give me the silk!"

Dorothy gave her the silk. Eugene stood apart. He possessed his fine pride and graceful self-poise again, and though his blood boiled he would not, being a man, wrestle with his sister for another man's bride.

Dorothy moved towards the door, her fair curls drooping over her agitated face. Eugene made a motion in her direction, and when Madelon would have thrust him back again, he only said, with a half-smile, "I would crave the lady's pardon; you would not prevent that." And then he bowed low before Dorothy Fair, and besought her to pardon, if she could, his unseemly conduct, and believe that it had for motive only the highest respect and esteem for her.

And Dorothy swept her curls farther over her face, and could not make the dignified response of offended maidenhood that she should, but courtesied tremblingly and fairly fled out of the house.

Eugene, with his Shakespeare book under his arm, went also out of the house and over across the field, to a piney wood he loved, where all the trees, even in this warm flush of spring, whispered eternally of winter and the north, and there he stretched himself out beneath a tree, as melancholy as Jacques in the forest of Arden. Now that he had got the better of his impulse of mad passion and jealousy, he was ashamed, and stayed late in the wood, for he did not like to meet his sister's rightly scornful face.

When he went at last late for his supper, Madelon, as he expected, noticed him only by an angry flash of her black eyes, under drooping lids. She said not one word to him, and as the days went on treated him coldly; and yet she did not give to the matter its full seriousness of meaning.

Madelon, well acquainted with Eugene's caressing manner, thought simply that, seeing poor Dorothy's alarm, he had striven to soothe her with endearments and assurance that he would not hurt her, as he would have done with a child. As for Dorothy, Madelon credited her with the soft spirit which she knew she possessed. She scorned them both, and felt as jealous for Burr's sake as he himself could have done, that other hands than his had touched his bride's; and yet she did not dream of the full significance of it all.

She wrought a marvellous garland of red roses on Dorothy Fair's green silk, and scarcely left herself time to sleep that she might complete that and her stint of household linen. She had nothing to add to her own wedding-garments.

CHAPTER XXI

The weeks went past, and the Sunday before the day set for her wedding came again. She had seen Lot but three times in the interval. He had sent for her, and she had gone obediently, and remained a short time, pleading her work as an excuse to return home. Lot had not sought to detain her; he had vexed her with no vain appeals, but treated her with a sort of sad deference which would have perplexed her had she cared enough for him to dwell upon it.

Lot was said to be in no better health. He did not stir abroad on those warm spring days. Once he had put on his great-coat, and was for setting foot on the springing grass in the sunny yard, but Margaret Bean had remarked to him how she had heard, whilst purchasing a bit of cheese in the store, a man say that he guessed Lot Gordon wasn't much worse, only afraid of a wife that could use a knife. Margaret Bean had shaken in her starched petticoats as she said it, not knowing how the news might affect her master towards the monger of it; but she was disposed to risk a little rather than have a mistress over her.

Lot said nothing in response about the matter, but pulled off his great-coat and sank into his chair with a fit of coughing, and declared he felt not well enough to go out that day.

That last Sunday Madelon went to him without being summoned, in the early evening after supper. On her last visit, the week before, he had asked her, and she had promised to come.

The frogs were calling across the meadows as she went along; there was a young moon shining with frequent silvery glances through the budding trees, which tossed athwart it like foam, and the mists curled along the horizon distances. Madelon, moving along, was as the ghost of one who had belonged to the spring, as a part of its radiant hope and stir of life and youth in days past, but was now done with it forever. The spring sounds and sights, and all its sweet influence, seemed to tear her heart anew with memories of the visions of fair futures which she had forfeited. The loss of the sweet dreams which the spring awakens in the human heart is not one of the least losses of life. Though the spring be unfulfilled, it sweetens the year.

Just before Madelon reached Lot Gordon's house, she met Burr going to court Dorothy. They were to be married in two weeks more. Madelon and Burr exchanged a murmur of salutations and passed each other.

Madelon went directly into Lot's house, to his sitting-room, as she was used to do lately, and found Lot standing in the midst of the room, waiting for her, with a lighted candle in his hand.

"I heard your footstep when you came through that open

space, where the road has a hollow echo," he said; "and I have been waiting for you ever since."

"You could not hear me; it is a half-mile away," said Madelon.

"A half-mile! what's a hundred miles when 'tis the heart that listens, and not the ears? Come; I have something I want to show you."

Lot led the way and Madelon followed out of the room across the front entry, with its spiral of stair mounting its landscape-papered height, and Lot opened the door of the opposite room, the great north parlor. "Wait here a minute," he said to Madelon, and she waited in the entry after he entered until he called her to follow.

Lot had lighted every candle in the great branching candelabra upon the shelf, and the room was full of light. Madelon looked about her, and even her despairing calm was stirred a little. Never had she seen or dreamed of a room like this. She grasped no details; her bewildered eyes saw them all melting into each other, combining newly and vanishing like kaleidoscopic pictures — folds and gleaming stretches of crimson damask and velvet, the dark polish of precious woods, spots and arabesques of gold and the satin shimmer of wall-paper, lights and shades of steel engravings, and elegant and graceful lady-treasures of gilded books and work-boxes and vases on shelf and tables. There was even a little piano, the only one in the village, with slender, fluted legs, and a mother-of-pearl garland over the key-board.

"I have had this all newly furnished for you. I hope it may please you," said Lot; and he looked at Madelon with hollow, wistful eyes.

That brought her to herself. "It is very pretty," she replied, and turned away.

Lot sighed. "Well, I have something more to show you," said he, and went forlornly before her, stooping weakly and coughing now and then, into the great middle room of the house, which was fitted up with carven oak which Governor Winthrop might have used. Here, too, Lot lighted all the branches of the candelabra on the shelf; and the great buffet directly responded with the dazzling white glitter of silver from the cream-jugs and ewers and spoons thereon.

Then Lot threw open the fine carved doors of the cupboard, and the shelves were covered with precious blue china, brought from over seas, and wine-glasses like bubbles of crystal, and decanters as graceful as plumes.

"Do you like it, Madelon?" Lot asked; and Madelon replied, as before, that it was pretty.

Lot showed Madelon all the wealth of his house before they returned to the sitting-room. Much had been there from his father's day, but much had been added to please this bride, who looked at it more coldly and with less part in it than she would have looked at the treasures in a merchant's windows. She saw, unmoved by any pride of possession, great canopied bedsteads, and chests of drawers whose carven tops reached the ceiling, and mirrors in gilded frames. She saw marvellous stores of linen damask napery in such delicate and graceful designs, from foreign looms, as she had never dreamed. She saw an India shawl, and lengths of silk and satin and velvet, and turned away from it all to the obstinate contemplation and endurance of her own misery.

At last Lot led the way back to the sitting-room. He set the candle on the shelf, and gave a strange, beseeching glance around the room at his books. It was as if he besought, with the irrationality of grief, those only friends he fairly knew for help and sympathy.

Then he turned to Madelon and laid a hand on each of her shoulders, and looked at her. "No, there is no need now," he said, when she would have shrunk away from him; and something in his voice hushed her, and she stood still.

"Madelon," said Lot Gordon, "tell me true, as before God. You are a woman, and always, I have heard, a woman takes comfort and pleasure in life with such gear as I have shown you, alone, even if she has little else. Would not all this give you some little happiness, even as my wife, Madelon?"

Madelon looked at Lot and hesitated. She had a feeling that her word of reply would stab him more cruelly than her knife had done.

"Madelon, tell me!"

"Will you have the truth?"

Lot nodded.

"No, Lot."

"Madelon, I can buy you more than all this. Are you sure?"

"Yes."

Lot gave a great sigh. "Dearly bought possessions are worse than poverty, you hold," said he. "Then, Madelon, there is no sweetening in all this for your bondage?"

She shook her head. "I shall do my duty, as I have promised," she said. "All this is useless. Let me go, Lot."

"Madelon!"

She looked up in his face, and a strange awe came over her at the look in it. A more secret lurking-place than any of the little wild things that he loved to discover had the self in Lot Gordon, and Madelon saw it for the first time, and perhaps he, also.

"True love exists not unless it can do away with the desire of possession. I love you, Madelon," said Lot; and then he let go of her shoulders and went over to the mantel-shelf, and leaned against it, with his head bent.

Madelon, all bewildered and trembling, stared at him.

"I — don't think I know what you mean," she gasped out, finally.

"You are — free," said Lot.

CHAPTER XXII

That year, spring seemed to break over the village in a day, like a green flood. All at once people's thoughts were interrupted, and their eyes turned from selfish joys or pains by the emerald flash of fields and hill-sides in the morning sun, and the white flutter of flowering boughs past their windows like the festal garments of unexpected guests.

The first week in May, the cherry-trees were in blossom, and the alders and shad bushes were white in the borders of the woods against the filmy green of the birches. The young women got out their summer muslins, and trimmed their bonnets anew; their faces, all unknown to themselves, took on a new meaning of the spring, like new flowers, and the young men looked after them as they passed as if they were strangers in the village.

On the afternoon of Wednesday, in the first week of May, Eugene Hautville strolled across-lots over to the village. Through the fields north of the Hautville place there was an old foot-path to the former site of an old homestead, long ago burned to the ground and its ashes dissipated on winds long died away. The oldest inhabitants in the village barely remembered the house that used to stand there. The slant of its roof crossed their minds dimly when they spoke of it: they could not agree as to whether it had faced north or south. It might have seemed almost fabulous, had it not been for the thicket of old lilacs purpling with bloom every spring, which had first grown before its windows, and the perennial houseleek which had clustered round the door.

Then, too, east of where the house had stood there was an old apple orchard, the trees thereof bent to the ground like distorted old men, and, when spring came, bearing scarcely one bough of pink bloom, among others shaggy with gray moss like the beard of age.

Then, also, the lane still remained which had stretched, in days gone by, from the northward of the old house to the highway. The lane had divided the fields of the old landowners, and had been the thoroughfare for the dwellers in the house when they went to meeting and to mill.

The Hautvilles often used it in the summer-time for a short-cut to the village. Eugene went along this foot-path, which was in its way a little humble track of history of simple village life, passed the site of the house, and then struck into the lane. It stretched before him like a shaft of green light. The afternoon sun shone through young willow-leaves, transparent like green glass. Low overhead hung rosy tassels from out-reaching boughs of maples. Between the trees, the flowering alders seemed gleaming out of sight before him like the white skirts of maidens. Here and there the ground was blue with violets. Eugene picked some half mechanically, as he went along, and made a little nosegay, with some sprigs of alder. He was half through the lane, and had just emerged from a clump of alders, when he saw Dorothy Fair coming. She gave a start when she saw him appear with a great jostling of white branches, and made as if she would have fled; then she held up her head with gentle dignity and advanced, lifting her lady-skirts with dainty fingers on either side. Mistress Dorothy, being weary of fine needle-work upon her bridal linen, had come out a little way to take the air, and naturally enough had chosen for her walk this sweet lane, which opened upon the highway a stone's-throw below her house.

If Eugene Hautville, at sight of her, felt a quaking of his spirit, and would also fain have fled, he made no sign, but walked on proudly like a prince, with a bold yet graceful swing of his stalwart shoulders. And when he and Dorothy met, he bowed low before her, and she courtesied and he bade her good-day quite clearly, and she murmured a response with pretty, prim lips; and they would have passed on had not both, as if constrained by hands of force upon their necks, raised their faces and looked of a sudden into each other eyes with that same old look which they had exchanged in the meeting-house long ago.

Dorothy Fair wore on that day a thin wool gown of a mottled blue color like a dapple of spring violets. It was laid across her bosom in smooth plaits, and showed at the throat her finely wrought lace kerchief. The sun was so warm that she had put on her white straw hat with blue ribbons, and her soft curls flowed from under it to her blue belt ribbon. She wore, too, her little black-silk apron, cunningly worked in the corners with flowers in colored silks. Dorothy looked up in Eugene Hautville's face, and he looked down at her, for a force against which they had come into the world unarmed constrained them. Then she bent her head before him until he could see nothing but the white slant of her hat, and caught at her silk apron as if she would hide her face with that also.

Eugene stood still looking at her, his face radiant and glowing red. "Dorothy!" he stammered, and then Dorothy straightened herself suddenly, though she kept her face averted, flung up her head, caught up her blue skirts again, and made as if she would pass on without another word. Eugene, with his face all at once white, and his head proudly raise, stood aside to let her pass. "'Tis a warm day for the season," he said, with his old graceful courtesy. But Dorothy looked up at him again as she neared him in passing, and her sweet mouth was quivering like a frightened baby's, and the tears were in her blue eyes, and no man who loved her could have let her go by; and certainly not this fiery young Eugene. Suddenly, and with seemingly no more involvement of wills or ethics than the alders in their blossoming, the two were in each other's arms, and their lips were meeting in kisses.

This fair and demure daughter of Puritans might well, as she stood there in her lover's embrace, being already, as she was, the betrothed bride of another, have been accounted fickle and false, but perhaps in a sense she was not. Never had she forgot or been untrue to her first love-dreams, which Eugene had caused, but had held to them with that mild negative obstinacy of her nature which she could not herself overcome. Now it was to her as if she were reconciled to her true lover, and was faithful instead of false; and less false she surely was to her own self.

Right contentedly had she loved for a time Burr's love for her and his tenderness, and had been stirred thereby to passion, but now she loved this other man for something better than her own sweet image in his eyes.

Never a word she said, but her hat slipped down on her shoulders, hanging by its blue strings, and she let her head lie on Eugene's shoulder, with a strange sense of wontedness and of remembering something which had never been.

And, also, all Eugene's fond words in her ear seemed to her like the strains of old songs which were past her memory. Burr's, although she had listened happily, had never seemed to her like that.

They stood together so for a few minutes, while the alder-flowers shook out sweetness, as from perfumed garments, at their side, and a bee who had left his hive and winter honey, and made that day another surprise of spring, hummed from one white raceme to another and then was away, disappearing in the blue air with a last gleam of filmy wing as behind a sapphire wall.

Neither of the lovers had knowingly heard the bee's hum, but when it ceased the silence seemed to make an accusing sense audible to them. They let each other go and stood apart guiltily, as if some one had entered the lane and was spying upon them.

Dorothy spoke first, without raising her pale little face, all drooped round with her curls. "What shall I do?" she said, like a child. She was trembling, and could scarcely control her tongue.

Eugene made no reply. He stood looking moodily at the ground, where his nosegay of violets and alders was all scattered and trampled.

Suddenly he had the feeling as of a thief in another man's garden, and a shame before Dorothy herself came over him. Eugene Hautville's principles of honor, in spite of his fiery nature, read like a primer, with no subtleties of evasion therein. Here was another man's betrothed, and he had wooed her away! He had kissed her lips, which were vowed to another. He had wronged her and Burr Gordon also. Strangely enough, Dorothy's own responsibility never occurred to him at all; he never dreamed of blaming her for falsity either to himself or Burr. That little fair trembling creature, clad like a violet in her mottled blue, seemed to him at once above and below all questions of personal agency. She bloomed like a flower in her garden, infinitely finer than those who wrangled around her and strove to gather her, and yet in a measure helpless before them.

In a moment Dorothy answered her question negatively herself: "I will not marry Burr," she said, without raising her head, and yet with that tone of voice which accompanies a lift of chin and stiffening of the neck muscles.

Eugene looked at her, and extended his arms as if he would take her to him again; then drew them back. "I do not know what to counsel you," he said, slowly. Then his eyes fell before the sudden shame and distress in Dorothy's.

"You do not know what do counsel me!" she cried. "Then you do not — care —" Tears rolled over her cheeks, and Eugene gathered her into his arms again, and laid his cheek against her fair head, and soothed her as he would have soothed a child. "There, there," he whispered, "it is not that, it is not that, sweet. I would die for you, I love you so! It is not that, but you are the promised wife of another man. How can I turn a thief even for you, Dorothy? How can I bid you be false, and forswear yourself? There's honor as well as love, child."

"But love is honor," said Dorothy.

"Not for a man," said Eugene.

Then she clung to him softly and modestly, and sobbed, and he kissed her hair and whispered in one breath that she was all his own, and in another that he knew not what to do, and was near distracted between his love and his sense of honor, until Dorothy said something which set him pleading for his rival whether he would or no, for the sake of stern justice.

"I am afraid of him, I am afraid of Burr," Dorothy whispered in his ear. "How could I have married him, when I was so afraid, even if you had not come?"

"Afraid?"

"*You — know — what — they said — Burr did!*"

Eugene held her away from him by her slender arms, and looked at her. "You did not believe that?"

"He would not tell me he was innocent, even when I begged him so."

"You knew he was."

"Why did he not tell me, when I begged him so?" she said, and the soft unyielding in her tone was absolute.

"Dorothy!"

"I am so afraid — you don't know," she whispered, piteously.

"But — you know Burr was cleared."

"Yes, I know, but even now he will not tell me on the Bible, as I asked him, that he is innocent."

"Dorothy, he *is* innocent," Eugene said, with solemn and bitter emphasis of which she knew not the full meaning.

"Then why does he not swear that he is, to me?" Back went Dorothy always, in all reasoning, to the starting-point in her own mind.

"I tell you he is, child. It has been proven so."

"Then why —" Dorothy began, but Eugene interrupted her in her circle. "There is no more cause for you to fear him than me," he said almost harshly, in his stern resolve to be just. Then Dorothy turned on him with sudden passion. "I am afraid," she cried out, "I shall always be afraid; even if he were to swear to me now that he is innocent, I shall always be afraid, for I coupled him with that awful deed once in my thoughts, and I cannot separate him from it forever. He will always hold the knife in his hand; even if it were not for you, I should be near mad with fear. I bid black Phyllis stay by the door when he comes."

"Dorothy!"

"Yes, I do. What my mind has once laid hold of, that it will not let go. I cannot separate him from my old thought of him. I have tried to be faithful, and true, but even had he sworn to me that he was innocent, the fear would have remained. Save me from him — oh, Eugene, save me!"

But Eugene put her quite away from him, and looked at her almost sternly. His honor held the reins now in good earnest. The suspicion of Madelon, which he had never owned to himself, became a certainty. He defended his rival as strenuously as he would have defended himself, since it involved truth to himself. "I swear to you, Dorothy Fair," he said, "that Burr Gordon is innocent, and that your fear of him is groundless."

Dorothy looked at him with dilated eyes. She said not a word, but her mind travelled its circle again.

"It is so," said Eugene; "I know it."

Still Dorothy looked at him.

"All my heart is yours," Eugene went on, "but I would rather it broke, and yours too, before I counselled you to be false to a man for a reason like that."

A flush came over Dorothy's face. She pulled her straw hat from her shoulders to her head, and tied the blue strings under her chin. She gathered up daintily a fold of her blue mottled skirt on either side. "Then I will marry Burr this day week," she said. "I will endeavor to be a good and true wife to him, and I pray you to forget if you can what has passed between us to-day."

She said this as calmly and authoritatively as her father could have said it in the pulpit, and courtesied slightly, then went on down the lane and out into the open beyond, with a soft tilt of her blue skirts and as gently proud a carriage as when she walked into the meeting-house of a Sabbath.

Eugene said not a word to stop her, but stood staring after her. All his study of his Shakespeare helped him not to an understanding of this one girl, whom he saw with love-dimmed eyes. This sudden abetting on her part of his resolve gave him a sense of earthquake and revolution, yet he did not call her back or follow her.

He proceeded through the lane to the highway, then a few yards farther to the store, to get his Boston weekly paper. The mail had come in. On this warm spring day the loafers on the boxes and barrels within the store had crawled out to the bench on the piazza and sat there in a row. All mental states have their illustrative lives of body. This shabby row leaned and lopped and settled upon themselves, into all the lines and curves and downward slants of laziness, and with rank tobacco-smoke curling about them, like the very languid breath of it. However, when Eugene Hautville drew near, there was a slight shuffling stir; a drawling hum of conversation ceased, and when he entered the store their eyes followed him, bright with furtive attention. The mill of gossip had ground slowly in this heavy spring atmosphere, but it had ground steadily. They had been discussing Madelon Hautville and the breaking off of her marriage with Lot Gordon. It was village property by this time, and all tongues were exercised over it.

"Why ain't Lot Gordon goin' to marry her?" they asked each other, and exchanged answering looks of dark suspicion. The reason for not marrying which Lot used every means in his power to promulgate — his fast-failing health — gained little credence. The story came directly from the doctor's wife that Lot Gordon was no worse than he had been for the last ten years, and was likely to live ten years to come. Margaret Bean was said to have told a neighboring woman, who told another, who in her turn told another, and so started an endless chain of good authority, that Lot Gordon had never coughed so little as he did this spring, and "ate like a pig." He was, it is true, never seen on the highway, but there were those who said he was abroad again in his old woodland haunts.

"Guess he didn't change his mind about havin' Mad'lon Hautville 'cause he was so much worse than common," they said; "guess when the time drawed near he was afraid." Margaret Bean was, furthermore, on good authority reported to have intimated that never, if Madelon had come to that house while she was in it, would she and her husband have gone to bed without the scissors in the latch of their bedroom door.

Lot Gordon, who had forsworn himself to save Madelon, was now, by his last sacrifice for her, bidding fair to prove what her own assertions had failed to do — her guilt. He crept out secretly into cover of the woods, now and then, on a mild day; he could not deny himself that. But otherwise he stayed close, and coughed hard when there were listening ears, and complained like any old woman of his increasing aches and pains. Still his cunning availed little, although he did not dream of it.

He went not among the gossips himself, and no one as yet had ventured to approach him with the rumor that was fast gaining ground.

No one had ventured to broach the matter to the Hautville men, for obvious reasons. "I wouldn't vally your skin if that fellar overheard what you was sayin' of when he come up the road, Joe Simpson," one loafer drawled to another, when Eugene left the store that afternoon and had disappeared going the long way home.

"Hush up, will ye!" whispered the other, glancing around pale under his unshaven beard as if he feared Eugene might yet be there. The Hautville men, however, hearing nothing, and saying nothing about the matter to each other, had always, among themselves, a subtle exchange of uneasy thought concerning it. If one sat moodily by and moved out of her way without a word while Madelon prepared a meal, the others knew what it meant. They also knew well the meaning of each other's glances at her, and sudden lowering of brows. Madelon herself did not know. When she had come home that Sunday night, and announced that she was not going to be married at all, she had not understood the sharp questioning, and then the stern quiet that followed upon it. She had told them simply that Lot said that his lungs were gone; that he had ascertained the fact himself through his own knowledge of medicine; that he could only live a wreck of a man, if at all, and, knowing it was so, had made up his mind that he would not marry.

Lot had indeed told her so, and had made her believe it, doing away with much of the force of his giving her up for the sake of his love. It is difficult in any case for one to understand fully the love to which he cannot respond, for involuntarily the heart averts itself from it like an ear or an eye, and misses it like the highest notes of music and colors of the spectrum.

Madelon had stared dumbly at Lot when he told her she was free, and for a moment indeed had struggled with a consciousness which would have stirred her at least into pity and gratitude and remorse, which she had never known, had not Lot recovered himself and spoken again in his old manner. He tapped himself on his hollow chest. "After all," he said, "'tis best you are not seduced like most of your sex into making the accessories of life supply the lack of the primal needs of it, into taking sugar instead of bread, and weakening your stomach and your understanding. 'Tis best for you and best for me, and best for those that might come after us. Treasure of house and land and fine apparel and furnishings may be a goodly inheritance, but our heirs would thank us more for power to draw the breath of life freely, and you would do better without a gown to your back, or a shoe to your foot, and a mate that was not half a dead man; and I should do better alone in my anteroom of the tomb than with another life to disturb the peace of it, and rouse me to efforts which will send me farther on."

Madelon had stared at him, not knowing what to say, with compassion, and yet with growing conviction of his selfish ends, which disturbed it.

Lot tapped his chest again. "My lungs are gone," he said, shortly; "I need no doctor to tell me. I know enough of physics myself to send the whole village stumbling, instead of racing, into their graves, if I choose to use it. My lungs are gone, and you are well quit of me, and I of a foolish undertaking, though of a charming bride. Now, go your way, child, and take up your maiden dreams again, for all me."

Madelon looked at him proudly, although she was half dazed by what she heard. "I care nothing for all the fine things you have shown me," said she, "and I have told you truly always that I do not care for you, but I will keep my promise to marry you unless you yourself bid me to break it."

"I bid you to break it," said Lot, steadily, and his eyes met hers, and his old mocking smile played over his white face. Then suddenly he bent over with his racking cough, and Madelon made a step towards him, but he motioned her away. "Good-night — child," he gasped out.

Then Madelon had gone home and told her father and brothers, and thought their strange reception of the news due to anything but the truth. She had told them that she was guilty of wounding Lot Gordon almost to death. That they should now be rendered uneasy by suspicions, when she had given them actual knowledge, was something beyond her imagination. She fancied rather that they considered Lot had treated her badly, or else that she had a longing love for Burr, and, perhaps, had herself broken off her match with his cousin on that account. She strove hard to bear herself in such a manner that they should not think that. She put on as gay a face as she could muster, and even took, beside the dress, a little blue-silk mantle to embroider for Dorothy Fair's wedding outfit, and sang over it as she worked.

Still, in a way, although her pride led her to it, her singing and

her gayety were no pretence, for Madelon, through much suffering, had reached that growth in love which enabled her to see
over her own self and her own needs. That knife-thrust she had
meant for her lover had stilled forever the jealous temper in her
own heart, and she fairly dreamed as she embroidered Dorothy's
bridal mantle some dreams of happiness that might have been
Burr's; so filled was she with purest love for him that his imagination possessed her own.

CHAPTER XXIII

It was told on good authority in the village that Parson Fair had paid all Burr Gordon's back interest money on his mortgage, and so released him from the danger of foreclosure; and then on equally good authority it was denied. There was much discussion over it, but one day the loafers in the store arrived at the truth. Parson Fair had indeed offered to pay the interest, and Burr had declined. He had also refused to live with his bride in his father-in-law's house, and when Parson Fair had, with his gracefully austere manner, intimated that he should be unwilling to place his daughter in such uncertain shelter, had replied harshly that Dorothy should have a roof over her head of his own providing while he lived; when he was dead it would be time to talk about her father's.

When Burr had gone to Lot Gordon and offered to part with a small wood-lot of his, with a quantity of half-grown wood thereon, at two-thirds of its real value to pay the interest, Margaret Bean had listened at the door, and thus the story.

"It is a sacrifice of a full third of its value, you know well enough," Burr had said, standing moodily before his cousin. "If I could wait for the growth of the wood, 'twould bring much more, but I'll call it even on the interest I owe you, if you will. This is the last foot of land I own clear."

For answer Lot had bidden Burr open his desk and bring him a certain paper from a certain corner. Then Margaret Bean had opened the door a crack, and had with her two peering eyes seen Lot Gordon take his pen in hand and write upon the paper, and show it to his cousin Burr.

"Very well," said Burr, "I will go home and get the deed of the wood-lot," and motioned towards the door, which drew to in a soft panic as if with the wind.

"Stop," said Lot; and Margaret Bean paused in her flight, and laid her ear to the door again. "I don't want your woodland," said Lot. "The interest is paid without it. It is your wedding-gift."

"Why should you do this? I did not ask you to," Burr returned, almost defiantly; and Margaret Bean had felt indignant at his unthankfulness.

"You can take from your kinsman what you could not take from Parson Fair," replied Lot. "I hear you will not go to nest in Parson Fair's snug roof-tree, with your pretty bird, either."

"I will die before I will take my wife under any roof but my own," cried Burr, fiercely, "and I want no gifts from you either. I am not turned beggar from any one yet. You shall take the woodland."

Lot waved his hand as if he swept the woodland, with all its half-grown trees, out of his horizon. "And yet," he said, "I thought 'twas what you left the other for. I should have said 'twas but your wage that was offered you;" and he smiled at his cousin.

"What do you mean, Lot Gordon?"

Lot looked at him with sharp interest. "Was there another leaf of you to read when I thought I was at the end," said he, "or were you writ in such plain characters that I put in somewhat of my own imaginings to give substance to them? Are you better, and worse, than I thought you, cousin? Do you love this flower that has her counterpart in all the gardens of the world, that is as sweet and no sweeter, that you can replace when she dies by stooping and picking, better than the one which has thorns enough to kill and sweetness enough to pay for death, and whose bloom you can never match?"

"I don't know what you mean," Burr said, impatiently and angrily; and Margaret Bean outside the door wagged her head in scornful assent.

"Then you loved Dorothy Fair better than Madelon Hautville, and 'twas not her place and money that turned you her way," said Lot, as if he were translating; and he kept his keen eyes on the other's face.

Burr's face flashed white. "What right have you to question me like this?" he demanded.

"But you would not take the price, after all," said Lot, as if he had been answered, instead of questioned. Then he looked up at his cousin with something like kindness in his blue eyes. "It proves the truth of what I've thought before," he said, "that oftentimes a man has to sting his own honor with his own deeds to know 'tis in him."

"My honor is my own lookout," Burr said, harshly.

"And you've looked out for it better than I thought," Lot returned.

Burr made another motion towards the door. "I can't stand here any longer," he said. "I'll go for the deed." Margaret Bean, moving as softly as she could in her starched draperies, fled back to the kitchen.

"Wait a minute," Lot said.

"Well," returned Burr, impatiently.

Lot got up, went over to the mantel-shelf, and stood there a minute, leaning against it, his face hidden. When he looked at Burr again he was so white that his cousin started. "Are you sick?" he cried, with harsh concern.

Lot smiled with stiff lips. "Only with the life-sickness that smites the child when it enters the world, and makes it weep with its first breath," he answered.

"If you want to say anything to me, Lot, talk like a man, and not a book," Burr cried out, with another step towards the door; and yet he spoke kindly enough, for there was something in his cousin's face which aroused his pity.

"It is not —" began Lot, and stopped, and caught his breath. Burr watched him half alarmed; he looked in mortal agony. Lot clutched the carven edge of the mantel-shelf, then loosened his fingers. "If," he said, brokenly, looking at Burr with the eyes of one who awaits a mortal blow, "you want — Madelon — it is not — too late. She — I know how she feels — towards you."

Burr turned white, as he stared at him. "She — she was going to marry you!" he said with a sneer.

"Do — you know why?"

Burr shook his head, still staring at his cousin.

"It was the price of — your — acquittal."

Burr did not move his eyes from Lot's face. He looked as if he were reading something there writ in startling characters, against which his whole soul leaped up in incredulity. "My God, I see!" he groaned out slowly, at length. And then he said, sharply, "But — you were going to marry her. Why did you give her up?"

"I loved her," Lot said, simply. His white face worked.

"But now — you — ask me to —"

"I love her!" Lot said again, with a gasp.

Burr strode forward, quite up to his cousin, and grasped his hand warmly for the first time in his life. "Before the Lord, Lot," he said, huskily, "'twas you, and not me, she should have fancied in the first of it."

"It is neither you nor me, nor any other man, that she will ever love as he is," Lot said, shortly, straightening himself, for jealousy stung him hard.

"What do you mean?"

"Woman reverses creation. She is a sublimated particle of a man, and she builds a god from her own superstructure, and clothes him with any image whom she chooses. She chose yours. Live up to her thought of you, if you can."

Burr dropped his cousin's hand, and surveyed him with that impatient wonder which he always felt when he used his favorite symbolic speech. "There's no question of my living up to the thought of any woman's but my wife's," he said, bitterly, and turned away.

"There's no knowing to what stature even a Dorothy Fair may raise a man in her mind. You may not be able to grow to that."

"It is all I shall attempt."

Then Lot spoke again, in that short-breathed voice of his, straining between the syllables. "Be sure — that you do — what — you will not — regret. Honor is not — always what we — think it."

"I have my own conception of it at least, and that I live up to.

'Tis high time," said Burr, with a kind of proud scorn of himself in his voice.

"Madelon Hautville — loves — you."

"She does not, after all this."

"She does!"

Burr stood straight and firm before his cousin, like a soldier. "If she does," said he, "and if she loved me with the love of ten lives instead of one, and I her, as perhaps I do, this last word of mine I will keep!" Then he went out with not another word, and presently returned with the deed of his little wooded property, which, however, his cousin Lot finally persuaded him to keep, as Margaret Bean gathered at the door, whither she had ventured again.

The loafers knew it all by nightfall, the news having been brought to the store by old Luke Basset, who had gotten it from Margaret Bean's husband. In a day or two they knew more from the same source. Lot Gordon had engaged his cousin to improve the Gordon acres which had been lying fallow for the last ten years. He had offered him a good salary. He wanted to carry out some new-fangled schemes which he had got out of books. Burr was going right to work; he had hired a man from New Salem to help him.

People began to think better of Lot Gordon than they had ever done, and they looked at Burr with more respect. Many had considered that Dorothy Fair was not going to "do very well." "Guess if it wa'n't for her father, and the chance of Lot's dying, she'd have a pretty poor prospect," they had said. Now they agreed that "Maybe Burr Gordon won't turn out so bad after all. Maybe he'll settle right down and go to work, and pay off his mortgage, when he gets married, and get a good living, even if Lot should hold out some time to come."

They watched Burr as he swung up the street to Parson Fair's in the spring twilights, with admiration for his stalwart grace, and growing approval for those inner qualities which outward beauty sometimes but poorly indicates. They approved also of the temperate hours which he observed in his courting, for no one within eye-shot, or ear-shot, but knew when Parson Fair's front door closed behind him. Burr, during the last weeks before his marriage, never stayed much later than half-past nine or ten at his sweetheart's house, and, in truth, was not sorely tempted to do so. Mistress Dorothy in those days behaved in a manner which might well have aroused to rebellion a more ardent or a less determinately faithful lover. She had the candles lit early in the beautiful spring twilights, and then she sat and stitched and stitched upon her wedding finery, bending her fair face, half concealed by drooping curls, assiduously over it, having never a hand at liberty for a lover's caress, or an eye for his smiles. Then, too, when Burr took leave, she stood before him with such a strange effect of terror and hauteur that he could do no more than touch her lips as if she had been a timid child, and bid her good-night. Had Burr Gordon, in those days, been less aware of his own unfaithfulness and weariness, and less fiercely resolved not to yield to it, he might well have perceived Dorothy's. As it was he confused her coldness with his own, and attributed it to the change in his own heart, and not to that in hers. And even had he suspected it he would not have made the first motion for freedom, so desperate was his adherence to falsity for the sake of truth.

Burr Gordon had at stake in this last more than any temporal good or ill of love. He had at stake his whole belief in himself, and he was also actuated by another motive which he scarcely admitted in his own thoughts.

Convinced he was that Madelon Hautville, believing as she did that he had forsaken her for honest love of another, would hold him in utter scorn and contempt were she to discover him false to Dorothy as she had been to her; and his very love of her love, strangely enough, kept him true to her rival.

So he went to see Dorothy, and found no fault with her coldness. The wedding preparations went on, and at last the day came.

CHAPTER XXIV

The wedding was to be at eight o'clock in the evening, and nearly all the village was bidden to it — even many of the Unitarian faction who had been Parson Fair's old parishioners. At half-past seven o'clock the street was full of people. The village women rustled through the soft dusk with silken whispers of wide best skirts. Young girls with spring buds in their hair flounced about with white muslins, and fluttering with ribbons, flitted along. The men, holding back firmly their best broadcloth shoulders, marched past in their creaking Sunday shoes. Before eight o'clock the fine old rooms in Parson Fair's house were lined with faces solemnly expectant, as the faces of simple country folk are wont to be before the great rites of love and death.

The women sat with their mitted hands folded on their silken laps, their best brooches pinning decorously their fine-wrought neckerchiefs, their bosoms filled with sober knowledge and patient acquiescence. The young girls sat among them very still, with the stillness of unrest, like birds who alight only to fly, their soft cheeks burning, their necks and arms showing rosy through their laces, their little clasped fingers full of pulses, and their hearts tumultuous and stirred to imagination by the sweet surmise and ignorance of love. They looked seldom at the young men, and the young men at them, as they sat waiting. Still there were some who had learned in city schools the suavities which cover like clothes the primal emotions of life, and they moved about with exchanges of fine courtesies, while the others looked at them wondering.

When the tall clock in the south room struck eight, there was a hush among these few who had learned to flock gracefully, chattering like birds, bearing always the same aspect to one another, without regard to selfish joys or pains. The lawyer's wife, in a grand gown and topknot of feathers, which she was said to have worn to a great party at the governor's house in Boston, composed to majestic approval her handsome florid face, and stood back with a white-gloved hand on an arm of each of her daughters, slender and pretty, and unshrinkingly radiant in the faces of the doctor's college-bred son and his visiting classmate. The doctor's wife, also, who had come of a grand family, and appeared always on festive occasions in some well-preserved splendor of her maiden days, which had been prolonged, drew back, spreading out with both hands a vast expanse of purple velvet skirt. She quite eclipsed as with a murky purple cloud the two meek elderly women and a timid young girl who sat behind her. They immediately peered around her sumptuous folds with anxious eyes lest they might lose sight of the bridal party; but the bridal party did not come.

A passageway was left quite clear to the space between the windows on the west side of the room, where it was whispered the bride and groom were to stand, and the people all pressed back towards the walls; but no one came. A little hum of wondering conversation rose and fell again at fancied stirs of entrance. Folk hushed and nudged each other a dozen times, and craned their necks, and the clock struck the half-hour, and the bridal party had not come.

In a great chair near the clear space between the windows sat the bridegroom's mother, with a large pearl brooch gleaming out of the black satin folds on her bosom. Her face, between long lace lappets, looked as clearly pallid and passively reflective as the pearls. Not a muscle stirred about her calm mouth and the smooth triangle of forehead between her curtain slants of gray hair. If she speculated deeply within herself, and was agitated over the delay, not a restless glance of her steadily mild eyes betrayed it.

People wondered a little that she should not be busied about the bridal preparations, instead of waiting there like any other guest; but it was said that Dorothy had refused absolutely to have any helping hands but those of her old black slave woman about her. It was known, too, that Dorothy had only once taken tea with Burr's mother since the engagement, and everybody speculated as to how they would get on together. Dorothy had, in truth, received the rigorously courteous overtures of her future mother with the polite offishness of a scared but well-trained child, and the proud elder woman had not increased them.

"When she comes here to live I shall do my duty by her, but I shall not force myself upon her," she told Burr. Burr's mother had not seen any of the dainty bridal gewgaws, but that she kept to herself. People glanced frequently at her with questioning eyes as the time went on; but she sat there with the gleam of her personality as unchanged in her face as the gleam of the pearls on her bosom.

"Catch her looking flustered!" one woman whispered to another. After the clock struck nine a long breath seemed to be drawn simultaneously by the company; it was quite audible. Then came a sharp hissing whisper of wonder and consternation; then a hush, and all faces turned towards the door. Burr Gordon, his face stern and white, stood there looking across at his mother. She rose at once and went to him with a stately glide, and they disappeared amid a distinct buzz of curiosity that could no longer be restrained.

"They've gone into the parson's study," whispered one to another. Some reported, upon the good authority of a neighbor's imagination, that Parson Fair had "fallen down dead;" some that Dorothy had fainted away; some that the black woman had killed her and her father.

Meanwhile, Burr and his mother went into Parson Fair's study. There stood the minister by his desk, with his proudly gentle brow all furrowed, and his fine, long scholar-fingers clutching nervously at the back of his arm-chair. He cast one glance around as the door opened and shut, then looked away, then commanded himself with an effort, and stepped forward and bowed courteously to the woman in her black satin and pearls. Elvira Gordon looked from one to the other, and the two men followed her glances, and each waited for the other to speak.

"Where is she?" she asked, finally.

"She is up in her chamber," replied Parson Fair, in a voice more strained with his own anxiety than it had ever been in the pulpit over the sins of his fellow-men. "I know not what to say or do — I never thought that daughter of mine — she will not come —"

Then Elvira Gordon cast a quick, sharp glance at her son, which he met with proud misery and resentment. "It is quite true, mother," he said. "We have both tried, and she will not come."

"Perhaps a woman —" said Parson Fair. "I wish her mother were alive," he added, with a break in his voice.

"I will go and see her if you think it is best," said Mrs. Gordon. In her heart she rebelled bitterly against seeming to plead with this unwilling bride to come to her son. Had she not felt guilty for her son, with the conviction of his own secret deflection, she would never have mounted the spiral stairs to Dorothy Fair's chamber that night. Parson Fair led the way, and Burr followed. The people stood back with a kind of awed curiosity. Some of the young girls were quite pale, and their eyes were dilated. Folk longed to follow them up-stairs, but they did not dare.

At the door of Dorothy's chamber crouched, like a fierce dog on guard, the great black African woman. When the three drew near she looked up at them with a hostile roll of savage eyes and a glitter of white teeth between thick lips. The parson advanced, and she sprang up and put her broad back against the door and rolled out defiance at him from under her burring tongue.

But he continued to advance with unmoved front, as if she had been the Satanas of his orthodoxy, which, indeed, she did not faintly image. She moved aside with a savage sound in her throat, and he threw the door wide open. There sat Dorothy Fair before them at her dimity dressing-table, with all her slender body huddled forward and resting seemingly upon her two bare white arms, which encompassed her bowed head like sweet rings. Not a glimpse of Dorothy's face could be seen under the wide flow of her fair curls, which parted only a little over the curve of one pink shoulder. Dorothy wore her wedding-gown of embroidered India muslin; but her satin slippers were widely separated upon the floor, as if she had kicked them hither and thither; and on the bed, in a great, careless, fluffy heap, lay her wedding-veil, as if it had been tossed there.

Elvira Gordon, at a signal from Parson Fair, entered the room past the sullen negress, who rolled her eyes and muttered low, and went close to the girl at the dressing-table.

"Dorothy!" said Mrs. Gordon.

Dorothy made no sign that she heard.

"Dorothy, do you know it is an hour after the time set for your wedding?"

Dorothy was so still that instinctively Mrs. Gordon bent close over her and listened; but she heard quite plainly the soft pant of her breath, and knew she had not fainted.

Mrs. Gordon straightened herself and looked at her. It was strange how that delicate, girlish form under the soft flow of fair locks and muslin draperies should express, in all its half-suggested curves, such utter obstinacy that it might have been the passive unresponsiveness of marble. Even that soft tumult of agitated breath could not alter that impression. When Mrs. Gordon spoke again her words seemed to echo back in her own ears, as if she had spoken in an empty room.

"Dorothy Fair," said she, with a kind of solemn authority, "neither I nor any other human being can look into your heart and see why you do this; and you owe it to my son, who has your solemn promise, and to your father, whose only child you are, to speak. If you are sick, say so; if at the last minute you have a doubt as to your affection for Burr, say so. My son will keep his promise to you with his life, but he will not force himself upon you against your wishes. You need fear nothing; but you must either speak and give us your reason for this, or get up and put on your wedding-veil and your shoes, and come down, where they have been waiting over an hour. You cannot put such a slight upon my son, or your father, or all these people, any longer. You do not think what you are doing, Dorothy."

Mrs. Gordon's even, weighty voice softened to motherly appeal in the closing words. Dorothy remained quite silent and motionless. Then Burr gave a great sigh of impatient misery, and strode across to Dorothy, and bent low over her, touching her curls with his lips, and whispered. She did not stir. "Won't you, Dorothy?" he said, gently, then quite aloud; and then again, "Have you forgotten what you promised me, Dorothy?" and still again, "Are you sick? Have I offended you in any way? Can't you tell me, Dorothy?"

At length, when Dorothy persisted in her silence, he stood back from her and spoke with his head proudly raised. "I will say no more," he said; "I have come here to keep my solemn promise, and be married to you, and here I will remain until you or your father bid me go, with something more than silence. That may be enough for my pride, but 'tis not enough for my honor. I will go back to your father's study, Dorothy, and wait there until you speak and tell me what you wish."

Burr turned to go, but Parson Fair thrust out his arm before him to stop him, and himself came forward and grasped Dorothy, with hardly a gentle hand, by a slender arm. "Daughter," said Parson Fair in a voice which Dorothy had never heard from his lips except when he addressed wayward sinners from the pulpit, "I command you to stop this folly; stand up and finish dressing yourself, and go down-stairs and fulfil your promise to this man whom you have chosen." The black woman pressed forward, then stood back at a glance from her master's blue eyes.

Dorothy did not stir; then her father spoke again, and his nervous hand tightened on her arm. "Dorothy," said he, "I command you to rise" — and there was a great authority of fatherhood and priesthood in his voice, and even Dorothy was moved before it to respond, though not to yielding.

Suddenly she jerked her arm away from her father's grasp, and stood up, with a convulsive flutter of her white plumage like a bird. She flung back her curls and disclosed her beautiful pale face, all strained to terrified resolve, and her dilated blue eyes "I will not!" she cried out, addressing her father alone, "I will not, father. I have made up my mind that I will not."

Then, as Parson Fair said not a word, only looked at her with stern questioning, she went on, shrill and fast, "I will not; no, I will not! Nobody can make me! I thought I would, I thought I must, until this last. Now when it comes to this, I can do no more. I will not, father."

"Why?" said Parson Fair.

"I would have kept my promise, father. I would have kept it, no matter if — I would have been faithful to him if he —" Suddenly Dorothy turned on Burr with a gasp of terror and defiance. "I would never have done this, you know," she cried; "it would never have come to this, if you had spoken and told me you were innocent."

"What do you mean, child?" said Parson Fair, sternly.

"He would not tell me that he did not stab his cousin Lot," replied Dorothy, setting her sweet mouth doggedly. Her blue eyes met her father's with shrinking and yet steadfast defiance.

"Dorothy," said he, "do you not know that he is innocent by his cousin's own confession?"

"Why, then, does he not say so?" finished Dorothy. "How do I know who did it? Madelon Hautville said she was guilty, then Lot

Gordon; and Burr would not deny his guilt when I asked him. How do I know which? Madelon Hautville was trying to shield him; I am not blind. Then Lot liked her. How do I know which?" Suddenly she cried out to Burr so loud that the people in the entry below heard her, "Tell me now that you are innocent, and either your cousin Lot or Madelon Hautville guilty," she demanded. "Tell me!"

Burr, white and rigid, looked at her, and made no reply. "Tell me," she cried, in her sweet, shrill voice, "tell me now that you did not stab your cousin Lot, and Madelon Hautville spoke the truth, and I will keep my promise to you, even if my heart is not yours."

Parson Fair grasped his daughter's arm again. "No man whom you have promised to wed should reply to such distrust as this," he said. "Dorothy, I command you to go down-stairs and be married to this man."

Then Dorothy broke away from him with a wild shriek. "No, I will not marry this man with his cousin's blood on his soul! I will not, father; you shall not make me! I will not! Night and day I shall see that knife in his hand. I will not marry him, because he tried to kill his cousin Lot. I will not, I will not!" The black woman pushed between them with a savage murmur of love and wrath, and caught her mistress in her arms, and crooned over her, like a wild thing over her young.

"There is no use in prolonging this, sir," Burr said to Parson Fair.

The elder man looked at him with a strange mixture of helpless dignity and sympathy and wrath. "You know that I have no share in this," he said, and he glanced almost piteously from Burr to his mother. "I could never have believed that my daughter —"

"We will say no more about it, sir," responded Burr. "I hold neither you nor your daughter in any blame." Then he offered his arm to his mother, and the three went out and down-stairs, and the black woman clapped to the chamber door with a great jar upon her mistress, whose calm of obstinacy had broken into wailing hysterics which betokened no less stanchness. Parson Fair, Burr Gordon, and his mother, at the foot of the stairs among the curious wedding-guests, looked for a second at one another.

The parson's fine state seemed to have deserted him. There were red spots on his pale cheeks. His long hands twitched nervously. "I will — inform them," he said, huskily, at length, but Burr moved before him. "No, sir; I will do it," he said.

Then he strode into the great north parlor, where the more important guests were assembled, and where he and Dorothy were to have been married. He stood alone in the clear space between the windows, and knew, as the eyes of the people met his, that they had heard Dorothy's last wild cry, and knew why she would not marry him. He stood for a second facing them all before he spoke, and in spite of the shame of rejection which he felt heaped upon him by them all, and a subtler shame arising from his own heart, in spite of the fact that he could not offer any defense, or do aught but bend his back to the full weight of his humiliation, he had a certain majesty of demeanor. Revolt at humiliation alone precipitates the full measure of it, and the strength which survives defeat, even of one's own convictions, is of a good quality. Silence under wrongful accusation gives the bearing of a hero.

There was a hush over the assembly so complete that it seemed as if the very personalities of the listeners were drawn back from self-consciousness to give free scope for sound. When Burr spoke, everybody heard.

"The marriage between Dorothy Fair and myself is broken off," was all he said. Then he went out of the room as proudly as if his bride had been by his side, through the entry to the study. Parson Fair and his mother were there. "They know it," he announced, quite calmly; then he took his fine wedding-hat from the table.

"Where are you going?" his mother demanded, quickly.

"To walk a little way." Burr turned to Parson Fair. "I beg you not to feel that you must deal severely with your daughter for this," he said, "for she does not deserve it. She was justified in asking what she did, and in feeling distrust that I did not answer."

"If a wife's faith cannot survive her husband's silence, then is she no true spouse, and 'twas the part of a man not to answer," said this Parson Fair, who had all his life followed in most roads the lead of his womankind, and not known it, so much state had he been allowed in his captivity.

"She was justified," said Burr, "and I beg you, sir, not to visit any displeasure upon her. I have not at any time been worthy of her, although God knows had she not cast me off, and did not this last, with what I remember now of her manner for the last few weeks, make me sure that her heart is no longer mine, I would have lived my life for her, as best I could; and will now, should she say the word."

With that, Burr Gordon thrust on his wedding-hat, and was out of the study and out of the south door of the house.

CHAPTER XXV

In the yard was drawn up in state, behind the five white horses, the grand old Gordon coach, which had not been used before since the death of Lot's father. Lot had insisted upon furnishing the coach and the horses for his cousin's wedding. The man who stood by the horses' heads looked up at Burr in a dazed way when he came out of the house and spoke to him.

"When my mother is ready you can take her home, Silas," said Burr. "Then drive over to my cousin's, and put up the coach and the horses."

The man gasped and looked at him. "Do you hear what I say?" said Burr, shortly.

The man gave an affirmative grunt, and strove to speak, but Burr cut him short. "Look out for that bad place in the road, before you get to the bridge," he said, and went on out of the yard. The road was suddenly full of departing wedding-guests, fluttering along with shrill clatter of persistently individual notes, like a flock of birds.

Burr, out of the yard, passed along through their midst with a hasty yet dignified pace. He said to himself that he would not seem to be running away. He looked neither to the right nor left, except to avoid collisions with silken and muslin petticoats, yet he was conscious of the hush of voices as he passed, and knew that they all recognized him in the broad moonlight.

When he reached the lane which led across-lots to the old place, he plunged into it by a sudden impulse. He went half-way down its leafy tunnel; then he stopped and sat down on a great stone which had fallen off the bordering wall.

Great spiritual as well as great physical catastrophes stun for a while, and there is after both a coming to one's self and an examining one's faculties, as well as one's bones, to see if they be still in working order. Burr Gordon, sitting there on his stone of meditation, in the moonlit dapple of the lane, came slowly to a full realization of himself in his change of state, and strove to make sure what power of action he had left under these new conditions.

His first thought was a cowardly one — that he would sell out, or rather give up his estate to his cousin, take his mother, and turn his back upon the village altogether. He knew what he had to expect. He tasted well in advance the miserable and half ludicrous shame of a man who has been openly jilted by a woman. He tasted, too, the covertly whispered suspicion which had perhaps never quite departed, and which now was surely raised to new life by Dorothy's loud cries of accusation. He knew that he was utterly defenceless under both shame and suspicion, being fettered fast by his own tardy but stern sense of duty and loyalty. It seemed to him at first that he would be crippled beyond cure in his whole life if he should stay where he was; and then he felt the spring of the fighting instinct within him, and said proudly to himself that he would turn his back upon nothing. He would brave it all.

There was a light wind, and now and then the young trees in the lane were driven into a soft tumult of whispering leaves. Burr did not notice when into this voice of the wind and this noise as of a crowd of softly scurrying ghosts there came a crisp rustle of muslin and a quick footstep up the lane. He only looked up when Madelon Hautville stopped before him and looked at him with incredulous alarm, as if she could not believe the evidence of her own eyes.

Dressed like a bride herself was Madelon Hautville, in a sheer white gown, which she had fashioned for herself out of an old crape shawl which had belonged to her mother, and cunningly wrought with great garlands of red flowers. She was going to Burr Gordon's wedding, not knowing the lateness of the hour; for her brother Richard had played a trick upon her, and set back the clock two hours, when to his great wrath she would not stay at home. The others were half in favor of her going, thinking that it showed her pride; but Richard was sorely set against it, and watched his chance, and slipped back the hands of the clock that she should be too late to see the wedding of the man who had forsaken her.

Madelon looked at Burr, and he at her, and neither spoke. Then, when she saw surely who it was, she cried out half in wonder and half chidingly, as if she had been his mother reproaching him for his tardiness: "What are you doing here, Burr Gordon? Do you know 'tis nearly eight o'clock, and time for your wedding?"

"'Tis nearly ten," said Burr, "and there is no wedding."

"Nearly ten?"

"Yes."

"But 'twas not eight by our clock."

Burr took out the great gold timepiece which had belonged to his father, and held it towards her, and she saw the face plainly in the moonlight.

"What does this mean?" she said; and then she cried, half shrinking away from him, "Are you married then? Where is she?"

"Dorothy Fair is at home in her chamber, and I am not married, and never shall be."

"Why — what does this mean, Burr Gordon?"

"She will not have me, and — no blame to her."

"Will not have you, and the people there, and the hour set! Will not have you? Burr, she shall have you! I promise you she shall. I will go talk to her. She is a child, and she does not know — I can make her listen. She shall have you, Burr. I will go this minute, and talk to her, and do you come after me."

Madelon gave a forward bound, like a deer, but Burr sprang up and caught her by the arm. "Why do you stop me, Burr Gordon?" she cried, trying to wrest her arm away.

"Do you think I have no manhood left, Madelon Hautville, that I will let you, *you* beg a woman who does not love me to marry me?"

"She does love you, she shall love you!"

"I tell you she does not!" Burr spoke with a bitterness which might well have come from slighted love, and, indeed, so complex and contradictory are the workings of the mind of a man, and so strong is the bent when once set in one direction, that not loving Dorothy Fair, and loving this other woman with his whole heart, he yet felt for the moment that he would rather his marriage had taken place and he were not free. His freedom, which he knew was a shame to welcome, galled him for the time worse than a chain, and he felt more injured than if he had loved this girl who had jilted him; for something which was more precious to him than love had been slighted and made for naught.

"She does — you are mad, Burr Gordon! She was all ready to marry you. She came to me to help on her wedding-clothes. She was all smiling and pleased. How could she be pleased over her wedding-clothes if she did not love you? She does, Burr! She is a child — I can talk to her. I will make her. Let me go, Burr! You wait here, and not fret. Oh, how pale you look! I tell you, you shall have her, Burr!"

"I tell you, Madelon, she does not love me, and I will not have you go."

Madelon stood looking at him, her face all at once changing curiously as if from some revelation from within. She remembered suddenly that old scene with Eugene, and a suspicion seized her. "There's somebody else!" she cried out, fiercely. "There's no truth in her. If she thinks — she shall not — nor he — I will not have it so!"

"For God's sake, Madelon, don't!" said Burr, not fairly comprehending what she said. He sat down again upon the stone, and leaned his head upon his hands. In truth he felt dazed and helpless, as if he had reached suddenly the mouth of many roads and knew not which to take. The intricacy of the situation was fairly paralyzing to an order of mind like his, which was wont to grasp, though shrewdly enough, only the straight course of cause and effect. He revolved dizzily in his mind the fact that he could not tell Madelon the reason which Dorothy had given for her rejection of him, and the conviction was fast gaining upon him that it was not the true and only reason. He held fiercely to his loyalty to

Madelon, and his shammed loyalty to Dorothy, and his slipping clutch of loyalty to himself, and knew not what to say nor what course to take.

Madelon, as he settled back upon the stone and bowed his head, made towards him one of those motions which the body has kept intact from the primitive order of things, when it was free to obey Love; then she stood back and looked at him a moment, while indignation and that compassion which is the very holiness of love swelled high within her. Then suddenly she leaned forward against him in her white robes, with the soft impetus of a white flowering tree driven by the wind, and put her arms around him, and drew his unhappy head against her bosom, and stroked his hair, and poured out in broken words her wrath against Dorothy Fair, and her pity for him. And all this she did in utter self-despite and forgetfulness, not caring if he should discover how great her love for him still was, believing fully that his whole heart had belonged to the other girl, and was breaking for her, and arguing thence no good for herself.

"She shall never marry him, that I swear to you, Burr," she cried, passionately, "and in time she may turn to you again; there is no faith in her."

Burr listened a while bewildered, not fully knowing nor asking what she meant, letting his head rest against her bosom, as if he were a child whom she comforted.

"Burr, you shall have her, you shall have her yet!" she said, over and over, as if Dorothy were a sweetmeat for which he longed, until at last a great shame and resolution seemed to go over him like a wave, and he put her away and rose up.

"Madelon," he said, "you don't know. Listen. You will scorn me after this — you will never look at me again, but listen: Dorothy must never know, for all the slight of this last must come from her and not from me, since she is a woman and I a man; but you shall know the whole truth. I never loved Dorothy Fair, Madelon, not as I love you, as God is my witness. She was pretty to look at, and I liked — but you cannot understand the weakness of a man that makes him ashamed of himself. I left you, and — I went — courting her because she was Parson Fair's only daughter, and I was poor, and that was not all the reason. I liked her pretty face and her pretty ways well enough, but all the time it was you and you alone in my heart; and, knowing that, I left you, though I was a man. I turned Judas to my own self, and denied and would have sold the best that was in me. Now you know the truth, Madelon Hautville."

Madelon looked at him. Her lips parted, as if her breath came hard.

Burr made as if to pass on without another word, but she held out her hand to stop him, though she did not touch him.

"Stop, Burr," she said, with a strange, almost oratorical manner, that he had never seen in her before. It was almost as if she mounted before his eyes a platform of her own love and higher purposes. "Listen to me," she said. "That night when I was in such terrible anger with you that for a second I would have killed you, I put it out of your power forever to do anything that could turn me against you again. I broke my own spirit that night, Burr. The wrong I would have done you outweighs all you ever have done or ever can do me. There is no wrong in this world that you can do me, if I will not take it so; and as for the wrong you may have done yourself — that only makes me more faithful to you, Burr."

Burr stood looking at her, speechless. It was to him as if he saw the true inner self of the girl, which he had dimly known by half-revealings but had never truly seen before. For a minute it was not Madelon Hautville in flesh and blood who stood before him, but the ghost of her, made evident by her love for him; and his very heart seemed to melt within him with shame and wonder and worship. "Oh, Madelon!" he gasped out, at length.

But Madelon turned away then. "You must go home now," said she, "and I must. Good-night, Burr."

"Good-night," said Burr, as if he repeated it at her bidding.

Then they passed without touching each other. Madelon went home down the lane, across the fields, and Burr went out in the silent street, whence all the wedding-guests had departed, and homeward also.

CHAPTER XXVI

In this little Vermont village, lying among peacefully sloping hills, away from boisterous river-courses, there was small chance of those physical convulsions which sometimes disturb the quiet of generations. The roar of a spring freshet never smote the ears of the dwellers therein, and the winters passed with no danger of avalanches. From its sheltered situation destructive storms seldom launched themselves upon it; the oldest inhabitant could remember little injury from lightning or hail or wind.

However, there is no village in this world so sheltered in situation that it is not exposed to the full brunt of the great forces of human passion, when they lash themselves at times into the fury of storm. It was here in this little village of Ware Centre, which could never know flood or volcanic fire, as if a sort of spiritual whirlpool had appeared suddenly in its midst. The thoughts of all the people, lying down upon their pillows, or rising for their daily tasks, centred upon it, and it was as if the minds of all were prone upon the edge of it, gazing curiously into the vortex.

The Sunday after Burr Gordon's disastrous wedding-day the faces of all the people on their way to meeting wore the same expression, in different degrees of intensity. One emotion of strained curiosity and wonder made one family of the whole village. The people thought and spoke of only one subject; they asked each other one question — "Will any of them be at meeting?" The Unitarian church was nearly deserted that Sunday, for Parson Fair's former parishioners returned to their old gathering place, under stronger pressure, for the time, than religious tenets.

It was a burning day for May — as hot as midsummer. The flowers were blossoming visibly under the eyes of the people, but they did not notice. They flocked into the meeting-house and looked about them, all with the same expression in their eyes.

When Burr Gordon and his mother entered, a thrill seemed to pass through the whole congregation. Nobody had thought they would come. Mrs. Gordon, gliding with even pace, softly murmurous in her Sunday silk, followed her son, who walked with brave front, although he was undeniably pale, up the aisle to their pew. He stood about to let his mother enter, meeting the eyes of the people as he did so; then sat down himself, and a long glance and a long nudge of shoulders passed over the meeting-house. Burr and his mother both knew it, but she sat in undisturbed serenity of pallor, and he stirred not a muscle, though a red spot blazed out on each cheek.

Madelon Hautville sat in the singing seats, but he never looked at her nor she at him. There were curious eyes upon her also, for people wondered if Burr would turn to her now Dorothy Fair had jilted him; but she did not know it. She heeded nobody but Burr, though she did not look at him, and when she stood up in the midst of her brothers and sang, she sang neither to the Lord nor to the people, but to this one weak and humiliated man whom she loved. The people thought that she had never sung so before, recognizing, though ignorantly, that she struck that great chord of the heart whose capability of sound was in them also. For the time she stood before and led all the actors in that small drama of human life which was on the village stage, and in which she took involuntary part; and the audience saw and heard nobody but her.

Burr, stiff as a soldier, at the end of his pew, felt his heart leap to hope and resolve through the sound of this woman's voice in the old orthodox hymns, and laid hold unknowingly, by means of it, of the love and force which are at the roots of things for the strengthening of the world. With weak and false starts and tardy retrogrades he had woven around his feet a labyrinth of crossing paths of life, but now, of a sudden, he saw clearly his way out. He trampled down the scruples which hampered and blinded him like thorns and had their roots in a false pride of honor, and recognized that divine call of love to worship which simplifies all perplexities. He would take that girl singing yonder for is wife, if she were indeed so generous-minded after all, not now, but later, when there could be no possibility of slight to Dorothy Fair. His honest work in the world he would do, were it in the ploughshares or the wayside ditches, with no striving for aggrandizement through untoward ways, and so would he humbly attain the full dignity of his being.

When Madelon Hautville stopped singing not one in the meeting-house had seen Burr Gordon stir, but the soul in him had surely turned and faced about with a great rending as of swathing wills that bound it.

Parson Fair preached that morning. Great had been the speculation as to whether he would or not. When he stood up in his pulpit and faced the crowded pews and the steely glances of curious eyes through the shifting flutter of fans, he was as austerely composed as ever; but a buzzing whisper went through the audience like a veritable bee of gossip. "He looks dreadful," they hissed in each other's ears, with nudges and nods.

All the principal participants in the village commotion were there except Lot Gordon and Dorothy Fair. Dorothy had not come, in spite of her father's stern commands, and sterner they had been than any commands of his to his beloved child before. Dorothy had cowered before her father, in utter misery and trepidation, after the company had left that wedding-night, but yielded she had not — only fallen ill again of that light fever which so easily beset her under stress of mind.

That Sunday morning, striving to rise and go to meeting as her father said, and being in truth willing enough, since she had a terrified longing to see Eugene Hautville in the choir and ascertain if he were angry or glad, she fell back weak and dizzy on her pillows, and the doctor was called. Dorothy's fever ran lightly, as all ailments of hers, whether mental or physical, were wont to do; and yet she had a delicacy of organization which caused her to be shaken sorely by slight causes. A butterfly may not have the capacity for despair, but the touch of a finger can crush it; and had it more capacity, there would be no butterflies.

It was a full month before Dorothy was able to go out of doors, and all that time the gossips were cheated out of the sight of her, and her father was constrained to treat her with a sort of conscience-stricken tenderness, in spite of her grave fault. Her mother had never risen from a fever which seemed akin to this; and Dorothy, in spite of his stern Puritan creed, was yet dearer to him than that abstraction of her which he deemed her soul.

Looking at the girl, flushed softly with fever, her blue eyes shining like jewels, as she lay in her white nest, he knew that he loved her life more fiercely than he judged her sins. He would turn his back upon her and go out of her chamber, his black height bowed like a penitent, and down to his study, and wrestle there upon his knees for hours with that earthly and natural love which he accounted as of the Tempter, yet might after all have been an angel, and of the Lord. And when Dorothy came weakly downstairs at last, with the great black woman guarding her steps as if she were a baby, he found not in himself the power of stern counsel and reproof which he had decided upon when she should have left her chamber.

All the neighbors knew when Dorothy Fair first stepped her foot out of doors, and told one another suspiciously that she did not look very sick, and that they guessed she might have come out sooner, and gone to meeting, had she been so minded.

And in truth the girl, beyond slight deflections in the curves of her soft cheeks, and a wistful enlarging and brightening of her blue eyes, as in thoughtful shadows, was not much changed. The first Sunday when she appeared in the meeting-house she wore, to the delight and scandal of the women, one of the new gowns and hats of her bridal outfit. Dorothy Fair, in a great plumed hat of peach-blow silk, in a pearly silk gown and pink-silk mitts, in a white-muslin pelerine all wrought with cunning needlework, sat in the parson's pew, and uplifted her lovely face towards her father in the pulpit, and nobody knew how her whole mind and fancy were set, not upon the sermon, but upon Eugene Hautville in the singing-seats behind her. And nobody dreamed how, as she sat there, she held before her face, as it were, a sort of mental hand-mirror, in which she could see her head of fair curls, her peach-blow hat, and her slender white-muslin shoulders reflected from Eugene's dark eyes. The fall of every curl had she studied well that morning, and the folds of the muslin pelerine over her shoulders. And when the congregation arose for the hymns and faced about towards the singers, then did Dorothy let her blue eyes seek, with an innocent unconsciousness, as of blue flowers, which would have deceived the very elect, Eugene's face.

But his black eyes met hers with no more fiery glances. Eugene never even looked at her, but sang, with stern averted face, which was paler and thinner than Dorothy's, though he had had no illness save of the spirit. In vain Dorothy sought his eyes, with her blue appealing ones, during every hymn; in vain once or twice during the sermon she even cast a glance around her shoulder with a slight fling of her curls aside, and a little shiver, as if she felt a draught. Eugene never looked her way that she could see.

When the long service was over, Dorothy, with sly, watchful eyes, quickened her pace, and strove so to manage that she and Eugene should emerge from the meeting-house side by side. But he was striding far ahead, with never a backward glance, when she came out, lifting daintily her pearly skirts. Burr was near her, but him she never thought of, even to avoid, and his mother's stately aside movement was not even seen by her. She courtesied prettily to those who met her face to face, from force of habit, and went on thinking of no one but Eugene.

Again, in the afternoon, Dorothy went to meeting, though her pulses began to beat, with a slight return of the fever, and again she strove with her cunning maiden wiles to attract this obdurate Eugene, and again in vain. That night Dorothy lay and wept awhile before she fell asleep, and dreamed that she and Eugene were a-walking in the lane and that he kissed her. And when she awoke, blushing in the darkness, she resolved that she would go a-walking in the lane on every pleasant day, in the hope that the dream might come true.

And Mistress Dorothy Fair, with many eyes in the neighbors' windows watching, went pacing slowly, for her delicate limbs as yet did not bear her strongly, day after day down the road and into the lane, and, with frequent rests upon wayside stones, to the farther end of it. And yet she did not meet Eugene therein, and her dream did not come true.

But it happened at last, about the middle of the month of June, when the great red and white roses in the dooryards were in such full bloom that in another day they would be past it and fall, that Dorothy and Eugene met in the lane; for there is room enough in time for most dreams to come true, and for the others there is eternity.

That afternoon Dorothy had gone forth as usual, but she said to herself that he would not come; and half-way down the lane she ceased peering into the green distances for him, and sat herself down on a stone, and leaned back against the trunk of a young maple, and shut her eyes wearily, and told herself in a sort of sad penitence that she would look no more for him, for he would not come.

The grass in the lane was grown long now, with a pink mist over the top of it; the trees at the sides leaned together heavy with foliage, and the bordering walls were all hidden under bushes and vines. Everywhere on bush and vine were spikes and corymbs of lusty blossoms. Birds were calling to their mates and their young; the locusts were shrilling out of depths of sunlight. Dorothy, in the midst of this uncontrolled passion of summer, was herself in utter tune and harmony with it. She was just as sweet and gracefully courtesying among her sisters as any flower among the host of the field; and she had silently and inconsequently, like the flower, her own little lust of life and bloom which none could overcome, and against which she could know no religion. This Dorothy, meekly leaning her slender shoulders against the maple-tree, with her blue eyes closed, and her little hands folded in her lap, could no more develop into aught towards which she herself inclined not than a daisy plant out in the field could grow a clover blossom. Moreover her heart, which had after all enough of the sweetness of love in it, opened or shut like the cup of a sensitive plant, with seemingly no volition of hers; therefore was she in a manner innocently helpless and docile before her own emotions and her own destiny.

She sat still a few minutes and kept her eyes closed. Then she thought she heard a stir down the lane, but she would not open her eyes to look, so sadly and impatiently sure was she that he would not come. Even when she knew there was a footstep drawing near she would not look. She kept her eyes closed, and made as if she were asleep; and some one passed her, and she would not look, so sure was she that it was not Eugene.

But that afternoon Eugene Hautville, who had gone all this time the long way to the village, felt his own instincts, or the natural towardness of his heart, too strong for him. Often, watching from a distance across the fields, he had seen a pale flutter of skirts in the lane, and knew well enough that Dorothy was there, and had turned back; but this time he walked on. When he came to Dorothy he cast one glance at her, then set his face sternly and kept on, with his heart pulling him back at every step. Dorothy did not open her eyes until he had fairly passed her, and then she looked and saw him going away from her without a word. Then she gave a little cry that no one could have interpreted with any written language. She called not Eugene by his name; she said no word; but her heart gave that ancient cry for its lover which was before all speech; and that human love-call drowned out suddenly all the others.

But when Eugene stopped and turned, Dorothy blushed so before his eyes that her very neck and arms glowed pink through her lace tucker and sleeves. She shrank away, twisting herself and hiding her face, so that he could see naught of her but the flow of her muslin skirts and her curling fair locks.

Eugene stood a minute looking at her. His dark face was as red as Dorothy's. He made a motion towards her, then drew back and held up his head resolutely.

"It is a pleasant day," he said, as if they were exchanging the everyday courtesies of life; and then when she made no reply, he added that he hoped she was quite recovered from her sickness.

And then he was pressing on again, white in the face now and wrestling fiercely with himself that he might, as it were, pass his own heart which stood in the way; but Dorothy rose up, with a sob, and pressed before him, touching his arm with her slender one in her lace sleeve, and shaking out like any flower the rose and lavender scent in her garments.

"I want to speak to you," she said, and strove in vain to command her voice.

Eugene bowed and tried to smile, and waited, and looked above her head, through the tree branches into the field.

"I want to know if — you are angry with me because — I would not — marry Burr," said Dorothy, catching her breath between her words.

"I told you that you had no reason — that he was not guilty," Eugene said, with a kind of stern doggedness; and still he did not look at her.

"I could not marry — him," Dorothy panted, softly.

"I told you you had no reason," Eugene said again, as if he were saying a lesson that he had taught himself.

"Are you angry — with me because I could not marry him?" Dorothy asked, with her soft persistency in her own line of thought, and not his.

Then Eugene in desperation looked down at her, and saw her face worn into sweet wistfulness by her illness, her dilated eyes and lips parted and quivering into sobs, like a baby's.

"I am not angry, but I encourage no woman to be false to her betrothal vows," he said, and strove to make his voice hard; but Dorothy bent her head, and the sobs came, and he took her in his arms.

"Are you angry with me?" Dorothy sobbed, piteously, against

his breast.

"No, not with you, but myself," said Eugene. "It is all with myself. I will take the blame of it all, sweet," and he smoothed her hair and kissed her and held her close and tried to comfort her; and it seemed to him that he could indeed take all the blame of her inconstancy and distrust, and could even bear his self-reproach for her sake, so much he loved her.

"I would not have married Burr — even if — he had told me — he was innocent," Dorothy said, after a while. She was hushing her sobs, and her very soul was smiling within her for joy as Eugene's fond whispers reached her ears.

"Why?" said Eugene.

"Because — you came first — when you looked at me in the meeting-house," Dorothy whispered back. Then she suddenly lifted her face a little, and looked up at him, with one soft flushed cheek crushed against his breast, and Eugene bent his face down to hers. They stood so, and for a minute had, indeed, the whole world to their two selves, for love as well as death has the power of annihilation; and then there was a stir in the lane, a crisp rustle of petticoats and a hiss of whispering voices; and they started and fell apart. There in the lane before them, their eyes as keen as foxes, with the scent of curiosity and gossip, their cheeks red with the shame of it, and their lips forming into apologetic and terrified smiles, stood Margaret Bean and two others — the tavern-keeper's wife and the wife of the man who kept the village store.

For a second the three women fairly cowered beneath Eugene Hautville's eyes, and Margaret Bean began to stammer as if her old tongue were palsied. Then Eugene collected himself, made them one of his courtly bows, turned to Dorothy with another, offered her his arm, and walked away with her out of the lane, before the eyes of the prying gossips.

CHAPTER XXVII

It was four o'clock that summer afternoon when the three women — Margaret Bean, the tavern-keeper's wife, and the store-keeper's wife — who had followed Dorothy and Eugene into the lane to pry upon them set forth to communicate by word of mouth the scandalous proceedings they had witnessed; and long before midnight all the village knew. The women crept cautiously at a good distance behind Dorothy and Eugene out of the lane, and watched, with incredulous eyes turning to each other for confirmation, the pair walk into Parson Fair's house together. Then they could do no more, since their ears were not long enough, and each went her way to tell what she had seen.

All the neighbors knew when Eugene Hautville left Parson Fair's house that afternoon, but their knowledge stopped there. Nobody ever discovered just what was said within those four walls when Dorothy — who, soft plumaged though she was, had flown in the faces of all her decorous feminine antecedents and her goodly teaching — confronted her father with her new lover at her side.

It was safe enough to assume, for one who knew her and them well, that the two men did finally turn and protect her and shelter her each against himself, and his own despite, as well as one another. After that Eugene Hautville was seen every Sunday night and twice in the week going into Parson Fair's house, and the candles burned late in the north parlor.

The banns were published in a month's time. Some accounted it unseemly haste, after the other banns which had come to naught, and some said 'twas better so, and they blamed not Parson Fair for placing such a flighty and jilting maid safe within the pale of wedlock — and they guessed he was thankful enough to find a husband for her, even if 'twas one of the Hautvilles.

However, Eugene was held in somewhat more of esteem than the others, since he had in his own right a snug little sum in bank which had come to him from an uncle whose name he bore. When it was known that Eugene had bought the old Squire Damon place, a goodly house with a box-bordered front walk, and a pillared front door, and would take his bride home to it, public favor became quite strong for him. Folk opined that he would, even if he was a Hautville, make full as good a husband as Burr, and that Dorothy Fair would have the best of the bargain all around. While many held Dorothy in slight esteem for her instability and delicacy, and thought she was no desirable helpmeet for any man, some were of the opinion that she had shown praiseworthy judgment and shrewdness in jilting Burr for Eugene.

Dorothy this time made small show of her wedding, and was married in her father's study with only the necessary witnesses and no guests. Eugene Hautville had chafed. Dorothy also, with her feminine desire for all minor details of happiness, was aggrieved that she could never now appear before the public gaze in all the splendor of her wedding-gear. But Parson Fair stood firm for once, and would have it so.

All the watchful neighbors saw was, after nightfall and moonrise, Parson Fair's door open, and the bride and groom appear for a second in a golden shaft of light which flashed into gloom at the closing of the door, and left there two shadows, as if the story of their life and love had already been told and passed into history. And then the neighbors saw them move up the road with long vanishing flutters of the bride's white draperies, and the great black woman, steadying a basket against her hip, in their wake, following her mistress like a faithful dog, with perhaps the most unselfish love of all.

The black woman favored Eugene more than she had ever favored Burr, perhaps because she was a true slave of love, and leaned with the secret leanings of her mistress's heart against all words of mouth, obeying her commands with a fuller understanding of them than Dorothy herself.

When this new lover came a-courting, the African woman had always greeted him at the door with that wide, sudden smile of hers, at once simple, like a child's, and wild, like the grin of an animal; and her voice, in her thick jargon, was nearly as softly rich to him as to Dorothy. Moreover she kept no longer jealous watch at the door of the room where the lovers sat, and was fond of treating the young man with little cakes which she made with honey, whose like was to be eaten nowhere else in the village.

After Dorothy and Eugene were wedded they faded into comparative insignificance in the thoughts of the villagers, which were then centred upon Burr Gordon and Madelon. The curtain went down upon Eugene and his bride as upon any pair of wedded lovers in his Shakespeare book.

Burr was in exceedingly ill repute, but he did not himself know it. Many of his old friends treated him coolly, but he attributed that to the embarrassed sympathy and constraint which they naturally felt towards him in his position. He thought they avoided him because they knew well that he would suspect even friendliness lest it contain a pity which would hurt his pride; and he thanked them for it. But the truth was, that outcry of Dorothy's against him on the wedding-night had lashed up into a hurricane all the suspicions which Lot's avowal had stilled. They did away easily enough with the force of Lot's statement, for there are many theories to furnish skin-fits for every difficulty, if one searches in the infinity of possibilities.

Lot's true reason none fathomed, for it was beyond their sounding-lines of selfish curiosity; but they found another which seemed to meet the needs of the case as well.

Lot, they said, had bargained with Burr to give up all claim to Madelon, and he would set him free by confessing an attempt at suicide. Margaret Bean, it was reported, had seen the letter which Lot had written to Burr in prison. When Madelon, who, half crazed by anxiety about her lover, had wrongfully accused herself to save him, had seen him turn to her rival and scorn her after his release, she had accepted Lot in a rage of pride and jealousy, as he had planned for her to do. The breaking off of the marriage betwixt her and Lot they mostly attributed to the simple cause he had mentioned — his failing health — though some thought that he had hesitated about marrying into the Hautville family when it came to it.

Suspicion had been for a time somewhat hushed against Madelon, the more so that she had been seen, since Dorothy had jilted Burr, to pass him with scarcely a nod, and was popularly supposed to hold an Indian grudge against him, and to be still anxious to wed his cousin Lot.

However, the tide soon turned again. On the Sunday after the banns between Dorothy and Eugene had been published, Burr had been seen to walk home openly with Madelon from evening meeting; and it was soon known that he was courting her regularly.

Then darker whispers were circulated. People said now that they were accomplices in attempted crime. That black atmosphere of suspicion and hatred, which gathers nowhere more easily than in a New England town, was thick around Burr and Madelon. They breathed, though as yet it was in less degree, the same noxious air as did the persecuted Quakers and witches of bygone times. The gases which lie at the bottom of human souls, which gossip and suspicious imaginations upstir, are deadlier than those at the bottoms of old wells. Still Madelon and Burr knew nothing of it, nor Burr's mother, nor Lot, nor any of the Hautville men. The attitude of Madelon's father and brothers towards herself and Burr had done much to strengthen suspicion. High voices and strange remarks had been overheard by folk strolling casually, of a pleasant evening, past the Hautville house.

In truth, at first old David Hautville and all his sons except Eugene had risen against Burr and Madelon, all their pride in arms that she should return to this man who had once forsaken her for another. But later they had yielded, for their pride was undermined by their own gloomy convictions as to Madelon, which they confided not to one another. However, the boy

Richard still greeted Burr surlily, with a fierce black flash under frowning brows, and scarcely spoke to Madelon at all until the day before her marriage. That was set some two months after Dorothy's.

Burr and Madelon, during the days of their betrothal, were as closely beset by spies on every hand as a party of Madelon's old kindred might have been, encamped in a wooded country, where every bush veiled savage eyes and every tree stood in front of a foeman, but they did not know it. Folk knew when Mrs. Gordon went to visit her son's betrothed, though 'twas on a dark evening. They knew what she wore, and how long she stayed. They knew when Madelon returned her visit; they knew, to remember, in many cases, more details of their daily lives than Burr and Madelon themselves.

Madelon had few wedding preparations to make. The wedding-garments which she had stitched with sorrow for her marriage with Lot would serve her now. She employed her time in increasing still further the household stores of linen for her father's and brothers' use, when she should be gone, and in making a great stock of sweet-sauce, jelly, and cordials from the fruits and berries of the season.

One afternoon in late summer, when the high blackberries were ripe, Madelon set forth with a great basket on her arm. A fine cordial, good for many ills, she knew how to make from the berries, and had planned to brew a goodly quantity this year. She went down the road a way, then over some bars, with her hands on the highest and a spring like a willow branch set free, across a pasture where some red cows were grazing, then over another set of bars, into a rough and shaggy land sloping gradually into a hill. Here the high blackberries grew in great thorny thickets, and Madelon pressed among them warily and began picking. She had not picked long — indeed the bottom of her basket was not covered — when she heard a rustle in the bushes behind her and looked over her shoulder hurriedly, and there was Lot Gordon.

Lot came forward from a cluster of young firs, parting the rank undergrowth with the careless wonted movement of one who steers his way among his own household goods. Well used to all the wild disorder of out-doors was Lot Gordon, and could have picked his way of a dark night among the stones and bushes and trees of many a pasture and woodland. Moreover, Lot, uprising from the great nest which he had hollowed out for himself from a sweet fern growth under the balsam firs, exhaling their fragrant breath of healing, and coming into sight, made better show than he had ever done in his own book-walled study.

Here, where the minds of other men swerved him and incited him not, where only Nature herself held him in leading-strings with unsearchable might or was laid bare before his daring eyes and many a secret discovered, Lot Gordon gained his best grace of home. The balsam firs framed him with more truth than the door of his own dwelling. To Madelon, as he came out from them, he looked more a man than he had ever done; for all unconsciously to her mind of strong and simple bent, he had seemed at times scarce a man but rather some strange character from a book, which had gotten life through too strong imagining.

Moreover to-day his likeness to Burr came out strongly. Madelon saw the cant of his head and swing of his shoulders, with a half sense of shame that he was not Burr, and yet with a sudden understanding of him that she had never felt before. She had not seen him since her betrothal to Burr. She thought to herself that he was thinner, and that the red flush on his cheeks was the flush of fever and not of the summer sun.

"How do you do, Lot?" she said. Madelon's cheeks were a splendid red; her green sunbonnet hung by its strings low on her neck, and her head, with black hair clinging to her temples in moist rings, was thrust out from the green tangle of vines like a flower. When Lot did not answer at once, but stood pale and trembling, as if an icy wind had struck him, before her, she pulled the pricking vines loose from her dress, and came out. "How do you do, Lot?" she said, again. Still Lot did not answer, and after a minute she turned with impatient dignity as if to enter her fastness again; but then Lot spoke.

"Like mankind," he said, "'tis not well, and it tends to death, but we were born with a lash at our backs to do it."

Madelon knit her brows impatiently, for this was his old talk, that savored to her of ink and parchment and thoughts laid up in studied guise, like mummies. Then she noted his poor face, and again the look like Burr, which caused her heart to melt with the fancy of her love in like case, and she said, with that gracious kindness which became her well, that it was a pleasant day, and the smell of the balsam fir was good for him.

But Lot looked at her with his great eyes set in hungry hollows, and answered her in that stilted speech which she liked not, trying to smile his old mocking smile with his poor lips, which only trembled like a child's when tears are coming. "There are rivers of honey and gardens of spices, and branches dropping balm," said Lot, "where a man can walk but his soul cannot follow him. His soul waits outside and strives to taste the sweet when he swallows it, and smell the balm and the spices when he breathes them in, but cannot; and that is only good for a man which is good for his soul."

"I don't know what you mean," said Madelon, shortly.

"I mean that I am outside all the good of this world, since the one good which I crave and cannot have is the gate to all the rest," said Lot. Then suddenly he cried out passionately, lifting up his face to the sky, "O God, why need it be so? Why need a man be a bond-slave to one hunger? Why need this one woman be the angel with the flaming sword before all the little pleasures I used to taste and love? Why need she come between me and the breath of the woods, and the incense of the fields, and their secrets which were to me before my own, so I can take no more delight in them?"

Madelon looked at him half in pity, half in proud resentment. "If it is so," she said, "it was not of my own accord I came; you know that, Lot Gordon. I meant no harm to you, and the harm that I did you brought upon yourself. I would not have come here to-day if I had known you were here and that it would disturb you."

"You could not have helped coming," said Lot. "I have been here since morning, and you have been here all the while."

"Why do you talk so, Lot Gordon?" cried Madelon, angrily, for Lot's covert meanings fretted her straightforwardness beyond endurance. "You know that I have just come here!"

"You came here when I did," said Lot, "when the fields were dewy. You held up your skirts and stepped daintily. I went ahead and you followed, high-kilted, pointing your steps among the wet grasses like a dove. Had I looked over my shoulder I could have seen you, but I looked not lest the power of flight might be in you like the dove."

"I shall go away if you talk like this. I will not stay here and listen to it; you know I was not here," said Madelon, and she paled a little, for she almost thought, used to his fanciful talk though she were, that Lot had gone mad.

"We walked towards the sun," persisted Lot, "but you were in my shadow and needed not to cast down your eyes. I saw some red flowers, but I did not pick them for you, and I heard you stop and break the stems as you came after. When we reached the shade of the firs there I sat down, but I left the space there, where the needles are smoothest and thickest, for you, and there you sat too, all day."

"Lot Gordon!"

"You need not mind, Madelon, for all day I looked not over my shoulder once. I saw not your face, nor touched your lips, nor your hand, nor even the fold of your dress. I harmed you not, even in my dreams, dear."

Madelon, standing quite free of the clinging blackberry vines, held up her dark head like an empress, and looked at him. In truth she felt little pity for Lot Gordon then, for she liked not being made to follow other than Burr even in a man's dreams. Still, when she spoke it was not unkindly, for in spite of this jealousy of herself for Burr, and in spite of her inability to understand such worship of herself, when she was spent in worship of another, she remembered how she had nearly taken the life of this man, and how he had striven to shield her, though against her will, and on hard and selfish conditions, and how he had at last sacrificed himself to set her free.

"Lot," said she, "there must be no more of this. I am almost your cousin's wife. You have no right." And then she repeated it passionately. "I say you have no right to love me like this, if I do not love you, Lot Gordon. I will have no other man but Burr think me at his heels. I will follow him till the day of my death, but no other. I would only have married you to save his life — you know that. You know I never loved you. You have no right."

"The right of love is every man's who sets not himself before it," returned Lot, with sad dignity. "I will not yield that even for love of you, Madelon; but myself shall be pushed yet farther out of sight, I promise you, and you shall be pestered no more, child. Go on with your berry-picking."

A great mound of rock uplifted itself like the swelling crouch of some fossil animal among the sweet ferns and the wild scramble of vines. Lot sank down upon it panting for breath. He leaned his head wearily forward between his hands, his elbows resting on his knees.

Madelon looked at him hesitatingly; she opened her mouth as if to speak, then was silent. She looked at the high vines, black with fruit, then at the field beyond, as if half minded to go away and leave them.

Finally she fell to picking again without a word. Lot coughed once, but he did not speak. Madelon kept glancing at him as she picked. Compunction and pity softened more and more her fiery heart, the more so since she felt the guilt of happiness in the face of the woe of another upon her. Finally she said, with that fond reversion to the little homely truths and waysides of life with which the feminine mind strives often to comfort, that she would put up for him a jug of her blackberry cordial, and furthermore that she hoped his cough was better. She said it with half-constrained kindness, not looking up from her berry-picking; but Lot lifted his head and thanked her and said the cough was nearly cured, with eagerness to respond to grace, like a child who has been chidden.

Then he watched her with bright eyes as she picked, his breath coming hard and quick. "Madelon!" he said, and stopped.

"What, Lot?"

"You remember — the gewgaws which I — showed you, Madelon — the feathers and ribbons and satins, and the other things? You cared not for them then. Will you have them now, for your wedding-gift?"

"No, Lot," said Madelon, quickly. "I thank you, but I cannot take them; I have enough."

"Why not?"

"I have enough."

"There is no need for you to tell me why," said Lot. "A woman like you would almost veil herself from her own eyes for the sake of a lover, so great is her jealousy. The thoughts and the dreams with which I bought the gewgaws profane them in your eyes while I am alive."

"I do not need them, and I cannot take them, Lot," said Madelon, steadily.

Lot said no more. He leaned his head upon his hands again. Madelon could hear his panting breath. She resolved that she would go away across the fields, down the road a piece, to another berry patch that she knew of. Still she did not go. One of those impulses which seem to come from authority outside one's self, or else from some hidden springs of motion which we know not of, had seized her. She looked at Lot and moved softly away a few steps, holding her skirts clear of the vines. Then she paused and looked again, and was away again. Her face was resolute and wary, as if she saw something which she feared and loathed, and yet would brave. Then she went close to Lot, and stood still over him a minute.

"Lot," she said.

He looked up at her, wonderingly. "Are you sick, Madelon?" he cried, and would have risen, but she motioned him back and spoke, turning her face away the while.

"Once I asked Burr to give me the kiss that I would have killed him for," said she, in a voice so sharpened by her stress of spirit that it might have come out of the flames of martyrdom. "Now I ask you to give me the kiss that I almost took your life for."

"Madelon!"

"It is all I can do to make amends," said she. Then she looked full at him, and did not shrink when she met his eyes, though her face grew white before the mad longing in them.

Lot stood up and leaned towards her, and she stood waiting. Then he threw out his hands, as if he would push her back, and turned away. "You owe me no amends," he said, hoarsely. "The wound that you gave me was my just desert for striving to take what you were not willing to give."

"Your life is your life," said she, steadily, "and I almost took it away from you. I would do this in token of repentance for that and whatever other harm I have done you unwittingly."

"You owe me no amends, and I will take none," said Lot, again.

Then he faced about towards her, and she started and looked at him, wondering and half in awe, for suddenly the love in the heart of the man showed itself in his face like a light, and it was almost as if she saw, unbelieving and denying, her own transfigured image in his eyes.

"Good-bye, Madelon," said Lot.

"Good-bye," she returned, faintly, and looked at him for the first time in all her life without the thought of Burr between them.

But that Lot did not know, and stood a moment gazing at her as a man gazes at one beloved under the shadow of long parting, striving to gain possession of somewhat to hold and cherish aside from the conditions of the flesh. Then he said good-bye again, and went away, with that soft winding glide of his through the underbrush which he might have learned from the wild dwellers in the woods, and was out of sight through the violet glooms of the firs.

CHAPTER XXVIII

The night before Madelon was married, as if by some tacit understanding of peace and harmony, the Hautvilles came together for a concert in the great living-room. Not one had said to another, "This is Madelon's last night at home, and we have been wroth with her; let us bury the hatchet, and raise our voices with one accord in our old songs;" but one impulse had seemed to move them all, as one wind moves the forest trees who are kin to one another, and they were all together at twilight, even Eugene and his bride.

Burr Gordon came also, but he and Madelon did not sit apart that evening. The weather was cool, even for late September, and an early frost was threatened. A great fire blazed on the hearth. Burr and Dorothy, on the settle in the chimney-corner, listened to the Hautville chorus, and Burr looked always at Madelon and Dorothy at Eugene. The Hautvilles stood together before the fire, old David with his bass-viol at his side, like the wife of his bosom; Louis holding his violin on his shoulder, like a child, pressing his dark cheek against it, and Eugene and Abner and Richard and Madelon uplifting their voices in the old songs and fugues.

The doors and windows were shut. Nobody heard nor saw Lot Gordon when he crept like a fox round the house, and came under a window and rested his chin on the sill and remained there looking at Madelon. She wore that night a soft gown of crimson wool, which clung about her limbs and her bosom, and showed her bare throat swelling with song into new curves which were indeed those of music itself. Lot, as he looked at her, saw her with the full meaning of her beauty as never Burr could, and as she could never see herself, for there is no looking-glass on earth like a vain love when it rises above the slight of its own desire. Greater praise than she would ever know again in her whole life went up for Madelon outside that window, as she sang, but she neither knew it nor missed anything when Lot went away.

At ten o'clock the concert ceased. Lot slunk away noiselessly, and soon Eugene and Dorothy went home, and Burr, lingering for a good-night kiss or two in the door.

Madelon set bread to rise that night, and fulfilled her little round of nightly tasks for the last time. Her father and brothers went to bed and left her there — all but Richard. He remained in a corner of the settle, his slim length flung out carelessly, his head tipped back as if he were asleep; but his black eyes flashed bright under their lids at his sister whenever she did not look at him. Madelon said not a word until her tasks were done; then she came and stood in front of Richard, and looked at him, frowning a little, for her pride was stung at his treatment of her, but holding out her hand. "Can't you bid me good-night, Richard?" said she, and tried to smile at him with that old loving comradeship which he had disowned.

The boy maintained his sullen silence for a moment, and Madelon waited. Then suddenly he cried, "Good-night," with sharp intonations, like the response of a surly dog, and sprang up and thrust something hard into her hand, with such roughness that it hurt her, and she started.

"'Tis a wedding-present for you," Richard said, savagely, with averted face. "I thought the one I gave you before would not serve for two weddings. Though there be but one bride, there should be different gifts."

Madelon gave one look at Richard; then she opened her hand, and there on her reddened palm lay a little gold pencil, which the boy must have spent all his little savings to buy. Madelon held it out to him. "Take it back," said she; "I want no presents with words like that to sweeten them."

Richard's clenched hand hung by his side. He shook his head sullenly.

"Take it!" said Madelon; but he made no motion to do so.

"Then I shall let it fall on the floor," said Madelon.

"Let it," returned Richard, and forthwith the little gold pencil rolled on the floor under the settle, and Madelon turned away with a white face. But before she had reached the door Richard was at her side and his hand on her arm. "Oh, Madelon!" he said, striving to keep the sobs back. Then Madelon turned and laid a hand on each of his shoulders, and held him away, looking at him.

"Why did you speak to me like that?" said she; and then, without waiting for an answer, drew the boy's head down to her bosom, and held it there a moment, stroking his hair. "If ever you are sick after I am gone," said she, "I will come and take care of you; and if you don't get good things to eat I will see to that, too;" and then she kissed Richard's dark head, and put him away gently, bidding him with a tender laugh "not to be a baby," and went over to the settle and picked up the little gold pencil, and praised it and said she would treasure it all her life.

And then she bade Richard follow her into the best room, and opened the carved oak chest and displayed six beautiful shirts made of linen, which she had herself spun and woven and wrought with finest needlework in bands and bosoms, for a parting gift to him, because he was the nearest of all her brothers, though she must not say so. "The others have shirts enough," said she; "I have seen to that, for I have meant to do my duty to you all, but none of the others have bosoms and wristbands stitched like these, and the linen is extra fine."

That night Richard would not go to his chamber, which he

shared with his brother Louis, lest he wake and spy his face flushed with tears, but crept stealthily back down-stairs, and, all unbeknown to any one, lay all night on the settle in the living-room. He slept little, and often waked and wept in the darkness like a child rather than one of the fiery Hautville brothers.

When wrath with a beloved one is stilled in the human heart and love takes its place, it is with a threefold increase, a great rending of spirit, and a cruel turning of weapons against one's self. Richard was one who would always deal with entireties, being capable of no divisions nor subtleties of praise or blame. Whereas his anger had been fierce against his sister that she should love and marry the man who had flouted her, now it was turned wholly against himself for his injustice and ill-treatment of her. He racked himself with the memory of his surly words and looks; and those six shirts of fine linen, with the cunning needlework in band and bosom, seemed the veritable scriptural coals of fire on his head. Also good and simple reasons for his sister's course came to him as he lay there and influenced him still more. "She had it in her mind to kill him, though 'twas the other she struck," he said to himself; "'tis only fit that she should make amends to him for that and keep his house for him, and bake and brew and spin and weave for him." Richard in the darkness nodded his head in agreement with his own argument, and yet he hated Burr as well as ever, and the next morning when he saw him stand beside his sister before Parson Fair, he clenched his slender brown hands until the sinews stood out, and his black eyes still flashed hostility at him. Yet when he looked at Madelon's face his own softened, and he set his mouth hard to keep back the quiver in it. Madelon wore not the silk of green and gold in which she had planned to be wedded to Lot; that she could not bring her mind to do, since the old wretched dreams and imaginations seemed to cling to the garment and desecrate it for this. She wore instead a sober gown of a satin sheen with the rich purplish-red hue of a plum, which set off the dark bloom of her face by suggestion rather than contrast; but all the boy Richard noted of her costume was his little gold pencil slung on the long gold chain around her neck.

Madelon and Burr were married quite early in the morning, in the best room of the Hautville house, and nobody outside the two families was bidden to the wedding. After the marriage the bride tied on a white-muslin apron and passed cake and currant wine; and the great Hautvilles sitting in sober state around the room, Elvira Gordon in her black satin and pearls, pretty Dorothy, and Parson Fair partook.

Then the bride went up to her chamber and put on a pelisse of stuff like her gown, lined with canary-colored satin, and a little cap of otter and a great muff which she had fashioned herself out of skins which her brothers had brought home, and took over her arm, since the day was frosty, a long tippet of otter which she could wind round her throat, if need be, and came down all equipped for her wedding-journey.

In front of the Hautville house stood waiting a smart chaise with a fine young horse in the shafts, and the bride and groom came out and got in and drove away. But first, while Burr was gathering up the reins, David Hautville's hoarse voice through the open door besought him to wait, and presently the old man came striding forth with the skin of a mighty bear which he had slain single-handed years ago, and which had been his chiefest treasure next to his viol ever since, kept beside his bed, whence no one dared remove it. He flung it up into the chaise, and tucked it well in over his daughter's knees. "Oh, father, I will not take your bear-skin!" Madelon cried, and the tears came into her eyes, for this touched her more than anything; and the memory of aught that she had ever lacked in tenderness towards them all seemed to smite her in the face.

"'Tis a sharp day for the time of year, and there'll be a frost to-night," was all old David Hautville said, and strode back into the house, keeping his face well turned away.

The horse that Burr drove was a young animal that he had purchased lately. It was of the stock of the Morgans, and stood with the faithfulness of a sentinel; but when the signal to start was given stepped out proudly as if to a battle charge, with eager tossings of heavy mane and high flings of knees and hoofs; and yet, when fairly on the road, never broke the swift precision of his course.

"He's got a fine horse there," Abner Hautville said, in his emphatic bass, as he watched them out of sight; and he further declared that for his part he would be willing to trade the roan for him. Then the boy Richard turned upon him, with a cry that was something between a sob and an oath: "Yes, trade off the roan and all we've got left to him, I'll warrant ye will!" he choked out. Then he was gone, pelting off madly across the fields, with his bold and innocent young heart, that had as yet known no fiercer passion than this for his sister, all aflame with grief and angry jealousy, as of one who sees his best haled off before his eyes, and still with awed submission to a power which he recognizes and under-stands not.

CHAPTER XXIX

As Burr and Madelon, setting forth on their wedding-journey, drove down the village street, they met many whom they knew; and had it not been for their self-engrossment they could not have failed to notice and wonder at the cold greetings they received, and the many averted faces which greeted them not at all.

Indeed, Burr did remark upon it when they met Daniel Plympton, who nodded with a surly air and turned his fat and pleasant countenance resolutely away, with a gesture that seemed to belie his own identity.

"What's come across Dan'l?" he said, laughing, for at that time coldness from the outside world seemed but provocative of amusement. Then he sang out gayly to the Morgan horse, and they flew along the road, under the outreaching branches, red and gold and russet, past old landmarks and houses and more familiar faces which bore strange looks towards them, and yet surprised them not, for a strangeness was over all the old sights and ways for them both. To the bride and groom, riding through the village where they had been born and bred, and whence all their earthly imaginations had sprung, came an experience like a resurrection. They saw it all: the paths their feet had trodden, the doors they had entered, the friends they had known from childhood, but all seemed no longer the same, since their own conditions of life had changed; and change in one's self is the vital spring of change in all besides.

As they rode along old associations lost their holds over them in their new world, which was the outcome of the old, and would in its turn wax old again. Burr looked at his own home, as he went by, as if he had never seen it; even his memory of himself and his childhood days was dim, and he and Madelon, glancing at Lot's windows and having his image forced, as it were, upon their consciousness, regarded it as they might have done an actor in some old drama of history in which they also had taken part, but which had long since passed off the stage.

They left the house behind and were swiftly out of sight, over the crest of a long hill with a great spread of golden maple branches closing after them like a curtain, and neither of them dreamed in what straits Lot Gordon lay behind his vacant windows — and all through this love and bliss and paradise of theirs.

The smart chaise and the Morgan horse had scarcely disappeared before Margaret Bean came hurriedly out of Lot Gordon's house and went rattling in her starched draperies towards the village; and soon after that the doctor was seen driving thither furiously in his tilting sulky, while windows were opened and spying heads thrust out all along his course.

An hour later everybody knew that Lot Gordon, some said by a fall in climbing over a stone wall, some said by a severe fit of coughing, had caused his old wound to beset him again with danger of his life. That night, indeed, the tide of rancorous gossip swelled high. The spirit of persecution and righteous retribution which finds easy birth in New England villages was fast getting to itself feet and hands and tongue and a whole body of active powers.

A stormy bridal night had Burr and Madelon known had they been at home; and had Lot Gordon died during the next three days, in which he lay in imminent danger, there had been fleet horses on the track of the swift Morgan, and the wedding-journey had come to a close.

Yet the Hautville men heard nothing of the bitterness which was gathering towards Madelon and Burr, for people, fearing their fierce tempers, hesitated until the time was come to disclose it to them. Even old Luke Basset dared not carry news to them. The tongues were always hushed when one of them drew near; and as for Eugene, who, having a wife, might perhaps have discovered it, he and Dorothy took the stage coach for Boston the day after the marriage, and were paying a visit at Dorothy's aunt's there.

After three days Lot Gordon was reported to be no longer hovering between life and death, and yet it was said on good authority, through the doctor's wife in fact, that he might at any time, by an injudicious step or a harder coughing-spell, end his life through the opening of that old wound, for which they held either Madelon or Burr, or perhaps both, accountable; and public indignation swelled higher and higher. It was resolved that when the bridal couple returned a constant espionage should be kept upon them, and in case of Lot's death active measures should be taken.

"We ain't goin' to have a man murdered to death in our midst by no French and Injuns nowadays and let it slide," proclaimed a fiery spirit in the store one night. Then when the door opened and Abner Hautville, dark and warlike in his carriage as any fighting chief, appeared, the man asked ostentatiously for a "quart of m'lasses, and not so black and gritty as the last was nuther," transferring the rancor in his tone to an inoffensive object with Machiavellian policy.

However, Margaret Bean's husband was in the store that night, and heard it all. He had been sent thither for a half-pound of ginger, and told not to linger; but linger he did, disposing his old bones with a stiff fling upon a handy half-barrel and listening to every word with a shrewd sense, for which no one would have given him credit, that he could by repetition and enlargement, if necessary, appease his wife's wrath at his delay. The workings of the human mind towards selfish ends even in the simplest organization have an art beyond all mechanism, and can astonish the wisest when revealed.

Nobody who saw old man Bean pottering homeward that night, his back bent with age, yet moving with a childlike shuffle, carrying his parcel of ginger with tight clutch lest he drop it, like one whose weariness of body must make up for feebleness of mind, dreamed what a diplomat he was in his humble walk of life, and what an adept still in doubles and turns and twists and dodges towards his own petty ends.

A sweeter morsel than any sugar old man Bean, overborne with a sense of naughtiness and disobedience, like a child, carried home to his wife to quiet her chiding tongue.

Hardly had he entered the door when he heard afar the swift rattle of her starched skirts, like a very warning note of hostility, and cut in ahead of her reproaches with a triumphant manner.

"Pretty doin's there's goin' to be," said he; "never was nothin' like it in this town. That's what I stayed for. Thought ye'd orter know."

"What do you mean?" asked Margaret Bean, staring.

"Ye know what the doctor says about *him*?" The old man jerked his head towards the door.

Margaret nodded.

"Well, they're goin' to have 'em both hung for murder the minute he draws his last breath."

"Can't till they're tried," said Margaret, with a sniff of scorn at her husband's lack of legal knowledge.

"Well, they're goin' to clap 'em into jail the minute they git home, an' keep 'em there till they can hang 'em," persisted old man Bean.

"They ain't."

"I tell ye they are!"

Old man Bean had a cup of tea, plentifully sweetened with molasses, made from the ginger which he had purchased, and went to bed happy and peaceful, as one who has worked innocently and well his small powers to his own advantage; and soon after that Lot also heard the news which he had brought.

Margaret Bean said to herself that it was her duty; and her duty, and a great devouring thirst of curiosity, overcame her natural fear of injuring the sick man.

Lot Gordon was still in bed, but propped up on pillows, with a candle on the stand at his side, reading one of his leather-covered books. Margaret Bean shrank back when she had delivered herself of her news, for the flash in Lot's eyes was like lightning; and she waited in trembling certainty as for thunder.

"I tell ye 'tis a lie!" cried Lot Gordon. "Do ye hear, 'tis a lie! Go yourself and tell them so from me. The wound has naught to do with this. It was naught but a scratch, for I had not courage enough to strike deep, much as I wanted to be quit of the world and the fools in it. Go you down to the store and tell the gossips that have no affairs of their own, and must needs pry on their neighbors so. Dare any one of them to turn knife on his own flesh for the first time and strike deeper! The next time I'll do better. Tell them so! The fools! Sodom and Gomorrah, and fire from Heaven for wickedness! Lord, why not fire from Heaven for damned foolishness, that does more harm to the world than the shattering of all the commandments into stone-dust!"

"I felt that 'twas my duty to let you know, sir," stammered Margaret Bean, backing farther and farther away from him.

"Tell the fools that I say, and I'll swear to it, and so will the doctor swear, that 'twas not the wound that has been my ailment, but my cursed lungs; but if 'twas 'twould be naught to them, for I struck the blow myself. I tell you that neither the one nor the other of them struck the blow — it was I. Do you hear? It was I!"

"Yes, sir," said Margaret Bean, trembling, her eyes big, her white face elongated in her starched cap ruffles.

"Go to bed!" said Lot, savagely, and the old woman scuttled out, glad to be gone.

Never before had Lot addressed her so. "I believe he did do it himself," she told her husband next morning, for she could not wake him to intelligence that night; "he's jest ugly 'nough to."

The next day at early dawn Lot's bell, which was kept on his stand beside the bed, in case he should be worse in the night and need assistance, tinkled sharply.

"Send your husband after the doctor," Lot ordered, peremptorily, when Margaret answered it; and presently early risers saw old man Bean advancing in a rapid shuffle towards the doctor's, and soon the doctor himself whirled past, his back bent to the rapid motion of his gig. The report that Lot Gordon was worse went through the village like wildfire. A crowd collected in the store as soon as the shutters were down; there was a knot of men before the lawyer's office waiting for him to come; and several hot-headed young fellows pressed into the stable and urged upon Silas Beers that he should keep the old white racer in readiness for an emergency that day, and also several others which, if not as fleet, had good staying powers.

When the doctor entered Lot Gordon's chamber Margaret Bean followed, tremblingly officious, in his wake, with a bowl and spoon in hand.

"I want to see the doctor alone," said Lot; and the old woman retreated before his coldly imperious order. "Stay out in the kitchen," ordered Lot, further, "and don't come through the entry; I shall hear you if you do."

"Yes, sir," replied Margaret Bean, and obeyed, nor dared listen at the door, as was her wont, so terrified was she lest Lot could indeed hear and had heard in times past.

The doctor, redolent of herbs and drugs, set his medicine-chest on the floor, and advanced upon Lot, who waved him back with a half-laugh.

"Lord, let's have none of that nonsense this morning," he said. "Sit down; I want to talk to you."

The doctor was gray and unshaven and haggard as ever, from a midnight vigil, the crumbs of his hasty breakfast were on his waistcoat; his eyes were bright as steel under heavy, frowning brows.

"Are ye worse? Has it come on again?" he demanded.

"No; sit down."

The doctor snatched up his medicine-chest with a surly exclamation.

"Where are you going?" asked Lot.

"Back to my breakfast. I'll not be called out for nothing by you or any other man after I've been out all night. If you want a gossip, get the parson; he's got time enough on his hands. A man don't have to work so many hours a day saving souls as he does saving bodies."

Lot laughed. "And neither souls nor bodies saved by either of you, after all," said he, "for the Lord saves the one, if he has so ordained it; and as for the other, your nostrums only work so long as death does not choose to come."

"Have it your own way; save your own soul and your own body, as ye please, for all me," said the doctor, who was adjudged capable when crossed of being surly to a dying man; and he made for the door.

"For God's sake stop," cried Lot, "and come back here and listen! I did not call you for nothing. The lives and deaths of more than one are at stake; come back here!"

The doctor clamped his medicine-chest hard on the floor. "Be quick about it, then," said he, and sat down in a chair at Lot's bedside.

Lot fumbled under his pillow and produced a folded paper which he handed to the doctor. "I want you to sign this," said he.

The doctor scowled over the paper, got out his iron-bowed spectacles, adjusted them, and read aloud:

"I, Justinus Emmons, practising doctor of medicine, do hereby declare that the death of Lot Gordon of Ware Centre will, when it takes place, be due to phthisis, and phthisis alone, and not in any degree, however small, to the wound inflicted by himself some months since. And, furthermore, I declare that his death will follow from the natural progress of the disease of phthisis, which has not in any respect been accelerated by his self-inflicted wound."

"You want me to sign this, do you?" said the doctor.

"I will call in Margaret Bean and her husband for witnesses," said Lot.

"You think I am going to sign this?"

"I want it in addition to the certificate of the cause of death which you will have to make out after my decease. 'Tis an unnecessary formality, but I would have it so," Lot returned.

The doctor dashed the paper on the bed. "If you think I am going to subscribe to a lie for you, or any other man, you're mistaken," he cried. "It was enough for me to hold my tongue when you made that fool statement of yours that wouldn't have deceived a man with the brains of an ox."

"My death will be due to phthisis; my left lung is almost consumed, and you know it," affirmed Lot.

"And I tell you," said the doctor, stoutly, "that your death from phthisis might not have occurred for ten years to come. Does a tree die because half its boughs are gone? When you die, you die of that wound. The evil was greater than I thought at the time. It takes less to kill a diseased man than a sound one."

"Then my death will be due to my disease and not to my wound, if it would not have killed a sound man," cried Lot, eagerly.

"I tell you, your death will be due to that wound that Madelon Hautville, with maybe your cousin at her back, gave you."

Lot's face glared white at the doctor. "I gave the wound to myself!"

The doctor laughed.

"I tell you, I gave the wound myself!"

"Take your wound into court, and see what they say."

"What do you mean?"

"I'll give any man who will stab himself in just the same place, with the knife held in just the same way, every dollar I have in the world."

"You can't prove it."

"I can prove it."

"I can do away with your proof," said Lot, in a strange voice. The doctor looked at him sharply.

"Then you will not sign this paper?" Lot said, presently.

"No, I will not; and I tell you, once for all, when you die I make out my certificate as it should be."

"How?"

"By a wound from a knife or other sharp instrument, inflicted by a person or persons unknown."

Lot's face, towards the doctor, looked as if death had already struck it; but he spoke firmly. "How long will it be, first?" he asked.

"I don't know."

"Approximate."

"A false step may do it."

"I can lie still!"

"A coughing-spell may do it."

"I will not cough!"

"More than that, a thought may do it, if it stirs your heart too much. I tell you as I should want to be told myself: your life hangs by a thread."

"Sometimes a thread does not break," Lot said, with a meditative light in his eyes.

"That's true enough."

"This may not."

"True enough."

"How long will you give it to last, before you sign this paper?"

"A year."

"Then you will sign this if I live a year from to-day?"

"No, I will not sign it, for you may have another stab on New-year's day, if you seem likely to live so long," said the doctor, shortly; "but I will promise you not to make out your certificate of death from this wound."

"How great a chance of life have I?" Lot asked, hoarsely, after a minute's pause.

"Small."

"Yet there is one?"

"Yes."

The doctor opened his chest, and began selecting some bottles.

"I want no more of your nostrums," said Lot.

"Very well," said the doctor, replacing the bottles. "I would not make out that certificate sooner than necessary — that is all."

"Dose death and go to the root of the matter," said Lot. "Then you won't sign this paper?"

"No," replied the doctor, with a great emphasis of negation.

"There is one thing you will do," said he.

"What?" asked the doctor, suspiciously.

"If I die within a year, to your truest belief, from any other cause than this wound now in my side you will say so."

"Of course I will do that," replied the doctor, staring at him.

"And you will in such a case let this wound drop into oblivion, you will hold your peace concerning it, 'forever after?'"

"Of course I will."

"Swear to it?"

"I swear. But what in —"

Lot smiled. "Some time, when you have leisure, write a treatise on 'Who killed the man?'" he said, as if to turn the subject, "and keep going back to first causes. You'll find startling results; you may decide that 'twas your duty to sign the paper."

"I have no time for treatises," returned the doctor, gruffly.

"You may trace the killing back to yourself."

"I'm not afraid of it. Good-day."

"Shake hands with me, doctor," pleaded Lot, with a curious change of tone, "to show you bear no grudge for the breakfast you lost."

The doctor stared a second, then went up to him with extended hand, looking at him seriously. He thought Lot's illness had begun to affect his mind.

"Keep yourself quiet, and you may outlive the best of us," he said, soothingly, as if to a child or a woman, shook Lot's lean hand kindly, repeated his good-day, and was gone.

Lot waited until he heard the outer door close. Then he tinkled his bell for Margaret Bean. "When are they coming home?" he asked, shortly, when she stood beside him.

"His mother said she was expectin' of 'em Saturday."

"Get my clothes out of the closet, will you," said Lot.

"You ain't a-goin' to get up?"

"Yes, I'm better; get the clothes."

When Margaret Bean had laid the clothes out ready for him, and was gone, Lot laid still a moment, reflecting, with his eyes on the ceiling. He wished to cough, but with an effort he checked it, gasping once or twice. "Saturday," he said, aloud. "To-day is Wednesday — three days. Can I wait?" He paused; then as if answering another self, he said, "No; I could die a thousand deaths in that time. I can't wait."

Lot Gordon got up, moving by inches, with infinite care and pains, dressed himself, crawled out of his bedroom into his library, which was adjoining, and sat down at his desk. Margaret Bean came timidly to the door, and inquired if he did not want some breakfast. She had to repeat her query three times, he was writing so busily, and then he answered her "no" as if his thoughts were elsewhere. The old woman hungrily eyed the paper upon which he was scribbling, and went away with lingering backward glances.

Lot Gordon, bending painfully over his desk, using his quill pen, with wary motions of hand and wrist alone, that he might not jar his wounded side, wrote a letter to the bride upon her wedding-journey.

"Madelon," wrote Lot, "I pray you to pardon what I have

done, and what I am about to do. The danger of blood-guiltiness and death have I brought upon you, and I now save you in the only way I know. I pray you, when you read this, and know what I have done, that you think of me with what charity you may, and that the love which caused the deed may be its saving grace."

Lot sat looking at what he had written for a moment, then tore it up, and wrote again:

"Madelon, — Alive I claimed nothing, dead I claim your memory, for the sake of the love for which I died."

And, after a moment, tore up that also.

And then he wrote again, with quivering lips, yet breathing guardedly:

> "Madelon, — The love that was set betwixt man and woman that the race might not die is one love, but there is another. That have I found and found through you, and bless you for it, though death be needful to its keeping. There is another birth than that of the flesh, through this so great love, which can upon itself beget immortality of love unto the understanding of all which is above. A greater end of love than the life of worlds there is, which is love itself. That end have I attained through this great love in my own soul which you have shown me, else should I have never known it there, and died so, having lived to myself alone, and been no true lover.
> "Lot Gordon."

And hesitated, reading it over; but at length tore that into shreds, and wrote yet again:

> "Dear Child, — I pray you when I am gone that you wear the pretty gowns and the trinkets which I offered you once, for I would fain give you for your happiness more than my poor life."

Tears of self-pity fell from Lot's eyes as he wrote the last; then he laughed scornfully at himself, and tore that up. "Self dies hard," said he.

He wrote no more to Madelon, but now to Burr:

> "Dear Cousin," he wrote, "I have this day discovered that my life is in imminent danger from the wound. If my death comes in that wise there will be trouble. I take the only way to save her, but I pray you, upon your honor, that you do not let her know, for even your love cannot sweeten her life fully for her if she knows; for love has taught me the heart of this woman. To you alone, for the sake of the honor of our blood, which has never been shed by our own hands before, I disclose this; for I would be set right in the eyes of one man

when I am dead."

Lot Gordon pondered long over that; but finally tore up that as he had torn the others, and gathered up all the fragments and crawled across the room with them, and threw them on the hearthfire.

Then, leaving them blazing there, he returned to his desk, and wrote:

"To all whom it may concern, or to all whom in their own estimation it may concern, this:

"I, Lot Gordon, of Ware Centre, being weary of life, which is a dream, have resolved to force the waking. Having once before attempted in vain to take my life, I now attempt it again, and this time not in vain, for my hand has grown skilful with practice. I take my life because of no wrong done me by man or woman, nor because of any vain love; I take it solely because my days upon this earth being numbered through my distress of the lungs, I have not the courage to see death approach by inches, and prefer to meet him at one bound. I have lived unto myself, with no man accountable, and I die unto myself, with no man accountable; and this is the truth with my last breath.

"Lot Gordon."

This last Lot folded neatly and addressed it "To my fellow-townsmen," and laid it in a conspicuous place on his desk, and then wrote on another sheet and put that in his pocket. Then he opened a drawer of the desk, and took out all the trinkets which he had offered Madelon, in their pretty cases, and with them in his hands crept out of the room, and up-stairs, into the chamber which he had caused to be decked out so newly and grandly when he had thought to marry her. There was a great carven chest in a corner of the room, which Lot unlocked, and took from thence all those rich fabrics which he had bought for Madelon. And then he laid them all — the silken stuffs and plumes and fine linens and jewels — out on the great bed, under the grand canopy, and placed on the top the sheet of paper on which he had last written, "For Madelon Gordon."

Margaret Bean had listened when Lot climbed the stairs. She heard him when he came down again, entered his library, and shut the door. She waited a long time. For some reason which she did not herself know she felt cold with terror. She would not let her husband leave her alone in the kitchen for a moment. At last, when it was nearly noon, she bade him keep close at her heels, and went to the library door and knocked, and when no answer came, knocked again and again and again, louder and louder and louder. Then she made her husband open the door, with fierce urgings, and peered around his shoulder into the room. Then she gave one great shriek, and caught the old man by the arm with a frantic clutch, and was out of the house with him and screaming up the street.

Saturday morning Burr and Madelon came riding into the village. As they passed up the street everybody whom they met saluted them with a manner which had in it something respectful, apologetic, and solemn. The lovers felt no wonder at such return of cordiality, seeing in everything but reflections of their own moods, and knew not what it meant until they reached home.

Then Elvira Gordon, meeting them at the door, told them that Lot was dead by his own hand, by a knife-thrust which crossed the old wound in his side; and she dwelt upon the reason for his deed: that he had been slowly dying from the disease of his lungs, and had not the courage to die by inches, which reason now all the town believed, since the doctor had said no word in contradiction, and never would, being mindful of his oath.

Madelon listened, white and still, saying not a word; and she said nothing when, up in their chamber, whither she went to take off her bonnet, Burr, who had followed, took her in his arms, and they stood together, looking at each other and trembling. Knowing not, and never to know, the whole which he had done for them, they yet knew enough. Suddenly, in the light of their own love another greater showed revealed; and each exalted the image of Lot Gordon above the other, and was acquaint with the spirit of what he had written and kept back; for love that so outspeeds self and death needs no speech nor written sign to prove its being.

THE END